While I Count
the Stars

While I Count the Stars

a novel

Valerie Banfield

For Mom,
lovely as lilacs in springtime

Where there are no oxen, the manger is clean,
but abundant crops come by the strength of the ox.

Proverbs 14:4

Chapter One

Spring 1940. "Hullo. Hola. You, up there, are you Señorita Savannah?"

"Who's asking?"

When the man raised his arm to shield his face from the sun, unkempt locks of his dark mane poked beneath his wide-brimmed hat. Probably one of the locals who heard about her plight. A gawker, a curious spectator. If only she'd not confided in Benita. Well, no, Benita wasn't exactly the culprit, it was the arrival of the others—the serious contenders—who presented the greatest problem. Who knew?

"Señorita Savannah?" the man asked again. He reached into his pants pocket, pulled out a piece of paper, and waved it at her.

Savannah wiped her sweaty brow with the tail of the ribbon that held her hat in place. A thorough inspection of the man's clothing identified him as a foreigner. Dark stains of perspiration dotted the heavy fabric at his underarms and chest. She looked at her own peasant blouse, its gauzy weightless material ready to catch the next breeze, an offering of relief from the warm summer air. If only these men tried to assimilate . . .

He started walking up the slope. "Señorita?"

Those shoes were unfit for a climb. Should he lose his footing, dark, damp soil would ruin his trousers. Savannah shook her head at the obvious. He, too, was a green one. Not what she ordered.

"Stay where you are," she said as she pushed the edge of her shovel into the soil and tucked her gloves into her skirt pockets. She peered at the visitor, assessing the good looks and strong build of what would certainly prove to be an unacceptable solution to her situation. The lovely smile and perfectly formed white teeth caught her by surprise. Too late, she turned her attention back to her feet.

When the heel of her right foot lost traction, her flailing arms overcompensated for the misstep, leaving her unbalanced body to toddle momentarily over her left leg. The slippery carpet of the hillside took her down, fast and hard. From the corner of her eye, Savannah watched the wind catch her hat and send it ahead of her. After three revolutions during which dirt smeared her cheeks, weeds clung to her hair, and the sun blinded her eyes, Savannah lost count of the number of rotations that followed.

Her body landed at the base of the hill, accompanied by an inharmonious, "Oomph." The sun's heat found its way through what had to be umpteen layers of mud, and rested on her face. She dared not open her eyes until she took inventory of her form.

"Señorita? Are you all right?" The voice carried mixed tones of astonishment and alarm.

The fingers he placed on her arm were tender and warmer than the sunshine—as if that were possible.

"Don't touch me." Her voice held little more than a whisper, but the venom with which she delivered her warning through clenched teeth forced the man to retract his hand.

She tested her fingers, hands, and arms first. Nothing broken. Her toes passed the wiggle test, as did her ankles and legs. If she managed to survive the fall with her back, neck, and shoulders intact, she could get rid of the visitor and get back to work. Regardless of her physical condition, time was short.

Savannah lifted one eyelid. A creased brow and worried lips—perfect and full . . . inviting—replaced his lovely smile and curious expression. When she opened her other eye, tiny orbs of light danced around the man's dark brown eyes.

"Señorita, are you all right?"

"I see stars."

"You see stars?" he asked, the furrows in his forehead growing deeper. He looked over his shoulder, as if he might see someone—anyone—who might help him deal with the lump sprawled at his feet. "Lie still. How many stars do you see?"

"You're number four."

"You see four stars?"

"No, you're number four."

"I look like a star?" he asked. His face took on a perplexed expression. Wasn't he listening?

The flickering lights swirled in slow motion as Savannah propped herself up on her elbows. She wrestled herself into a sitting position and stretched shoulders, testing her muscles and ligaments. She pushed her neck forward, sideways, and back. When the backward movement seemed to encounter a knot, she uttered, "Ugh."

"Please, Señorita. Are you all right?"

Savannah blinked her eyes several times, hoping to eradicate the dots of light from her view. She fastened her attention on the form in front of her: dark chocolate eyes framed by long black eyelashes, prominent cheekbones on a most pleasant face, and that smile—at the moment, tentative yet optimistic.

When her cheeks warmed at his attention, she adjusted her view downward. So much for trying to save the man's trousers, the knees of which bore the black hue of the rich soil on which he knelt. She extended her hand.

"Help me up?"

He looked sturdy and rugged from her view at the top of the hill. Standing next to the stranger, she measured her slight frame against his stocky form. Her visitor was muscular—and handsome in the way of the Costa Rican men. Yet he bore traits not consistent with those of the nationals. Not that it mattered. She'd have to send him on his way, just as she intended to do with the others. The other three . . . who just wouldn't go away. Could it get any more complicated?

"You are Savannah Hamilton, are you not?"

Was his a statement or a question? Savannah glanced at her untidy condition and swallowed her amusement. She intimidated him? Looking like this? When she ran her fingers through her tangles, she encountered leaves, dirt, and an uprooted flower. Her white blouse and coral-colored skirt wore large brown and black spots that might look rather nice on a painted pony.

He reached into his pocket and extracted a white handkerchief. As he lifted his hand, as if to wipe the mud from her face, she saw handsome stitching on the corner of the cloth, a tedious task contributed by some caring female. Judging from his youthful appearance, the embroiderer was probably his mother, or maybe a spinster sister.

Recognizing hers was not a kind thought, Savannah pulled her face away from the young man's hovering cloth, and wondered at her merciless judgment. When had she become so cynical? Before Daddy duped the family into joining his unorthodox and so-called mission to Central America, or after she discovered it was the prospect of making money that had motivated the dear man?

History was of no consequence. The task at hand had nothing to do with dear Daddy and everything to do with finding a means to stay in this place. She couldn't go back home. Not now. Hopefully, not ever.

Chapter Two

Micah stared at the paper he pulled out of his pocket. Had he misread? Misunderstood? He'd not bothered with a letter, as the message required an urgent response. His awkward introduction to Savannah Hamilton left him tongue-tied and baffled. He read the correspondence one more time:

Stranded American missionary of the female persuasion seeks to wed American male missionary who owns a good heart, good intentions, and proper visa status and documentation to share with future wife.

Twenty-three-year-old daughter of distinguished missionary seeks to remain in Costa Rica to continue the work of her dear, departed papa.

Only serious parties of good repute and with references need apply. Make inquiry in person at the Misión de Cacao, Muy Bella, Costa Rica.

Haste is required, as the authorities have given this new orphan ninety days to marry a suitable provider. Failing this, the devoted evangelical must depart her beloved country, abandon her service to those in need, and return, broken hearted, to the shores of North America.

Surely, the Good Lord has the power to stir the heart of just one man who owns the characteristics described above. Might it be you?

"Stay here a minute," Savannah said. She traipsed to the

yard in front of the mission house and spoke to a man who stood outside. She waved her hands and pointed at Micah before she strode into the building. The man gestured for Micah to join him.

"Do you have a name?" The middle-aged man wore a furrowed brow, an expression just short of a grimace, and an apron. In one hand, he carried a large pot by its handle. His other hand he extended toward Micah.

"Sí Señor. Micah Keller."

"I am Roberto Vargas, the cook."

The cook? Not what Micah expected. Not that anything was thus far. The young missionary woman worked the coffee and cocoa plants while the man took charge of the kitchen. What next?

"I am also the repairman, the temporary pastor, and the mission's liaison."

"Liaison? The mission requires a mediator? To interact with whom?"

Roberto chuckled when he said, "Should you manage to remain at Misión de Cacao for more than a day, the need will manifest itself." He looked over his shoulder before he said, "If you seek adventure, you will not be disappointed should Savannah decide to keep you here."

"Adventure?" Micah scoffed. "I do not seek adventure. I aim to save souls, to lead them to Christ. And . . . should she decide to *keep* me? As if I have no say in the matter? I came in good faith, although the request was, of itself, unconventional. I will not be ridiculed. Certainly not by a woman."

Roberto licked his lips and erased the hint of humor that lifted the edges of his mouth. "You look as if you could use some food and drink. Come this way."

Without waiting for a response, Roberto tossed the swill from his pot into a clump of weeds, turned around, and walked toward the largest of the mission buildings.

Micah perceived that it was God who directed him to respond to the young woman's advertisement. Micah had been certain that he was destined to abide in this place. So sure was he that the situation would work itself out, he embarked on the journey while lacking the funds for round-trip transportation. As Micah followed Roberto, he ran his hand through his hair, propped his hat back on his head, and fingered the few remaining coins he hid in his pants pocket. Perhaps he should have prayed a little more.

Chapter Three

He had a good appetite and passable manners, but he neglected to look her in the eye. Unlike the other hopeful gents gathered around the heavy wood table, with their lovelorn eyes and drooling mouths, Micah acted as if he might be anxious to return from whence he came. Good. Tomorrow morning suited Savannah just fine. Maybe he would take the others with him.

"¿Hablas español?" Simón asked the newcomer. The six-year-old shoved his jet-black hair out of his eyes, put both elbows on the table, and used his fists to support his chin.

In those fleeting moments when Savannah dared consider the prospect of motherhood, it was the image of Simón that came to mind. The bright, inquisitive, and happy rascal tested Benita's patience, will, and her stamina, much as Savannah had tested her mother—back in the days when she still had one.

"Más o menos," Micah replied.

More or less? What kind of an answer was that? Could the man speak Spanish or not?

"¿Cómo se dice . . . uh, how do you say 'I love Savannah' en español?" Simón asked.

Micah's neck and ears turned the color of a sun-ripened

tomato, and when he drew his napkin to his flaming face, he looked as if he might choke. Simón clanged his spoon against his plate and slipped away from the table before Benita could grab him. His not-so-innocent laughter chased him out the door.

"Manténte lejos del perro. No te ensucies," Benita called after her son.

"Why do you bother?" Savannah asked. "He will *not* stay away from the dog, and he *will* get dirty. You know that. And, we speak English here. Remember?" She tilted her head upward until the tip of her nose aligned perfectly with Benita's wide eyes.

Benita turned her discomfort on Roberto, who pretended not to notice the exchange. Cowards, both of them. Savannah scoured the faces gathered for the evening meal. Cowards. The lot of them.

Where were the men whom she sought? Not that she needed more than one, but identifying *the* one seemed almost more trouble than it was worth. The first three suitors—as if they met that description—were lovesick men searching for a gringo wife.

The illiterate Andrew might have a difficult time persuading the local government officials that he held the credentials of a minister, and therefore, had reason to settle in the area with a wife.

Andrew looked up, as if he sensed Savannah's scrutiny from her perch across the table. He considered himself superior to the two men who arrived soon after he did, but aside from his being polite, he had little to offer. The North American took more siestas than the Ticos, and failed to comprehend the value of a work ethic. He remained at Misión de Cacao while he sought employment with one of the large coffee plantations, or so he said each time Savannah broached the subject of his need to leave.

Second to arrive was Randall, who, at sixty-two, Savannah awarded the nickname Gramps. How absurd it was for him to think he might be an appropriate mate for her. Randall rested his elbows on either side of his dinner plate, an apparent means to protect his allotment of food from those sitting to his right and left. He kept his face cast downward as he shoveled rice and beans into his mouth.

He managed to help with light chores, but Savannah couldn't afford to feed the man. Although he was skinny as a string bean, Randall ate more than three grown men. He needed to go away very soon. Having conceded to Savannah's rejection of his proposal, he too, sought employment elsewhere.

When Charles, the transient American who popped into town every now and then, heard of her situation, he threw his hat into the ring, along with the other two. Charles, however, resided in the local jailer's cell as often as he wandered the streets picking pockets and drinking to excess.

Savannah pushed her plantains around her plate with her fork. Why was this so hard? She shook her head in dismay as she regarded the three men. A fine band of possibilities, they were.

She turned her gaze toward Micah, which prompted him to halt the spoon he held halfway to his mouth. He twisted his head far enough to return her stare, and won the dinner round when Savannah blinked first. Maybe he wasn't as timid as he first appeared.

Micah, however, did not meet her expectations, as he held too many of his own. His appearance suggested he carried on soft work to support himself. His fingernails were short and clean, his palms free of callouses. Swaths of sunburn on his cheeks and nose implied he worked indoors.

No doubt, Savannah was not the wife of Micah's choosing. She could be mistaken, but his bearing suggested he thought himself to be someone of authority, someone who would likely redirect her chores from the hillside to the kitchen. She could think of little worse than that possibility. A wife who obeyed her husband without question and who melted into obscurity on the home front? 'Twas not she.

Savannah conceded that not all women were doomed once they wed. She considered the unlikely roles Roberto and Benita established in their marriage. Perhaps Savannah could do likewise with a mate. Benita proved to be the worst cook in Costa Rica, and when Savannah's father threatened to fire her straightaway, it was Roberto who stepped up and offered to take over kitchen duties.

Father, who rarely disparaged others, accepted the pair's unorthodox roles with aplomb. Benita and Pablo, the couple's fifteen-year-old son, worked the crops, repaired fences and buildings, and cared for the livestock while Roberto prepared meals, laundered clothes, and kept the interior of the mission's buildings in fine shape.

It was clear that Micah held hopes for a union that Savannah could not—would not—meet. He, along with the other three, needed to go home. Decision made, Savannah gathered her dishes, took them to the sink, and walked outside.

Chapter Four

Savannah recoiled when Micah appeared on the veranda and cleared his throat. Best to get the conversation started.

"Why do you have to sneak up on me?" Savannah wailed.

"I didn't. I have a soft step. I didn't mean to alarm you."

Savannah crossed her arms and narrowed her eyes. "Before you say a word, why don't we agree that you made a mistake?"

"A mistake?" The woman thought to dismiss him? Shouldn't it be the other way around? The gall . . .

"I believe you owe me the courtesy of an interview," Micah said.

"An interview?"

"Yes. I'd like to schedule a discussion with you, day after tomorrow."

"Why wait? We can conduct one now."

"Not now. I need to finalize my thoughts for the message I intend to deliver tomorrow."

"Message? Tomorrow?" Savannah asked.

Micah pursed his lips at her apparent ignorance. Who was this woman? Or *what* was she—a Christian missionary or a heathen? So far, he'd witnessed more of the latter than the former.

"Tomorrow. The Sabbath?"

Comprehension washed over the woman's face. Indeed, his comments served as a reminder. Good heavens.

"The Sabbath. Of course. Why do you presume to deliver the message?" Savannah asked.

"If you seek a husband who is to serve as the patriarch of this mission, I suspect you should know how deep-seated his faith is. How better to demonstrate my spirituality, as well as my good intentions, than through a Sabbath message?"

The annoyance that darted from her gray eyes fueled Micah's resolve and quickened his temper. He would not leave here until he and Savannah Hamilton discussed her needs, his qualifications, and their mutual desire to save souls—although at this juncture he questioned the woman's character and motives. Micah bit his tongue at the stinging accusation his irritation formulated. He pulled in a long breath, clenched his jaw, and expelled the air through flared nostrils.

"Fine. You can deliver your sermon tomorrow. We'll meet the day after, and you can be on your way by noon." Savannah spun on her heels and started to walk away.

"A moment, please?"

The downturned edge of one side of her mouth spoke volumes. "What?"

"When does the service begin?"

"Ten."

"May I ask how many people you expect?"

"Around fo—" she mumbled as she walked away. "Have Roberto show you to your room. See you in the morning."

Micah dropped both hands to his sides. He hadn't been this perturbed since Ruth upended his world, and Ruth Benning didn't hold a candle to Savannah's fiery disposition.

~

At nine-thirty, Micah crossed the yard to the small chapel. When he pushed open the door, the wind kicked up and swirled heavy layers of dust throughout the dark room. He removed his hat and waved it through the air as he choked on the weightless assault.

After he propped open the door and waited for the air to clear, he ventured back inside and walked up the narrow aisle, formed by a pair of benches on either side. He stood behind the dais, as if he were speaking to the congregation. How might upwards of forty people worship in this near-empty sanctuary? Did the parishioners bring their own chairs?

Micah ran his thumb across the top of the lectern and studied the dark stain that collected on his skin. If this much dust could accumulate in a week's time, why didn't someone take responsibility to clean this house of worship? Weren't the good people who served at this mission acquainted with the terms reverence and holiness?

A heavy weight pushed down Micah's shoulders as his watch measured the minutes until the service started. Instead of reviewing his notes, he found a rag and started dusting. As he dusted, he prayed over each seat, all of which remained unoccupied as the hour struck.

At ten-fifteen, Micah walked out of the building and stood on the small porch, taking in the lack of activity throughout the premises. At quarter to eleven, Simón rounded the corner. He flinched with surprise, but drew his mouth into a wide grin when Micah nodded to him.

"Good morning, Simón. A peaceful Sabbath to you."

The child knitted his brow. "What do you mean to give

me? What is a piece of sabbish? Is that like succotash? I don't like succotash."

Micah pulled his damp collar away from his neck. Perhaps the boy needed a different word. "I meant to welcome you to worship. We worship on the Sabbath."

"Sabbath?"

"Yes. As the Bible calls it."

Simón's eyes widened as some level of comprehension found him. "The Bible. Mr. Hamilton had a Bible. He let me hold it."

"Are the others coming soon?" Micah asked.

"To the Bible?" Simón asked.

"To worship."

When confusion replaced the boy's smile, Micah said, "Would you please fetch the others?"

"Yes. You wait here." Simón disappeared, and with the exception of a dog barking, the property fell into silence.

At eleven, Micah stood at the lectern and surveyed those who occupied the wooden benches. Savannah sat on the end of the bench to the right, her hair in disarray. Her wrinkled clothes complemented her bare feet.

On the bench to Micah's left, Simón sat between Roberto and Benita. Pablo, who rubbed his bloodshot eyes with his fists, took the bench behind his family.

"Where are the others?" Micah asked.

"The others?" Savannah asked. "Andrew, Randall, and Charles went to town last night. They aren't here."

"And the rest?"

"What rest?"

"The rest of the forty."

"Forty?"

Simón's gleeful eyes bounded from Micah to Savannah as

the speed and volume of dialogue increased.

"Forty. Did you not say you expected forty people here this morning?"

"I did not."

"What, then, did you say?"

Savannah reached down and dusted off the top of her foot. She directed her response toward the ground when she murmured, "I said . . ."

"What? I can't hear you."

This time, she looked up and rested her annoyance on Micah's face. Those gray eyes held as much smoke as the room held dust.

"I said 'four-ish.' "

"Four-ish? You have a congregation of four?" Micah gripped the edge of the dais until his knuckles turned white. He unclenched his jaw when he detected fear in Simón's face. Benita took one of the boy's hands and patted it as she and Roberto exchanged mortified expressions.

"Things haven't gone well, in the spiritual sense, since my father departed," Savannah said as she smoothed her skirt. She upped her chin in what appeared to be an act of defiance. Or, perhaps it was a warning.

Micah ran his hand over his jaw, inducing it to relax. He smiled.

"Let's begin, then."

Chapter Five

Savannah poured generous servings of steamed milk and sugar into her coffee, and stirred the mixture with enough vigor to slosh the drink over the sides of her cup. Her anxiety over her circumstances prevented sleep the night before, and after dozing just as the sun poked its rays over the hillside, she arose with a headache and an equally sharp temper. She took her coffee outside and lowered herself into her favorite chair.

The mental "what if" list followed her to the veranda. What if Micah was the last man to answer her advertisement? What if the authorities followed up with their threats and sent her back to the States? What if this marked the end of her sun-soaked, flower-scented Costa Rican mornings?

A shudder gripped Savannah as she lifted her hot drink to her lips. This life could not come to an end. The second "what if" list—the one that kept her pacing in her room most of the night—forced its way to the surface. What if she kept Micah? Although it wasn't a list, per se, the question generated enough fodder to fill an encyclopedia.

At the sound of footsteps, she knew he'd arrived. Without turning to acknowledge him, she said, "If you're ready for your interview, please take a seat." She closed her eyes at her rudeness. Did she have to act this way? Yes. No. Maybe?

He stood over her and extended the carafe. "Would you like some more coffee? Warm up your cup?"

She squeezed her eyes shut, held out her cup, and nodded. After he filled her cup, he lowered the carafe to the barrel that sat in the space between the two chairs, and took a seat.

"Did you sleep well?" she asked. She would be civil, if nothing else. When she glanced at his face, Micah's dark eyes and kind demeanor fought with Savannah's desire to dislike the man. He was handsome and owned a comely smile, which he chose to share in spite of her cold tone.

The calm manner in which Micah reacted to yesterday's episode in the chapel took Savannah by surprise, as did his sermon. He delivered his message with practiced skill, and with the zeal and passion of someone who spoke to a crowd of thousands, not a reluctant congregation of five.

Regardless of what may have transpired in Micah's past to induce him to respond to her advertisement, he displayed spiritual depth and a fierce love of the Lord. That, Savannah had not anticipated; thus, the midnight pacing in her room.

"Quite, well," Micah replied. "And you?"

Savannah answered with a closed-mouth grin and a sip of coffee. She put her cup down.

"I promised you an interview. Shall we begin?"

"What would you like to know?"

"I want to know of your heritage. Keller is what? Austrian? German?"

"German. My father immigrated to America at the turn of the century."

"You don't look particularly German."

A broad smile spread across Micah's face. "You mean I look like the locals?"

"The Ticos? Well, you have to admit . . ."

"Early in his career, my father worked in San José."

"Here?" Savannah interrupted. "You father worked in the capital?"

"He was a doctor, but had an itch to travel. After his training and over the course of a few years, he worked his way from Texas to Mexico to Costa Rica. It was here that he met and married my mother."

"Were you born here?"

"Yes."

"You're a citizen?" Savannah sat taller in her seat. This would allow Micah to remain in Costa Rica forever. A highly favorable trait.

"I am. I lived here until I was four, at which time my parents moved to Texas. I studied at a divinity school in Austin and took a staff position there when I graduated. I also served as an unpaid assistant to the pastor of my church."

"When did you come back to Costa Rica?"

"It was at my mother's request. Since my father is deceased, my mother asked that I return with her. For the past few months, I've lived in Alajuela, where I was born. My mother plans to stay there, as my uncle has taken her into his home."

"Alajuela? That's awfully close to Poas. Don't you find that intimidating?"

"The volcano hasn't erupted since 1929. I choose not to worry."

"Why did you come?"

"Here?"

Savannah nodded.

"Your mission is in need of a pastor. It is my calling and my duty to preach."

"And the part about marrying the departed pastor's daughter?"

Micah's cheeks and neck warmed, but he held his gaze steady when he said, "I assumed anyone who might risk an unconventional and rushed marriage was motivated by a deep-seated need to serve the people at this mission." He raised his eyebrows and lifted the edges of his lips when he added, "I expected more than five people to have served as your motivation."

No, no, no. It was *not* Savannah's turn to blush. She would not let this man—charming as he was—usurp control of this interview. She cleared her throat.

"Have you ever been married?"

A flicker of unease crossed Micah's face before he answered. "I was engaged to marry."

Savannah tipped her chin and stared at Micah until he squirmed.

"The day of the wedding Ruth—my betrothed—and the best man fled the back door of the church and eloped." His pout seemed to say, "There, are you happy now?"

Savannah's hand flew to her open mouth. She tapped her finger against her lips while she tallied his pluses against his minuses. What did he do to make his bride run away? Would she, too, want to escape? In her case, however, she wouldn't know until after she said, "I do."

"I am ready to begin anew," Micah said, his tone serious. "Yes, I was jilted. I seek a new congregation, a new start. You are in need of a husband. Before I submit a formal proposal, may I interview you, Señorita?"

Savannah shifted in her seat, crossed and uncrossed her legs, and smoothed her skirt. Just as she determined Micah to be a suitable answer to her dilemma, he sought to question her? None of the others dared quiz her about her background, her faith, or her character.

"Me?" Her voice squeaked. Not a good start.

"Where were you raised?"

"Kansas."

"What brought you to Costa Rica?"

"The Dirty Thirties."

Micah scowled at her response. "The Dust Bowl?"

"That and the stock market crash in 1929 rendered our futures rather bleak. Father knew how to farm, but one cannot reap a crop from dust. When he heard of Costa Rica's lush vegetation, its gentle people, and their success with coffee and banana plantations, he brought us here."

"Us?"

She'd not intended to upturn that stone. "My mother, my brother, and me."

A shadow accompanied Micah's furrowed brow. "Your mother and your brother—are they late?"

"Dead? No. Mother grew tired of the poor start my father managed once we got here. She took my little brother and went back to live with her sister."

"She abandoned you?"

"I suppose you could say that. She wasn't happy here. My father and I, on the other hand, thrived in this place. I can't imagine living anywhere else."

"Please tell me about your late father."

Savannah sucked in her breath and said, "He's not really late . . . he's just departed."

"I don't understand."

"Departed. He departed Costa Rica and sailed back to North America."

"He's not dead? You're not—how did you describe yourself?—orphaned?"

"I've been abandoned. As if I were an orphan. Is that not similar enough for you to understand my plight?"

Indignation flashed in Micah's narrowed eyes. He blinked several times while he measured her news. In the ensuing silence, Savannah crossed her legs again. She pushed a lock of hair away from her face and waited.

"I see how you might feel orphaned, but I can't help but feel you employed deliberate phrasing in order to bring a prospective husband to do *your* bidding, and not necessarily the bidding of the Lord. Otherwise, why the intimations?"

"It was not my intention to deceive. My father's abandonment unsettled me, and in my haste to find a solution, I might have misconstrued my words. My purpose for the advertisement, however, is quite succinct. I need to find a suitable spouse who has the heart to keep this mission alive." Savannah swept her hands across the vast expanse as she asked, "It's magnificent here, is it not?"

"It is."

Micah grew silent as he lowered his gaze to the floor. Savannah's heart generated a distinct thud. He didn't want her. Just as she decided to accept the anticipated proposal, he intended to leave.

"Do you have any more questions for me?" Savannah asked. Her voice was playful, her smile coy and inviting.

Micah stood and said, "No. None at all."

∼

Micah wiped his damp forehead with his handkerchief, one of two his mother embroidered for him. He exchanged a worried glance with her as the small gathering waited for the last person to arrive. A nervous glimpse at his watch notched his angst to a higher level, but when his mother tugged at his shirtsleeve, he shook his head and mouthed, "Everything is fine."

He didn't know Savannah well enough to trust her promise. Was he to be made the fool—a public spectacle— here, too? It was bad enough in Texas, but in Alajuela, where others held his mother in high esteem, it would be unforgiveable. Micah looked heavenward and prayed, *Please, don't let me be the source of my mother's heartbreak.*

Micah, like the others, turned toward the sound of hooves against the cobblestone. When the traditional two-wheeled ox cart, with its colorful wheels and frame, came into view, his heart calmed at the sight, only to pick up its beat as he regarded the cart's lone occupant.

Roberto led the white and brown ox; Benita and her sons walked behind the cart in which his bride-to-be sat. Savannah wore her hair pulled back and adorned with a halo of tiny white flowers. Her cheeks and lips wore a splendid rose hue. This woman, this stranger, stole his breath and pushed aside his ever-present misgivings.

Micah ran his hand along the embroidered front of his tunic, a handsome gift hastily made by his mother when Savannah admitted she was not up to the task typically carried out by the bride. Her skills, she told him, lay in nurturing the coffee and cocoa crops, not in household chores. Roberto caught Micah's eye and rewarded him with a wide smile—one full of knowing. Too much knowing.

A short celebration followed the simple ceremony,

conducted by the evangelical pastor who married Micah's parents. Too soon, Micah kissed his mother on her forehead, exchanged hugs with his uncle's family, and led the way to a tired pickup truck.

He helped Savannah climb into the passenger seat, and lent a hand to Benita as she wiggled next to his bride. Roberto, Simón, and Pablo waited in the truck bed, Pablo having stretched into a prone position, his head cradled by a bag of coffee beans. As the sun fell below the horizon, Micah began the short journey back to Misión de Cacao.

Chapter Six

"That's it?" Micah asked.

"For today." Savannah shrugged. "The berries got a late start. We'll harvest more. Be patient."

Be patient? How did the residents of the mission intend to feed themselves? Feed the chickens, the goats? This coffee and cocoa enterprise was a joke, and without a congregation to provide for its pastor, his wife, and the resident caretakers, the financial forecasts for the immediate future were grim.

"Do you want me to go? I barter well," Savannah said.

"You barter well? The agent threatened to throw you in jail last time you tried to influence his price. No, I'll go."

Micah created a small explosion of dust when he slapped his hat against his thigh and climbed into the truck. The more he learned from Roberto, the more Micah appreciated that his role was not to re-establish what the departed-not-late Sherwood Hamilton nurtured and managed when he oversaw the mission, but to *establish* a viable operation. Misión de Cacao, at the present, housed neither a congregation nor a self-sustaining agricultural venture.

When he arrived at the broker's place of business, a small crowd waited outside the office door. One of the coffee farmers stood on the porch, punctuating his words with wild gestures.

"I'm telling you, the world isn't just watching Germany. They are suspicious of everyone of German heritage."

"That's nonsense," one of the others called out. "Some of us were born here. We're citizens."

"They claim our German ties will persuade us to aid the Führer's cause," the speaker on the porch replied.

"What German ties?" the second man asked.

"Coffee. They buy our coffee."

"So do the other European countries."

The man on the porch waved his hat in the air until he had the men's attention again. "Hans," he said as he pointed to the office door, "calculates that Germany buys upwards of forty percent of our crops."

Micah took a step back towards his truck. Forty percent? If things deteriorated with Germany's aggressive behavior, the coffee farmers risked losing forty percent of their income? His queasy stomach, already roiling at his present economic condition, churned.

He finished his business with the broker's assistant and double-counted the few colóns he collected for the paltry crop. After purchasing necessities—which included a number of last-minute substitutions—he shoved the meager remnants into his pocket and began the drive back to the mission.

Micah's mind wandered as much as his truck rambled down the road. He had no need to rush back; in fact, without a resolution to their predicament, and in light of the exchange at the broker's office, the need for solitude and quiet became urgent.

He pulled the truck to the side of the road, and finding no place to sit, he dropped the tailgate, and climbed aboard. With his arms behind his head, he gazed at the immense mass of blue overhead.

What had Savannah called Costa Rica? Magnificent. Yes, it was. Mild, green, lush, majestic, and more. The geography itself was reason enough to want to live here. But the people made the desire more so. The potential for Germany's behavior to induce strife and rift among the Costa Rican population sounded absurd, but Micah knew better. The Great War, appropriately named, was not far enough in the past to ease his anxiety. No one escaped the global reach of that event.

~

"Did you bring me something sweet?" Simón asked. He wore a look of anticipation as Micah dropped a small parcel into the boy's hands.

"Not this run. Sorry. Can you take this into the house?"

Savannah stood on the veranda and watched Simón's face and shoulders crumple in disappointment. Micah always brought Simón a surprise. Why not today? Had her penny-pinching husband turned into a miser? She tsk'd to herself as she walked to the truck.

"You didn't bring anything for Simón?" she asked. She set her jaw in an attempt to bury her annoyance. A sweet for the boy was such a small thing.

"I didn't have money to spare," Micah replied.

"You didn't get a fair price, did you? I should have gone and bartered. I knew it." She didn't mean to kick the tire. Well, yes she did. She didn't mean for Micah to see her do it.

He looked at her with an expression she couldn't read. Whatever it was, it looked like trouble.

"I got a good price. Something else came up. I'll put the

supplies away if you'll make coffee. We need to talk."

Savannah was unfamiliar with this particular side of Micah, although at present, the two still knew very little about each other. Interesting the way these lessons transpired. Some silly; some not so pleasant. What did coffee say about a conversation? Hmm?

As she started back toward the house, Micah said, "Wait. Let's have a cup of chocolate instead. Simón should have something sweet." Yes, Micah had a soft heart where Simón was concerned.

As she stirred sugar and chocolate into the warm milk, she envisioned Micah with a boy of his own. It was plain to see he had the makings of a good father. Unlike Savannah's own father, who held to hope more than effort, Micah stood ready to put in a good day's labor to make ends meet. Beyond that was his dedication to his pastoral calling.

Attendance on Sabbath still numbered six, including the pastor, but at least all arrived on time, clean and attentive, unlike their first such gathering. Savannah felt the skin around her eyes crinkle as the image brought a smile to her face. She had not given Micah a fair or kind introduction to Misión de Cacao. The man had a good heart . . . and a greater abundance of patience.

Simón skipped into the kitchen and took a seat at the table while Micah, who carried a box of supplies, lumbered in after him.

"Cocoa. Gracias Señorita Savannah."

"Who?" Savannah asked.

"I forgot. Gracias Señora Keller."

"Much better."

"Perhaps he should call you by the title most familiar to him," Micah said.

Savannah pulled her shoulders back at the odd remark, but Micah's solemn expression pushed back her retort. "Why don't you take that outside?" she said to Simón.

Once he was beyond hearing, Savannah lowered herself to a chair, poured mugs of cocoa for the two of them, and asked, "What happened today?"

"Some of the coffee farmers fear reprisal for the activity underway by Adolf Hitler. Some say it is likely that we will be banned from exporting to Germany."

"How much can that affect the growers here? We export to all of Europe."

"Germany buys forty percent of our annual yield."

Savannah choked on the cocoa and covered her mouth with her hand until she caught her breath. "I wasn't aware of that. Why, the entire country could suffer if an embargo is initiated."

"Nothing may come of it. It was all talk. Just the same, I want to prepare for extenuating circumstances."

Savannah didn't mean to scoff, but really, they lacked the wherewithal to prepare. "How is that possible?"

"We need to plant a variety of crops, not to sell, but to feed our families. Instead of a sweet treat for Simón, I purchased vegetable seeds."

"Seeds? You want to plant a vegetable garden?"

Micah nodded. "I hope the project is unnecessary, but I believe it is in our best interest to begin. Now."

"I suppose it's a prudent endeavor, but if we find ourselves with two tons of squash, we'll have to share it with the community."

"No, Savannah. No one can know about this. We cannot produce enough food for the community. If need arises and others discover we have resources, they will take them from us."

"You'd let the others starve?"

Micah answered her with an unwavering stare. Should she take solace in the moisture that collected in his dark eyes? He wanted to protect them.

"We must have a conversation with Roberto and Benita," Savannah said. "Their boys, too. But no talk of war around Pablo and Simón. Tell them we do this to feed ourselves if the coffee and cocoa crops are insufficient."

"I'll talk with them after dinner. Right now, I need to walk the property and determine the best location for our garden."

As Micah stood, Savannah reached for his hand. "You don't think Germany will bring the world into another war, do you?"

"They invaded Poland, and they turned against Russia, who used to be their ally. If the Germans continue to grab for power, who knows what havoc might follow?"

Chapter Seven

December 1941. Benita sent Simón to the chicken coop to gather eggs while the others hunched around the radio. The static, louder than the announcer's voice, scraped against Savannah's frazzled nerves while weariness wrapped around her blossoming frame. In just one month, she'd face a different fatigue, one of night feedings. She fidgeted in her seat but found little relief.

Given the events of the past few days, she didn't know whether she waited in hopeful expectation or dread. Perhaps a little of both. The distress on the faces of Roberto, Benita, and Pablo paled in comparison to Micah's obvious alarm.

"Shh," Pablo said. "Listen."

The pangs that flitted through Savannah's core had nothing to do with motherhood and everything to do with President Roosevelt's declaration of war with Japan. Another war? Japan retaliated against an embargo placed on its exports following its takeover of French Indochina—by bombing Pearl Harbor? The newsman's reports were inconceivable, horrifying. Hawaii conjured visions of palm trees, the expanse of ocean, the wonder of a peaceful country—much as one might describe this beloved Costa Rica. The similarities weighed on Savannah's heart.

Thirty-five-hundred dead or wounded, 350 aircraft destroyed or damaged. The Pacific Fleet was no more; and the Arizona? One couldn't find words. More than 1,100 lost. Pearl Harbor would never be as it was. It wasn't possible.

"Surely the United States and Japan consider Costa Rica neutral," Benita said. "Our declaration of war against Germany during The Great War was a farce, really. Nothing but a meaningless piece of paper that foreign countries didn't recognize. We're safe here."

Micah ventured a glance at Savannah before he answered, "Let's pray we stay out of the fray, but we need to be cautious and prepared."

When fists pounded on the door, Pablo went to investigate. He returned with Albert Shuler, the farmer who owned the property adjacent to the mission.

"Did you hear?" His voice was breathless, his face pained. "We joined the Allied forces."

Savannah knitted her brow. Reporters broadcast the news of the allegiance three days ago, December eighth. Everyone knew that.

"Yes," Micah said.

"No, you don't understand. There's more."

"Come in, Albert." Micah motioned to Benita to turn off the radio. "What have you heard?"

The elderly neighbor took in a deep breath and said, "They're building a concentration camp."

Micah shrugged a shoulder. "The Americans?"

"Them, too. Their president issued orders to detain all citizens of Japanese heritage. They're locking them up."

"No," Savannah said. "Roosevelt it too smart a president to have a knee-jerk reaction like that. You must have misunderstood."

Mr. Shuler pointed a finger at Savannah when he said, "Do you think I misunderstood this?" He pulled a newspaper out of his jacket. When he turned the headlines for all to see, Benita clutched her throat. Savannah couldn't see the reaction of the men for the tears that flooded her eyes.

~

"Randall? I thought you returned to the U.S." Savannah inspected the elderly man, one of the dismissed suitors who had answered her advertisement for a husband. He looked different—not his shaggy gray hair or his worn clothing—but his demeanor. Instead of the defeated frown and sagging shoulders of a reticent candidate, he regarded Savannah with something more akin to provocation. His pale blue eyes darted about the premises, as if he searched for something.

"Is Micah home?" Randall asked as he leaned to one side and peered over Savannah's shoulder so he could see inside the house.

She stepped sideways and forward, and closed the door behind her as she walked onto the veranda. The tone behind Randall's three-word question was strident, impatient.

"He's next door. Mr. Shuler needed help repairing the roof on his house."

"He'd better hurry so he can keep the rain out while he's rotting in jail."

Savannah stepped back at the suggestion. "Why do you say that?"

"I hear things. Shuler's got ties with the Nazis. Micah ain't doing you no favors by helping your neighbor. They'll think the two are conspiring."

Savannah put her hands on her hips and spit her answer.

"They're doing no such thing, and you know it. Everyone knows the internment camp is a joke."

"If you say so," Randall answered while he wore a satisfied smirk.

"What do you want?" Savannah asked. She crossed her arms, drawing Randall's attention to her swollen belly. In response to his condescending glower, she tipped up her chin.

This wasn't her first altercation with Randall Miller. The man was more than peeved when she notified him he was not the suitor she sought. He dallied at the mission for weeks, complaining that he needed to find work at one of the other farms before he could vacate the temporary quarters Savannah provided for him when he first arrived. It wasn't until Micah brought her home after their wedding that Randall left.

The last she'd heard, his new employer, who owned the banana plantation located a few miles away, fired Randall. She figured he'd gone home. Then again, judging from his unkempt appearance, he probably lacked the funds he needed for travel.

"Looking for a job." Randall stretched his neck again as he made a show of surveying the property. He acted haughty and superior, having forgotten about his own ragged appearance. "You got plenty that needs doing here."

The comment was an understatement, but did not convey the totality of the mission's current situation. They had the muscle needed to fill the potholes that challenged the integrity of the truck's suspension, and they bartered for what they needed to work the crops and mind the animals. They could patch things if they had the wherewithal on hand, but couldn't replace anything. What they lacked was money.

Dear old daddy, Sherwood Hamilton, didn't own a keen financial molecule in his person. Not only did the mission fail to make money under his tutelage, he left the operation with a fair amount of debt. Were it not for Micah's influence and promises of more timely payments, creditors might have booted the lot of them off the property.

In the months since Savannah and Micah married, they repaid everything. Which left them with nothing to spare. For now, their existence was hand-to-mouth. That they'd made it so far was a relief to Savannah. Now this man aimed to shame her by pointing out what they'd *not* managed to accomplish? She thought not.

"We have plenty of work, but we aren't in a position to hire anyone. Sorry." Savannah turned, as if to go back into the house.

"I didn't come to ask you, Señora. I came to speak to the man of the house." Randall narrowed his plucky blue eyes and curled the edge of his mouth in an expression of contempt.

Savannah set her jaw, sucked in air through her nose until her chest filled, and put her hands on her hips again. "Don't patronize me."

"Ooh, what big words you use. 'Don't patronize me,' she says. Such a clever woman." Randall leaned forward until his face was close enough for Savannah to smell the acrid odor of his decayed teeth.

"What's going on here?" Micah strode from the corner of the house and bounded up the steps to the veranda two at a time. He yanked off his hat and slapped it against his leg, creating a tiny dust storm as flecks of dirt fell to the floor. His hair and brow were damp with sweat; under his arms, rings of moisture stained his work shirt.

Randall glared once more at Savannah before he squared his shoulders and turned around to face Micah. When he replaced his condescending tone with something more appropriate for a job applicant, Savannah pulled her lips together and tapped the toe of her right foot against the floorboards. Micah didn't needs words to understand that message.

"Good day to you, Micah. I've come to speak with you about a job."

"She already told him no." All three adults turned toward the corner of the house. Simón, who must have been on tiptoe, stood at the edge of the veranda with his elbows planted on the floor and his chin resting on upturned hands. His stance looked cherubic, his face innocent and pensive. His words, though, levied his accusation right where he intended. Simón did not like Randall Miller.

"Is that true?" Micah asked Savannah.

"Yes, but he thought he needed to hear the answer from you," Savannah said. Randall refused to acknowledge her steady glare, but she gathered some satisfaction when he shuffled his feet.

"She's right. We can't take on anyone right now. Don't have the money for wages."

"I can work for room and board," Randall offered.

Room and board? Savannah could only hope the whites of her eyes were wide enough to remind Micah of the vast quantities of food Randall consumed. She relaxed when amusement flickered in Micah's eyes.

"You eat too much," Simón blurted.

Savannah had to drop her eyes to her feet. She needn't make fun of Randall.

With what appeared to be some effort, Micah took on a

solemn tone when he said, "Can't afford to feed anyone else. Not right now. We're sorry." Micah stepped toward the door, but Randall moved to block his path.

"You're making a mistake. You need me as much as I need a place to stay."

"What makes you say that?" Savannah asked.

"When the Nazi-haters come after your German husband, I can attest to his political activities—or not. I'm not just offering to work for you. I'm your insurance."

Savannah opened her mouth to give an angry reply, but Micah shoved Randall toward the steps before she could utter a word.

"You aim to have someone take you into their home because you threaten blackmail?" Micah stuck his fingers against Randall's chest and pushed. "First of all, I'm not German. I'm a citizen of Costa Rica—the United States too. I'm not a Nazi sympathizer. Everyone knows that. Get off this property."

"And don't come back," Simón yelled as Randall stepped away from the veranda and started walking toward the road.

Savannah wasn't fast enough to shield Simón from the crude gesture Randall shared as he left his angry audience behind.

Chapter Eight

Micah stood at the dais and studied the faces of those who gathered for the Christmas Eve service. The sparse attendance reflected the unspoken attitudes of the townsfolk. These days the majority of the area's residents treated those of German, Italian, or Japanese ancestry—and anyone remotely associated with them—with suspicion.

Before the declaration of war, the congregation had grown from the original five—Savannah, Roberto, Benita, Simón, and Pablo—to about twenty. Today? The only person brave enough, or perhaps nosy enough, to join the original five was Randall. Micah turned the man away when he sought employment; he would not reject anyone who entered the sanctuary to worship, whether his presence was that of a genuine worshipper or that of a man seeking evidence that authorities might construe as treasonous.

Micah's countenance lifted when he considered that the size of the congregation would increase at the first of the year. Babies counted, especially the one he and Savannah awaited.

Savannah sat next to Simón. She wore her long straight hair loose over her shoulders. The luminous summer sun left streaks of gold in her chestnut brown locks and stained her cheeks with a pink glow, both of which accentuated the startling quality of her pale gray eyes. Would their baby look like her, or would it carry Micah's dark hair and eyes? Would the child prove to be cautious and level-headed or an unconventional free spirit? Regardless of the little one's innate characteristics, Savannah's uninhibited inspiration would render the latter tendency rather likely.

When Savannah looked up and saw Micah shaking his head, while obviously taking inventory of her, she blushed. He looked down at this notes and prepared to begin the service.

A cool evening breeze invited itself into the open door, flitted down the aisle, and tousled Micah's hair before it conceded its influence to the wall at the back of the chapel. As he delivered his message and prayed with the small flock entrusted to his care, the distant sound of doors slamming and raised voices filtered into the room.

Randall inclined his head in the direction of the noise, shuffled in his seat, and coughed into his hand. When Pablo gave the man a sideways glance, which looked more like a warning, Randall folded his hands in his lap and directed his attention back to Micah. In return, Micah locked his gaze on Randall. The man's eye twitched and his cheek flinched. He knew something.

They were in God's house, celebrating the birth of the Savior. Micah would not let Randall Miller steal this sacred moment from his family, his congregation. Micah nodded to Benita, who took her place at the front of the chapel.

She lifted her voice in song. "Away in a manger," she began. "No crib for a bed. The little—"

The scream that carried from the neighbor's property lifted the hair on the back of Micah's neck, and served to

40

silence everyone in the chapel. He exchanged a worried look with Roberto. Pablo was already on his feet and halfway to the door.

"You'd better stay here," Roberto said. He placed a firm hand against Micah's shoulder, and although he dipped his head towards Randall, his directive excluded any mention of that particular threat. "Stay with the women. You don't want Savannah fretting over you." He turned toward Simón, who waited at the door, and said, "Son, you stay here with Pastor Micah and your mother."

Without a word to any of the others, Randall coughed into his hand again, sidestepped Simón, and walked out of the building. Micah stood at the door long enough to confirm that Randall headed back towards the road, and not in the direction of the neighbor's property or the mission homestead.

~

"Savannah, you need to sit down," Benita said for the hundredth time.

"I'm fine," Savannah answered as she paced in the kitchen. "You need to put Simón to bed. It's late."

"No," Simón wailed. "Not before Papá and Pablo come back."

"Come, little one," Benita said. "If you won't go to bed, come sit with me and be still."

Although the boy's face wore weariness, his furrowed brow spoke of his fear. His big eyes searched for comfort, for a promise that all was well on this Christmas Eve. Savannah folded one arm over the other and massaged her shoulders. Was all well? Roberto and Pablo had been gone for more than an hour, and although no one cried into the night air again, muffled sounds of vehicles moving and doors slamming continued to filter through the night air.

Micah's boots were heavy against the veranda's wood floor. Savannah heard his footsteps pause from time to time. She knew he wanted to join the men. He knew he needed to stay at the mission.

Why did Randall choose tonight to return to Misión de Cacao? Did he arrive for the Christmas service, or was he privy to the events unfolding next door? The refusal to hire Randall notwithstanding, was he neutral? Friend? Foe? Accuser? Spy? Who knew? Not to be trusted? That, Savannah knew.

When Micah's footsteps fell silent, Savannah walked to the door and listened to the quiet murmuring. She detected Pablo's tenor pitch and the deep resonant quality of Roberto's voice, but she could not discern the conversation.

Savannah stepped into the darkness and cleared her throat. "Please. Tell me."

Micah leaned close to Savannah and whispered into her ear. His breath was warm on her neck. "Go in. Tell Benita they've returned. Once Roberto assures Simón everything is all right, and after Benita puts the boy to bed, we'll talk. Go on. We'll be right in."

With the boy asleep in his bed, and Benita back in the kitchen, Roberto pulled in a deep breath and said, "The authorities arrested Albert Shuler. They've taken him to San José. Labeled him an enemy alien."

"What about his wife?" Savannah asked. "And the children?" Rosa, a Tico, was much younger than Albert; their children were all under the age of seven. The woman had to be terrified.

"They permitted his wife to call her family. She packed one suitcase for herself, one for each of their four children, and after her father arrived, they left with him."

Micah rubbed the side of his chin with his thumb while he took in the news. "What else?"

Pablo, who looked more angry than worried, said, "We stayed back, so we couldn't hear everything."

"You weren't hiding, were you?" Savannah asked.

"They knew we were there," Pablo replied.

"Albert asked who would care for the property in his absence," Roberto said. "They told him the government would appoint a local businessman to operate the plantation. If a suitable manager is not identified, the government will assume the task."

First an arrest based on unfounded accusations? Then the government appropriating the farm? This was outrageous. It was already difficult for Savannah to breathe, given the late stage of her pregnancy. The injustice done to her neighbors squeezed her chest until she feared she might choke.

"What about their home? Their possessions?" she asked.

"One of the officers said they would send a truck to pick up their personal belongings. He said they would put them in storage for safe-keeping." Pablo spit his next statement. "You believe that, of course."

Micah's dark eyes wore a look of defeat. "Shuler has a large, profitable farm. He has much to lose." Micah took in the meager collection of essentials that filled their kitchen. "We have nothing here. We can only hope and pray that the authorities leave us alone."

"Everything about this is wrong," Pablo said.

Benita put her hand over Pablo's fist, but the action did little to ease her son's angry countenance.

"What about Randall?" Savannah asked. "Do you think he knew something? Is that why he came tonight?"

Pablo shoved his chair away from the table and stood. He scoffed when he said, "He tried to hide behind one of the trucks, but we saw him. He watched the whole thing."

"He makes me uneasy," Roberto said.

"He had to understand why we didn't hire him. It's obvious we don't have anything to spare here," Micah said. "Randall might be self-centered and annoying, but he's not stupid."

"He may be smarter than you think," Pablo said.

"Why do you say that?" Micah asked.

"I followed Randall when he crept around the property and went behind the equipment shed. I saw one of the uniformed men pass something to him. Randall must not have thought that the man was trustworthy. He counted his payment before the two parted company."

Savannah didn't know whether the kick to her stomach came from Pablo's news, or in the form of a tiny foot against her womb. Regardless of the cause, the movement took her to her knees.

Chapter Nine

February 1942. Savannah studied the uniformed Tico troops who stood watch. Why the government chose this site was unimaginable. This place sat among San José's treasures, including the stately Teatro Nacional, the country's foremost architectural wonder. This entire situation was inexcusable.

Workers started and completed construction of the internment camp—this albatross—in record time. *La Tribuna* reported that the internment camp housed up to 400 men, all of whom held the now-infamous distinction of being of German, Italian, or Japanese descent.

Never mind that the list of potential Nazi and Japanese sympathizers compiled by the U.S. Embassy in San José included many who held Costa Rican citizenship. Never mind that the men on the list had businesses to run, property to maintain, and families who relied upon their provision. Never mind that many of them had never stepped foot in the countries of their ancestors.

Except for a few folks at the mission, and his mother and uncle in Alajuela, no one seemed to mind that the list included Micah Keller. No one seemed to mind at all.

Savannah, along with dozens of other women, sat in a long line of chairs. Three-week-old Alegría slept peacefully in her arms. The baby jerked at the sound of chairs scraping the floor, but didn't awaken. Her perfect full mouth imitated the motion of a babe nursing at her mother's breast.

"Tell me, does this resemble anything that the newspaper described?" asked the woman to her right.

Savannah offered a weak smile. Better not to have a conversation with someone whose husband was on the Black List.

"What did the reporter say?" the woman continued. "This place is like a dormitory with kitchens and dining halls. They called it 'very accommodating.' Those were the words. 'Very accommodating.' All lies. I see a stark institution enclosed by electrified fences. As if our husbands were cattle who might stray." The woman's voice seethed through her clenched teeth.

Savannah turned her body away from the angry visitor. They had much in common as far as their opinion of the events that led them here. Savannah, however, did not voice her anger. She didn't dare.

She stood when she saw him enter the visiting area. He looked handsome as ever, but a veil covered his delightful, loving eyes.

"You shouldn't have brought her here. This is not a place for an infant." Though he scolded Savannah, he reached for his daughter. "She's so beautiful." Micah closed his eyes and when he opened them, tears brimmed. "Are you all right? You look lovely, but tired."

"We're all fine. Well, not fine, but we're managing. Simón is my designated mother's helper. He's wonderful. So gentle, so loving."

Now it was Savannah who had to wipe her eyes. Tears came easily these days, days when she and her husband should have been basking in the joy of parenthood. Instead? She saw guards, fencing, wire, and distrusting glances passed among the jailers, the confined, and the visitors, alike.

"Why are you here, Micah? This is ludicrous."

"I don't know why my name was on the embassy's list."

"Neither do I. Don't they have to produce evidence that you are—what was their term?—an enemy alien?" Savannah wanted to spit as she spewed the two words from her mouth. Enemy? Alien? The man was passive as a lamb. And he held both Costa Rican and American citizenship. How was he an alien? How?

"Keep your voice down." Micah threw a wary glance toward the sentry standing closest to them. "Why am I on the list? I suspect it has more to do with my father than me."

"Your father? How? The man is dead." She hadn't meant to sound so cold, but Micah didn't seem to have noticed her terse tone.

"While he practiced medicine in Mexico and Central America, prosperous and well-connected people sought my father's services. Most regarded his medical training as superior to that of the locally trained physicians. I suspect some of his patients included outspoken individuals who were considered hostile to their governments."

"But you are not your father."

"The U.S. and others have chosen to assume that children inherit and hold to their parents' political bent."

Savannah compressed her lips, leaned closer to Micah, and asked, "I intend to get you out of here. I'll go back to the government offices every day until they hear my plea."

"You can't do that. They'll arrest you too."

The furious storm that enveloped Savannah's body threatened to explode into a vicious tirade, but Micah's imploring eyes seemed to penetrate her soul. As her respirations revved up and her nostrils flared, she bit the inside of her cheek. When the guard looked in her direction, Savannah dropped her eyes to the ground.

"Think of the baby. Become invisible." Micah lifted the tip of Savannah's chin and locked his solemn brown eyes on her. "Quit going to town altogether. Let Roberto and Benita go."

"But—"

"No 'buts.' Be invisible. Be mute. Besides, I don't know how long they will keep me here."

Savannah sat up in her seat. "You think they plan to release you? Then why are we having this conversation? It's about time. This entire event has been irresponsible, inhumane."

"Shh." Micah's eyes widened at the volume and venom with which she delivered her declaration. "That's not what I meant. I don't expect them to release me. I think they plan to move me."

When Savannah gasped, even the guard turned around. She covered her mouth with her fist.

"They've sent some of the men away. To the United States. I hear they plan to deport some to Germany in exchange for American prisoners of war."

"They wouldn't," Savannah said.

"Nothing is predictable in wartime. I suspect the rumors hold some truth." Micah glanced at the uniformed watchman, who had the power to end their visit on a whim. "If they send me away, I want you to go to my uncle's home. He will take care of you, as will my mother."

"I can't, Micah. I can't leave the mission. You know that. Roberto, Benita, Pablo, Simón. I am responsible for all of them. And besides, we have ample food there. The vegetable garden is teeming, and even that old banana tree is producing fruit. If this situation continues for any length of time, we may have nothing but the food your wise seed purchase provides for us. Please don't ask me to leave."

The guard pointed to Micah and gestured that he was to go back inside.

As Micah stood, he kissed Alegría's brow and handed her back to Savannah. "As long as Roberto is at the mission, you have my blessing. You must promise me you will go to Alajuela if he leaves."

"I will. I promise."

Micah pulled her into a fierce hug and nuzzled her neck. He kissed her gently on the lips, released his hold, and followed his keeper back into his 'very accommodating' prison.

~

Savannah waited in the truck, but only because Roberto threatened to walk to the internment camp to demand a visitation with Micah. She didn't need to add to Micah's worries. He didn't need to know she still accompanied Roberto to town when they sold their coffee and cocoa crop and purchased necessities for the mission.

Savannah endured more than a few stares from the Ticos, those people who used to greet her as a friend, a member of the community. Now she found herself on Muy Bella's unwritten Enemy Alien list. The power to the north, the country in which she was born, called it the Black List; her adopted Costa Ricans sometimes referred to it as the Proclaimed List. Regardless of the title, it provoked division among the residents. She'd never known people carried so much hatred, all of it driven by fear.

The official edict, the *Directiva de Accion Democratica Costarricence,* fed the fury. The proclamation printed in the June 28 issue of *Diario Costa Rica* sounded like sheer nonsense to Savannah, and fueled her refusal to heed both Micah and Roberto's directives not to leave the safety of the mission's compound. Why, the idea of hiding there was nothing less than self-imposed imprisonment. One detained resident was already too many. Besides, Savannah gave people more credit than those two worriers did.

This whole "Enemy Alien" affair was ridiculous. That's what the official proclamation was. Rubbish. She pulled out the worn document, which marked her place in the book she brought along to read while she waited for Roberto to run errands. She'd read and translated the article so many times she almost had it committed to memory.

BLACK LIST or "PROCLAIMED LIST" for COSTA RICA. To Costa Rican citizens and Allies of the War against the Totalitarians. Patriot Costa Ricans should not deal with people or businesses named in the Black List or "Proclaimed List." Do not buy from enemies of Democracy; the money you spend will be used to attack yourself. We must economically liquidate those who sympathize with the crimes of the Gestapo. War is death. Totally against them or with them.

Following the proclamation were four columns with the names of the accused, none of whom received any type of hearing. Micah's name fell toward the end of the second column. Her Micah. Why? Why was he on the list and not some of the others? Who had the power to choose? To accuse?

Savannah folded the paper and slipped it back into her book. She was too annoyed to read anything else. And tired. Alegría slept through the night most of the time, but now as her first tooth pushed its way to the surface, the baby wailed at night more than she slept.

The sun warmed the truck's interior while a gentle summer's breeze swept in one window and out the other. Savannah slouched in her seat and closed her eyes. She didn't remember resting her head on the bench seat, and when the squeak of the driver's door alerted her to Roberto's return, it was all she could manage to get out of the way as he slid into the truck, started the engine, and peeled away from the curb.

"What's wrong?"

"We have to get you back to the mission. Now." Roberto checked the rearview mirror repeatedly while he maneuvered the truck around vehicles and pedestrians.

Savannah sat up straight and craned her neck as she looked at the path from which Roberto retreated. When he braked to avoid hitting a large dog as it loped across the street, several men shouted from the sidewalk and raised their fists in the air. As Roberto accelerated, Savannah watched one of the men pick up a large bottle and hurl it at the truck. She covered her face with her hand and ducked as shards of glass spewed into the truck cab.

"Stay down," Roberto yelled. "Pray they don't follow us."

Savannah's empty arms weighed heavier than the alarm that hovered over the two travelers as they made their way back to the mission. Alegría. She had to reach her daughter. Where, though, might anyone find a safe haven in this war-torn world? Never in her life had she felt so vulnerable. And alone. *Micah, we need you.*

~

The noise in the streets was relentless. Every guard stood stock-still. Ready. Anxiety lined their faces. Clenched jaws twitched at every crack of glass and shout; their fingers hovered over the triggers on their guns.

They feared the citizens might direct their violence to the camp, and for good reason. Regardless of the catalyst that provoked the violence beyond the fenced perimeter, the site was a large target filled with detainees the government labeled enemies.

Perspiration dotted Micah's forehead at the same time his body shivered, as sirens, gunshots, and machine gun fire erupted into the air. The tense sentries ignored the internees' shouts as they begged an explanation. Who started a riot? Why? Who was in danger? Did the German and Japanese residents start the uprising, or were they the target of the aggressors?

Micah considered his plight as the world unraveled, not inside the camp, but outside. His wife and daughter were outside. Were they safe? He could only hope the disorder stayed within the confines of the city. Misión de Cacao was situated well beyond San José, but if this escalated, who might protect his family?

The local authorities knew the mission held nothing of value. Although the team that inspected the property claimed to seek evidence relating to the accused's subversive activities, everyone knew the search gave the inspectors opportunity to abscond with anything they desired. They were looters, thieves. Rumor among the detainees was that some officials seized not only personal property, but entire plantations and businesses. Just as his former neighbor, Albert Shuler, warned.

Aside from the dirt upon which Misión de Cacao rested, the premises offered little to quench the thirst of the greedy examiners. Micah found some comfort, if not a little humor, in Savannah's report that the team left empty-handed—but that was before this unexpected battle emerged in the streets of San José.

"Savannah, be careful," he said under his breath.

Micah paced until the value of that exercise proved as futile as his anxiety was powerless. From his place of incarceration, his only influence rested in his prayers—and that bequest was to give all control to the Lord.

Savannah stood in the doorway and held Alegría against her shoulder while she tried to soothe her daughter's cries. The little one seemed to sense the unsettled atmosphere that walked into the door with Roberto and Pablo after their trek into town. The fuss surrounding the instrument resting on the tabletop stoked Alegría's irritability and summoned a sense of shame. Savannah braced herself for the scolding.

"Where did you get that?" Benita whimpered and drew back against the wall, as if the radio might electrocute her. She looked at her husband. "Roberto?"

He shook his head without answering her and turned to Pablo. "Go to the window. If you see anyone—"

"I know," Pablo said.

Savannah absorbed Benita's angry stare while Simón inserted the cord into the socket and adjusted the radio until the static fell away.

"They'll throw all of us in jail if they hear about this," Benita said between clenched teeth.

"Then they'd better not hear," Roberto said.

His apparent defense of the situation took Savannah by surprise. Although he didn't voice an opinion, he knew the government's overreach was inexcusable. Still, this seemingly innocent situation smacked of dissident behavior. The consequences were dire.

"Where did you hide it?" Benita asked.

"I did it," Simón replied. "When the men came in their truck, I heard them talk about guns and radios. I hid it in the chicken coop. It stinks in there. They didn't look very hard." He finished his explanation with a shrug.

"Did you know about this?" Benita asked Roberto.

"Shh. Let's listen."

"It's a good thing you didn't have guns," Benita muttered under her breath.

Aside from the news gathered during Roberto's infrequent trips into town, those residing at the mission knew little of the events transpiring across the globe as countries fought each other. Savannah knew about the radio, but didn't dare risk its use. Until today.

Riots in San José? Where? Were the detainees safe or were they the object of the unrest? She had to know. She'd put the radio back as soon as she knew Micah was safe, and not a moment before . . . unless the authorities arrived at their doorstep first.

The person who delivered the local broadcast, in Spanish of course, spoke in a strident, excited voice, and at a speed that rivaled that of a 33⅓ rpm record played at 78 rpm. Savannah caught some of the words, but couldn't decipher the report in its entirety. What did U-boats have to do with San José?

By the time the short news clip ended, Savannah's head swam. Alegría, who must have sensed her mother's growing unease, yowled.

"Shh." Savannah whispered into her daughter's ear and rubbed the infant's back. "All is well. Shh." When Alegría quieted, Savannah settled into a chair while Simón unplugged the radio and hauled it back to its hiding place.

"You know I didn't understand the broadcast," Savannah said to Benita.

Benita leaned back in her seat and looked at Roberto for help, but it was Pablo who started to speak. Now seventeen, Pablo looked and acted more like a young man than a youth. Tonight his eyes wore the same angry sheen Savannah first saw when Pablo and Roberto witnessed the arrest of their neighbor.

Roberto put his hand on Pablo's shoulder and replied to Savannah's comment. "A German submarine torpedoed the San Pablo, a ship owned by the United Fruit Company."

With her free hand, Savannah covered her mouth with her fingers. "Where was the ship?"

Pablo's jaw twitched before he said, "Docked at Limón."

"The ship wasn't at sea? It sat at a dock on Costa Rica's Atlantic coast? But why? Why would they sink a ship—a fruit ship?" Bile rose in Savannah's throat. The Costa Rican government declared war with Germany, but this tiny country wasn't a threat to the Nazis. This didn't make sense. Was this despicable act simply a show of force?

"Twenty-four Costa Ricans died." Roberto's voice trailed off as he lowered his head.

Savannah exchanged a panicked look with Benita. "What

happened here?"

"A riot," Pablo said.

"It wasn't a rumor?" Savannah asked.

Roberto shook his head. "The reporter said that the Ticos were so angry that they looted the German-owned businesses."

"More than 120 businesses. Stripped bare," Pablo said. "Seventy-six injured; a hundred German and Italian residents arrested."

"What about the internment camp? Was anyone hurt?" Savannah asked.

"The broadcaster didn't mention the camp," Roberto replied.

"Tell her what the president said." Pablo looked at his father as he made the statement, and when Roberto stiffened, Savannah held her breath.

"President Guardia didn't call them riots. He called them demonstrations. He said they 'greatly pleased him' and that the 'fifth column would be exterminated.' "

"But," Savannah said as tears washed over her cheeks, "the Germans who live here aren't the fifth column. They are farmers, coffee growers. Pastors, husbands, and fathers. Like Micah. They aren't here to undermine the government. Is anyone—anyone at all—able to stop this madness?"

Chapter Ten

August 1942.

"Mamá? The teacher put a new pin on the map today." Simón carried a bowl of plantains to the table and went back to the counter to pick up a platter loaded with grilled vegetables.

Savannah regarded the pained expression that darted across Benita's face. While most parents thrilled at the promise of their children advancing in knowledge, the frequent updates regarding the world map in Simón's classroom were hardly welcome achievements. At the same time, as all were reluctant to risk bringing the radio from its hiding place, the situation left the adults at the mission starved for news.

The teacher kept track of the countries that joined the war—regardless of the side they supported. If Simón grasped the situation and retained the truth of the teacher's comments correctly, those countries that supported the Allies' efforts earned a red pin. A black pin represented their foes.

"What did you learn?" Benita asked as she dried her hands on a towel.

"She put a pin in Brazil. It's not far from here." Simón used his arms and hands to form a large circle. "Pretend this is the whole world." He let his circle fall away and raised one hand. He pointed to the area above his fingers and said, "Costa Rica is here." He pointed to another spot toward the bottom of his palm and said, "Brazil is here."

"Did she tell you what happened in Brazil?" Savannah asked.

"It was a red pin. Brazil is not a . . . ¿Cómo se dice enemigo en Inglés?"

"How do you say 'enemigo in English?' " Savannah repeated. How fitting was the Spanish word for enemy. It looked and sounded like 'not amigo,' not a friend. "The word is enemy."

"That's right. I forgot," Simón replied. "Professora said Brazil joined the war. It is not an enemy. The people who live there got mad, like they did here when the Germans sank the fruit boat."

"They had riots in Brazil?" Benita asked.

Simón nodded. "The Germans sank their boats too. Lots of them."

Savannah smashed a bit of soft plantain and slipped the top of the spoon between her child's lips. Alegría's eyes widened with pleasure as she swallowed the sweet fruit.

"Shh. Listen," Roberto said. "It sounds as if a vehicle is approaching. All of you stay here." He stepped onto the veranda, and while he waited in the doorway, Savannah heard the creak of metal as someone navigated down the pot-holed path.

Goose bumps gathered along the base of her neck as the unexpected visitor drew near. Few travelled at night, and the driver's decision to leave off his headlights suggested the visit held an untoward purpose or was intended to catch the residents by surprise. Neither likelihood sat well with

Savannah. When she glanced at Alegría, fear clutched her chest. This child, this innocent babe, sat quietly, her tiny mouth open for the next morsel of food. Between anxious glances toward the door, Savannah managed to feed Alegría tiny bits of plantain.

When the vehicle's motor stilled, Savannah expected to hear a door close and footsteps rushing toward the house. Instead, silence filled the night air. This visit wasn't official; it was covert. And probably illegal. Savannah did what she did best when anxiety washed over her. She picked up Alegría and started to pace.

Roberto stepped into the kitchen, put his fingers to his lips, and gestured for the visitor to come in. The caller kept his head down and his collar up, until Roberto closed the door and the window curtains. The man held a parcel in his arms.

Simón pushed away from the table and sped past Benita before she could grab him, but Roberto stopped his inquisitive son with a hand to each shoulder.

"What is it?" Simón whispered. "What did you bring?"

When the visitor turned his head, the shadows fell away. Savannah knew the face, but didn't recognize the behavior of the man who owned it. "Dr. Gutierrez?" she asked.

"Forgive me. I didn't know where else to go." He looked at everyone in the room and said, "Please, I don't have much time."

When the parcel moved, Simón stepped back so fast he landed on his backside. "Wh-wh-what is it?"

The sound emitted from beneath the covering was a whimper, a tiny mew.

"You brought me a kitten?" Simón asked as an excited glimmer filled his eyes. Roberto helped Simón to his feet, but held the boy in place.

Savannah's mouth fell open as understanding reached her hearing—and her heart. Recognition wrapped around Benita, too. She stood up, crossed the room, and took the small bundle from the doctor.

"Whose child is this?" Benita asked. She lifted the cloth and exposed the face of a tiny newborn.

Savannah recoiled at the sight. She'd never seen a baby so small before. Yet, further inspection confirmed that it had the characteristics of a full-term baby. Dark hair framed the perfectly formed features. In the dim light, the infant dared a blink at its audience. The eyes were dark, probing.

"She belongs to Lucia Greco."

"Marcelo's wife?" Roberto asked.

"Yes," the doctor replied. "The man who owned the bakery before—"

"Before his arrest," Savannah said. She knew of the situation. Police seized Marcelo Greco in the aftermath of the riots two months earlier. Looters destroyed his shop, his livelihood.

"Why are you here?" Savannah asked. "What's wrong with Lucia? Does she need a wet nurse?" She pressed Alegría closer to her bosom. Although she didn't plan to wean her baby any time soon, the idea of taking care of another woman's infant caught her off guard.

"Señora Greco refused to go to the hospital because she had no money. She thought they might turn her away, her being Italian and all. When a neighbor called for me, I went to the Greco's home. Or what was left of it. They had an apartment above the bakery." Dr. Gutierrez cleared his throat and pressed his lips together before he said, "She hemorrhaged. I couldn't save her, but I aim to save her daughter. Please. Take her."

Savannah stepped back. "Take her?"

"What kind of a future will befall this child, this *Italian* baby, if she is given over to a government who deems her an enemy? Please don't make me hand this infant over to the authorities." The physician's forehead furrowed. The man looked exhausted, disheartened, and utterly defeated.

"How can we take her?" Savannah asked. "When they come for Lucia's body, they'll expect to see a baby. How will you explain its absence?"

Dr. Gutierrez's shoulders slumped when he said, "She had two babies. Twins. The boy died with his mother. No one needs to know about the girl."

Savannah tightened her hold on her sleeping daughter. Lucia didn't get to hold her child, her children. Their father sat in an internment camp not far from here. Soon he'd learn that he'd lost his wife and his son. Wasn't it wrong to keep news of his daughter's birth from him? This tiny infant belonged to Marcelo Greco.

For more times than Savannah could count, she felt Micah's absence. What was the right thing to do for the father and for the baby? Savannah prayed, but she didn't know how to listen to God's answers very well. Micah did. He'd know what to do. But Micah wasn't here and the doctor had little time to spare before he had to notify people about Lucia's death.

"But how can we explain the baby's presence here?" Roberto asked.

"I'll say she's mine," Benita said. "Ours."

"Have you lost your mind?" Roberto asked.

Benita pulled her baggy dress away from her body. "Look at me. I'm large. I wear my clothes loosely. The baby is so small. We can tell people she came early. Look at her dark hair, her coloring. Not so different from me. It wouldn't be hard to deceive anyone. Not hard at all."

Deceive. Micah wouldn't like that description, its implications. Still, Savannah couldn't see Micah turning this baby away. The right thing to do was to take the child. Savannah was certain of that. The right thing to do after Marcelo Greco gained his freedom, would be to return the child to him. When Savannah looked at Benita, she buried the knowing that Benita would do no such thing.

When Roberto protested, Benita fired back in rapid Spanish, and for the next several minutes, she, Dr. Gutierrez, and Roberto exchanged more words and emotion than Savannah had the ability to follow, much less comprehend.

Simón stood silent during the discussion, but when Benita looked at Savannah and said, "It's settled," the youngster raised his arms toward the baby.

"I get to name her. I want to call her Paloma."

"Paloma?" Benita asked.

"Because she's tiny like a bird."

Savannah brushed the baby's cheek with her fingertip and said, "Paloma. Dove. It's perfect."

Dr. Gutierrez's troubled face failed to reflect any hint of satisfaction in placing the child with people who would care for her and love her. He thanked them awkwardly, put on his hat, and made his way back to his car.

As the sound of the vehicle's motor diminished, Pablo dashed into the kitchen. His clothes were dirty from his long hours of work at the coffee broker's compound.

"What's wrong?" he asked. His gaze tore from one person to another, but stalled when he saw Savannah nursing the baby. His eyebrows arched high on his forehead as he turned his head and focused on Alegría, who was asleep in Benita's arms.

Simón ran up to Pablo and tugged on the sleeve of his work shirt.

"Guess what, Pablo? Mamá had a baby while you were at work today. You have a new sister."

~

Few rumors circulated among the internment camp population, probably an end product of distrust. A wide chasm separated the detainees, with political bent defining the demarcation. While it seemed apparent to Micah that the Allies fought for freedom and justice, a number of the prisoners were quite vocal about their support of their homelands.

Among those incarcerated in San José, those of German descent—and those individuals whose businesses and properties were confiscated or destroyed following their arrests—were the most hostile and uncooperative. More than once, Micah chose solitude over conversation during those times in which the detainees had opportunity to interact with one another.

When Micah's jailer walked one of the inmates to the yard, the man sitting next to Micah leaned sideways, and in a low voice, he said, "They're sending some of the prisoners to concentration camps up north. Before the year's up."

"Up north? Where?" Micah asked. He reacted as if he hadn't heard of the possibility months ago. In his heart, Micah expected to be among the individuals selected for relocation, especially given his dual citizenship. Why not send a U.S. citizen back to the U.S.? Somehow, though, during the long delay between the first rumors and the news of the pending action, he'd pushed the concern aside.

"California. Maybe Texas." Anger simmered in the man's tone, in his closed fists, his clenched jaw. "I'm not going."

"As if you have a choice," Micah said.

"I do. I volunteered for repatriation. My family too. The U.S. will make the travel arrangements. It's that simple."

"You'd rather expose your family to violence, to invasion or occupation, than to wait out the war in the safety of the United States?" Micah considered Savannah and Alegría. If he had to choose between a concentration camp in the U.S. and a flat under attack or under siege somewhere in Europe, he'd exchange his freedom, and theirs too, for their safety.

"You make it sound as if this internment camp is a family holiday," the inmate said. "I'm hardly the only person who hates the U.S. and the Ticos for what they did to us. Open your eyes and look at the injustice." The man scoffed as he swept his gaze over the compound. "If I had a gun, I'd take down every single one of them."

"Keller," the guard yelled. "Tu visitante está a la espera." His visitor was waiting? Micah already knew that. The bigger concern? How long would Savannah have to wait—really?

The words of his fellow detainee spun around in Micah's head as the officer led him to the visiting area. When he saw Savannah's face, he donned the mask of confidence and relegated the inmate's gossip to a crevice in the far reaches of his mind.

She looked lovely, as always. And sad. She smiled for him, but her eyes said she wept for him. For them.

"Savannah, love. Where's Alegría? Is she ill?"

"She's cutting another tooth and she's miserable. The guards wouldn't give us more than a two minute visit if she started screaming." Savannah looked down. "I'm sorry. I know you wanted to see her."

"Don't be sorry. I'm grateful to see you." He was. He couldn't tell her this might be the last time he saw her until . . . well . . . until the world returned to some sense of order. Who knew how many months might pass between now and then?

Savannah sat up straight. "I have some cheerful news."

She didn't look cheerful; she looked pained.

"Really?"

"Benita and Roberto have a baby girl. Paloma."

"A baby? Why, that's wonderful, but why didn't you tell me before?" Micah studied the slight downturn of Savannah's brow. Why did his wife have to think before she answered what should be a simple question?

"They didn't know. She came as a surprise. Such a tiny thing." Savannah raised her gaze from her lap to Micah's face. Her smile was strained, fake.

"Is she well?" A fair question, but Micah fought to find the one that might explain Savannah's less than enthusiastic announcement.

"Yes. Just tiny."

"What then? Do you lack food, clothing? Is something amiss at the mission? Is Randall bothering you again? What?"

"No. Nothing. Everything is fine."

"You're not telling me something. I see it in your eyes."

She turned away at the remark. Micah needed to tread softly, but they had so little time.

"Please talk to me. What's wrong?"

"We're all fine. We're well." She locked her serious gray eyes on him when she said, "I promise."

"How can I pray for you if you won't confide in me? I'm

your husband. The one who loves you more than life. Savannah? Tell me."

"Keller. Se acabó el tiempo. Ven conmigo." The guard's *Time's up. Come with me* directive came far too soon. When Micah stood, he wrestled with the overwhelming desire to grab his wife and run from the camp. Whatever she held back from him exacted a distressful cost. How could he help her if she wouldn't disclose her needs? The more realistic, but bitter, question: How could he help her if she shared her burden? In this place, he could do nothing. Nada. When he glanced over his shoulder before the guard pushed him through the doorway, Micah's fortitude, like his heart, shattered into a million pieces.

Chapter Eleven

Two weeks after Paloma's birth, Dr. Gutierrez parked his car in front of the mission homestead and knocked on the front door. Savannah saw him, but it took several minutes for her to descend the hill, as she tested each downward step before she took another. Carrying Alegría on her back challenged Savannah's balance, but kept her hands free to tend to the coffee and cocoa crops.

When she reached the visitor, she dusted her hands on her skirt and wiped beads of sweat from her forehead.

"Is Señora Vargas here?" the doctor asked.

"No, she and Roberto went to the coffee broker's."

The man looked around, lowered his voice, and asked, "How is the little one? Is all well?"

"Paloma? She's fine." Savannah's bosom tingled at the thought of the wee one and her voracious appetite. "She's a hardy eater. She won't stay little for long."

"I'm happy to hear that."

The thought of the babe's dead mother and unaware father replaced the good report with an air of solemnity. "Were you able to handle the Greco's situation?" she asked.

The good doctor winced at the question and shuffled his feet. "All went as expected. It proved to be a difficult set of circumstances, but I believe the outcome is as best as we could have hoped." When Dr. Gutierrez looked at Savannah, his eyes held equal measures of gratitude and guilt. She understood.

"Can I help you with something today?" she asked.

Dr. Gutierrez pulled an envelope from his pocket and handed it to Savannah. "This is the birth certificate for Benita and Roberto's baby. I think they'll find everything in order."

Savannah hadn't considered the need for the paperwork, nor the implicit deception the doctor penned when he put his signature on the legal document. This certificate erased any hope of restoring the child to her father, should the opportunity ever present itself. A wave of misgiving descended on Savannah when she accepted the envelope. Her complicity in the act resounded as clearly as a judge who struck his gavel on the top of his desk. Case closed.

"I have one more thing I need to discuss with you," the doctor said. He gripped the band of his hat as his fingers tightened into a fist. "When I drove away from here that night, after checking on the Vargas' baby," he said as he looked at Savannah, as if he wanted to make certain she agreed with his tale, "someone was hiding in the bushes near your veranda."

Savannah couldn't swallow the knot that encircled her throat. When she remembered, she blew out a welcome speck of relief. "Pablo. It was Pablo. He came into the house just after you left."

"No. I saw Pablo walking along the road as I pulled away from the mission. This was someone else."

"Did you recognize him?"

"It looked like the older American who stayed here at the mission for a while. Before you and Señor Keller married."

"Randall." Savannah's shoulders fell. "I heard the man who runs Shuler's plantation hired him." If Randall was on the mission property, his purpose couldn't have been forthright. Perhaps he meant to steal some of the produce in the garden or eggs from the chicken coop, but what if he meant to spy on them? Randall's threat rang in Savannah's ears as clearly as if he'd spoken it yesterday: *When the Nazi-haters come after your German husband, I can attest to his political activities—or not. I'm not just offering to work for you. I'm your insurance.*

"I don't know that his presence means anything at all," Dr. Gutierrez said, although his tone convinced neither the teller nor the listener. "Who's to say whether he heard anything? Just mind yourself where he's concerned. We all have much to lose if he knows what happened that night."

"Yes. Thank you."

The doctor nodded, put on his hat, and went back to his car. Savannah watched him as he drove away, but closed her eyes as Randall's words echoed in her mind. What did he know?

~

Savannah heard a car door close somewhere in the distance. Rapid footsteps clapped against the wood floor of the veranda, followed by a fist pounding the front door.

She bolted upright and listened as the footsteps trailed away from the house and padded down the dirt path. A car door slammed, an engine turned over, and the sound of a motor faded.

More than once she conceded that she needed an escape plan. More than once, she failed to fabricate such a plan.

What was she to do now? Roberto and Pablo, her potential defenders, were fast asleep in the caretaker's quarters. Savannah and Alegría were alone in the main house. Alone and vulnerable.

Savannah crept out of bed and tiptoed toward the front door. Through the open window she heard . . . crying? A small voice. A whisper, and then a whimper.

When she dared open the door a crack, the moon rested its long brilliant reach over two tiny forms. One wiped fists at tearful eyes while the other opened her eyes wide, inspecting the stranger.

Savannah scanned the darkened landscape, but knew no one was nearby. The adult who banged on the door meant to abandon these two. Savannah looked at the crescent moon and the star-studded expanse overhead. While God's heavenly handiworks went about their predictable duties, His two-footed earthly creations ran amok. How could someone—anyone—even in wartime, forsake their children? She ached for their loss as much as the children feared their inexplicable circumstances.

She knelt on the floorboards and reached for the older child. "What's your name?"

The girl, who looked about three or four years old, tilted her head. Her puzzled expression suggested Savannah try again.

"¿Me puedes decir tu nombre?"

Once again, the girl angled her head. This time she arched her eyebrows. If she couldn't even say her name, how could Savannah hope to communicate with either of them? When another thought flitted into her mind, the implication caught her breath. Oh dear.

"Was ist dein Name?"

The girl's eyes lit up.

"Brigitte," she said as she hugged herself with her arms.

Savannah pointed to the younger child, who had longish hair but looked rather boyish. She needed to get them inside. One step at a time.

"Dein Bruder?"

Little Brigitte nodded. When her brother whimpered, she grabbed his hand.

"Rolf," she said. The boy's damp eyes implored his big sister to fix things. To take him back home. Savannah's heart ached.

"Sie haben einen anderen Namen? Einen Nachnamen?" The wrinkled forehead that met that question silenced any others that might follow. The little girl didn't know her other name, her last name, and Savannah had expended her paltry allowance of conversational German. No matter. She didn't need words to offer them food, a bed, and a strong measure of love.

She reached her arms towards Rolf and picked him up, and then she offered a hand to Brigitte. "Come. Come in."

~

"What do you mean, you have two more?" Micah pressed his thumbs against his temples, as if the action might reconfigure the words that just came out of his wife's mouth. If it weren't for the guard standing ten paces away, he'd take her by the shoulders and shake her. "Savannah?"

"Someone abandoned them. Left them at the mission in the middle of the night. What was I to do?"

"Take them to the authorities. That's what you *will* do. Think, woman. They'll charge you with harboring the enemy." His diatribe sounded preposterous even as he said it, but it was the truth. Some bureaucrat or extremist could use those children as pawns in a war game. Their presence at the mission put everyone at risk.

"What would the authorities do with them? The city doesn't have an orphanage. If it did, do you think the administrators would open their doors to two German children? Do you think the officials will house them with you men, here at the internment camp?"

"Of course not," he replied.

"Consider this. If something happened to me while you're detained here, what would become of Alegría? Would you want Benita and Roberto to turn her over to someone—some *authority*—in order to protect themselves?"

Micah clenched his teeth on that one. As much as it pained him to agree, Savannah was right. But "right" didn't keep his family safe; it put them at risk.

"You need to find the parents."

"We tried. Pablo found out who they were, but not before they fled the country. I can't toss the children aside as if they were merchandise. They've suffered enough trauma already."

Micah ran a hand through his hair and squinted past the chain link fence and the barbed wire. Government offices were a stone's throw away.

"Maybe we should advise the authorities of the mission's expanded services."

"I don't know what you mean."

"Perhaps you could meet with one of the local officials and tell him that Misión de Cacao has found a need to provide temporary housing for children whose parents have been detained by the government—or, in this case, abandoned by their parents. Ask for permission to put an advertisement in the newspaper. If they support the activity, you won't have to fear for your safety."

"And if they are opposed?"

"They won't oppose you. As you said, the men to whom you must speak will not have an alternative to offer the children. I'm at peace with the idea, but the task falls on your shoulders. Are you prepared to carry that load?"

He looked into Savannah's fair gray eyes. They didn't reflect the color of clouds on a stormy day, but held the sheen of molten silver, warm and luminous. Fetching, but at the same time, a source of his melancholy. He wanted to greet those eyes as each dawn unfolded and as nighttime marked the end of a day well spent—spent with his wife and child. Was there no end to this imprisonment?

"I trust you, and I want to protect those children. I'll do it," Savannah stated.

"What about food and clothing?" Micah asked. "Are the crops sufficient to feed everyone?"

"The vegetable garden is thriving, and we're blessed with abundance. The crops are better, as well. Coffee bushes are flowering more than in the past. God is a trustworthy provider, and we have all we need, Micah. He'll do the same for the children who come to us."

A heavy sigh escaped Micah's lips. Sometimes his burden stifled him, choked him. "I want to be there. To do my part." He hung his head. "I'm sorry for all this has done to my family."

Savannah dared brush his face with her hand. Micah glanced at the guard, who seemed to be in deep conversation with one of the internees. Instead of pulling away from his wife, he put his hand over hers, pulled her sun-kissed hand to his lips, and kissed her fingertips.

"Keller," the guard yelled. "Ven conmigo."

Micah smiled. "It was worth it, love."

As he turned to go, Savannah whispered, "Micah, do what you do best from this place. Pray for us. I love you as far as the east is from the west."

As the guard led Micah back to his quarters, emptiness joined forces with his compulsory solitude and pushed his spirit low. *As far as the east is from the west.* The psalmist's words.

Micah picked up his Bible, with its worn leather cover, and searched the pages until he found it. Psalm 103. Phrases caught his eyes as he skimmed the page: *He works justice for the oppressed. His kingdom rules over all.*

Micah listened to the sounds filtering into the camp from the busy streets of the capital city. As much as he yearned to be with his family, he conceded that God's holy hands held his loved ones in a much safer place than he ever could. Did the knowing make the separation from his family any easier? Micah's arms were so empty that they ached.

Chapter Twelve

November 1942. "Why do I need geography lessons?" Simón asked. He sat at the table in the kitchen, both elbows on the table, and a piece of paper resting in front of him. "Isn't Africa far away from Costa Rica?"

Savannah gathered a stack of bowls from the cupboard while Roberto spooned rice into a serving bowl. When Roberto declined an answer, Savannah looked up and said, "It is far away, but when the world is at war, we get caught up in everyone's messes."

"What happened in Africa?" Roberto asked.

"Professora said the Allies landed in French North Africa. She put pins in Algeria and Morano."

"Morocco?" Savannah asked.

"Maybe," Simón said. "I get mixed up. I thought France was in Europe so how can it be called French North Africa?"

Sometimes Savannah wished she'd studied to be a teacher. Between her haphazard language lessons with Brigitte and Rolf and her occasional assistance with Simón's schoolwork, she recognized how little she knew. She was most comfortable writing the sermons that Roberto delivered each week as he assumed Micah's pastoral duties—that, in spite of the minute size of the congregation.

"Sometimes a country controls a place that is beyond their borders," Roberto said. "France is in Europe, but the French also control French North Africa, which is—"

"In Africa," Simon interjected.

"Yes," Roberto said.

"Professora said Germany captured southern France. Is that France in Europe or France in Africa?"

"Europe. I think," Roberto said. He carried a pitcher to the table and put his hands on his hips as he looked at Simón. "I never thought about those countries either. War might force us to learn things we never wanted or needed to know. Let's hope this war teaches us not to have another one. It's unfortunate we didn't learn the last time around."

Savannah tried to imagine the world globe. Algeria and Morocco? She'd have to guess at their exact locations. Regardless, the tentacles of war seemed to be never-ending and far-reaching. The possibility of a quick finish was as remote as Benita learning how to cook.

Cooking. Not Savannah's favorite chore, but because only she could breastfeed Paloma, the three youngest children became her primary responsibility. Benita made a habit of taking Brigitte with her as she worked outside, but as Savannah and Roberto prepared dinner, they borrowed Simón to keep an eye on the tenacious trio.

Savannah looked at her ten-month-old daughter, now napping in a nearby corner. The rascal already required persistent supervision, and when she advanced from crawling to walking, Savannah suspected she would have to increase her attentiveness ten-fold.

"Roberto, Simón. Come here. Get Savannah." Benita's animated but happy voice, and Brigitte's laughter, came from somewhere beyond the back door. Savannah picked Alegría up from her blanket and glanced at a sleeping Paloma before she scurried after Simón and Rolf. Rolf's giggles erupted before she could see what caused the commotion.

Simón ran circles around a disinterested cow, while Rolf shrank against Roberto's legs. Benita lifted the rope that encircled the beast's neck and said, "Look what I found at the gate."

"You found a cow?" Savannah asked.

"It was tied there."

"Don't you think someone meant to retrieve her?" Savanna asked.

"No." Benita waved a piece of paper. "It says, 'Leche para los niños. La alimentación de la vaca.' "

"Milk for the children. Feed for the cow. It's a gift?" Savannah asked.

Roberto leaned his head toward Savannah and said in a low voice, "Although some of the people act badly towards you, most know you are a good woman. They won't voice an opinion because they are afraid. This is a fine gift for a fine lady."

Savannah walked to the cow and let Alegría run her excited fingers over the animal's reddish-brown muzzle. When the cow snorted, Alegría squirmed in enjoyment and her bare feet wiggled so much that Savannah had to wrap both arms around her girl. Rolf kept his grip around Roberto's leg, but Brigitte stepped forward far enough to tap the cow on the end of its nose.

"You're a brave girl, Brigitte." Savannah knew she didn't understand the words. Not yet. But until that time, they coped quite well with hand signals, facial expressions, and as many smiles as one could form in a day's time. Nighttime hugs and goodnight kisses served up a mountain of love that words couldn't begin to deliver. It wasn't easy, but it was so, so worth the effort and the sacrifices. If not for Micah's absence, and in spite of a world at war, Savannah's life overflowed with an abundance of love and joy.

By the time Benita settled the cow into her new quarters, and they all gathered for dinner, the rice was cold. No one cared. Pablo lumbered into the house, took off his hat, and joined the others at the table.

"Guess what, Pablo?" Simón asked. "Guess what Mamá found while you were at work."

"Another baby?" He fastened his wide eyes on his mother. "Mamá?"

Benita's shoulders bounced when she laughed.

"No," Simón replied. "A cow. We have a cow. "

"That's good news." Pablo grinned at his younger brother, but Savannah couldn't help but notice the young man's creased brow. Something troubled Pablo, and when the others went to check on the cow once more before bedtime, he kept his seat at the table.

"I need to talk to you," Pablo said. "Not now. After everyone's gone to bed, would you meet me on the veranda? Yours, not ours."

"Of course. Are you in some sort of trouble?"

"Me? No." He helped carry dishes to the sink before he walked the short distance to the caretaker's home.

Later, when the dusky sky darkened, Savannah took a seat on the veranda and waited. The scent of a promised rain filled the air. A good shower, a cleansing rain, would be good for the garden and the coffee and cocoa crops.

She watched as Pablo and his elongated shadow crossed the courtyard between the two buildings. When he took a seat next to her, she handed him a cup.

"Hot tea. Chamomile and hibiscus blossoms. It will help you sleep."

"Thank you." Pablo's voice was deep now. The young man sounded and looked more like his father with each passing year.

"How's the work at Shuler's place?"

"If we didn't need the wages, I wouldn't be there. It's not right working for the people who stole the plantation out from under Shuler."

She wouldn't disagree, but neither would she voice her agreement. Words changed nothing.

"I need you to tell me about Paloma."

Savannah's shoulder muscles stiffened. Her grip on the handle of her mug tightened. "What about her?"

"Whose child is she?" Pablo's voice, unlike Savannah's reaction, was calm.

"What do you mean?"

"Do you really think I believe the story about it being a surprise? The only surprise was in the fabrication of the story."

"Paloma belongs to your parents."

"So the birth certificate says. How did they get the doctor to forge the paperwork?" Pablo put his cup on the barrel resting next to the chair. "I don't even care about the papers. I want to know what happened. I want to know why."

"Don't you think you should have this discussion with your parents?" Savannah asked.

"I can't. I know they won't alter their story. I don't want to put them in a situation where they have to lie to me. Again."

"Why do you think the child belongs to someone else?" Savannah asked.

"You mean aside from the fact that the baby's hair is curly, her skin is darker, and her eyes are shaped so differently from anyone in my family?"

"Lots of Ticos have curly hair, Pablo. Don't let your suspicion get the best of you."

"Ticos have Spanish blood, Spanish ancestry. Paloma looks Italian. Not Spanish."

Savannah pressed her palm against Pablo's arm. "I've seen you with that baby. You wear your affection on your sleeve. Why are you asking me these questions?"

"What will happen to my parents when the truth is exposed? Will they go to jail or will the police simply break my parents' hearts when they take Paloma away from them?"

Pablo's intense delivery unnerved Savannah. Words failed.

"Randall knows. He knows about the doctor coming to the house and asking you to take care of the baby. He knows my mother offered to call it her own. He *knows*."

Savannah closed her eyes while the truth swarmed in her head like a host of angry bees. The rapid beat of her heart pounded angry accusations across her forehead.

"What does he want?"

"I don't know," Pablo replied. He brushed his hand over the top of the barrel. "You know what's painted here."

She didn't need daylight to remind her of the endless hours she and her father sat across from one another, maneuvering their pawns, knights, bishops and kings across the surface.

"A checkerboard."

"Randall's setting up the chess board. Putting the pieces into place and warning you that he intends to make the first move. I am not a good chess player," Pablo said.

"Neither am I."

~

"If the government gave your wife an opportunity to join you for the duration of your detention, would she do so?"

Micah blinked. What kind of a question was that? Why would any woman voluntarily commit herself—and her children—to confinement?

"Keller?" The uniformed officer tapped his pencil impatiently.

"I wouldn't want her to."

"What if you, your wife, and your daughter could move to a camp intended for families? One in which you could enjoy wholesome activities and the company of those like you."

"Those like me?"

"Germans. Like you."

"But I'm not German, sir. Neither is my wife. I'm a citizen of Costa Rica; we're both citizens of the United States."

"Semantics aside, you cannot deny you are of German ancestry."

"One of my parents was German," Micah replied, knowing the man had already reviewed the contents of the file sitting on top of his desk.

"So let me ask again. Would your spouse volunteer to join you during your . . ."

"Imprisonment?" Micah offered.

"This is hardly a prison. You receive good treatment here, don't you?" The man's arched eyebrows didn't leave room for an objection.

"My complaint lies with my detention. No one has charged me with a crime."

The officer brushed Micah's comment away with the flick of his wrist.

"The United States has erected a camp that allows detainees to live with their families. Your name is on the list of those who will relocate. It will be much simpler to have your wife and child travel with you, so if you can get her to sign the paperwork, we will process it along with yours."

Micah pushed his shoulders back and with some effort, kept his opinion of the offer to himself. Although rumors circulating among the detainees had merit, Micah didn't trust the man sitting in front of him to tell him the truth. The offer could disguise a forced repatriation of the three of them to Germany. Unbelievable but plausible. Micah needed to tread carefully.

"And if she chooses to stay here?"

"When she realizes she erred, it could take months to reunite you. You need to get her signature when she comes for her next visit."

"Anything else?" Micah asked.

The official ignored the question, looked at the guard who stood by the door, and said, "Get him out of here. Bring in the next one."

Chapter Thirteen

January 1943. "What do you mean, 'He's already gone'? Gone where?" Savannah's fury got the best of her, and although she won admittance to the office of the man in charge, she knew she did so with some risk.

The official, who stood at the window as she entered, looked as if he were inspecting his kingdom. He squared his shoulders and tipped up his nose before he took a seat at his desk.

"The letter your husband gave you was quite clear. You do know how to read, don't you?"

"I know how to read," Savannah said through clenched teeth.

The Tico feigned civility as he opened a drawer, thumbed through some files, and pulled out two sheets of paper. He regarded Alegría who, despite Savannah's too-tight grasp on her daughter, slept in her mother's arms. After folding the papers and securing them in an official envelope, he stretched out his arm and dangled his explanation in his fingertips.

"It takes two parents for a family to function properly," the man said.

"Then why did you arrest—"

The man continued to hold the papers within Savannah's

reach, but at the same time he gestured to the armed guard who stood by the office door.

"This is not the place for you to voice your opinion. As I started to say, we made an effort for you to be reunited with your husband, for you to live as a family unit, but you failed to respond."

Savannah didn't have the foggiest notion what the man meant, but as the guard stepped toward her, she chose to hold her tongue.

"We can help you make arrangements, but the task is much more difficult and time-consuming than it needed to be. Take this letter home. Read it this time. Once you've completed your paperwork, bring it back to me. You may tell the guards that I expect you, and they will bring you to me. Please be prepared to leave Costa Rica that same day. I'm certain your husband will be happy to hear you want to join him. Good day, Señora Keller."

As the man turned his back on her, the guard wrapped his free hand around Savannah's arm and steered her toward the door. When they reached the place where the visitors had to exit the compound, the guard spoke in a low voice when he said, "Your husband doesn't want you to follow him. He wants you and your daughter to be free. He knows you have much work to do for your family and the mission."

"How do you know that?" Savannah asked.

The guard lifted his face and regarded the line of visitors waiting to see their loved ones.

"I know lots of things, Señora. If you choose to stay in Costa Rica, you must be very careful." He opened the door and waited for Savannah to step to the other side. "You must go now. Please do not return."

~

If he hadn't seen it himself, Micah wouldn't have believed human beings had the capacity to treat each other this way. That the Costa Rican and United States governments precipitated this action infuriated him.

First they searched and confiscated luggage. Then they seized the passengers' legal documents: passports, work visas, birth certificates. Every form of identification.

The crew of the Puebla, an armed troop transport vessel docked at the port of Puntarenas, waited to take the internees to San Pedro, California. From there, authorities would process the individuals and make arrangements to send them to their final destinations. Wherever those might be.

The detainees included families with infants, small children, and pregnant wives. Before the crew herded them on board, soldiers separated the men. While some of women wept openly, children wailed. The sight fortified Micah's resolve. He'd done the right thing.

As he followed one of the soldiers, Micah turned at the sound of small feet racing over the deck. The little tow-headed boy cried out, "Papá!" Micah's stomach roiled when one of the soldiers grabbed the child and pinned the boy's scrawny arms to his sides while the youngster kicked and screamed. The boy's tears ripped Micah's soul to shreds.

The uniformed troops escorted the men below deck, to the forward-most part of the ship. There, soldiers divided the seventy or so men into three groups, and stuffed each group into a room that measured no more than seven feet by twenty feet—something more suited for storage than passengers. By his calculation, Micah's share of the space afforded to the twenty-two men in his room, was less than six and one-half square feet. He could only hope that the quarters given the women and children were more humane.

When it came time for the men to eat, which turned out to be twice a day, the men had no other option than to eat standing, or squatting. Since the room was too small for each man to squat at the same time, some of them made do with a corner of the shower room or the lavatory. Nothing in Micah's background prepared him for this nightmare.

As day turned into night, contempt and loathing replaced Micah's hoped-for accommodations. Did these military men underestimate the physical conditions of a ship docked in a tropical climate? The Puebla lacked a functioning ventilation system, and blackout rules forced the crews to seal every porthole after the sun set. This edict affected the men below, and the women and children in the cabins, alike. If they didn't leave port soon, their jailers would have to unload a good number of their human cargo in the form of dead bodies.

After a day of boarding, assignment of quarters, and a night of unbearable heat, Micah waited for the ship to leave port. It didn't budge from its mooring.

At noon on the second day, the crew selected him among those who volunteered to help serve meals to the women and children. That group, he would learn, received three meals each day—but the officers in charge neglected to give them enough time to eat.

The first day he helped with a meal, a whistle blew twenty-five minutes after the volunteers served the first bowls of food. Guards ordered the bewildered mothers, some with too many children to tend, or those with ill children or fussy eaters, to leave their food and exit the room so that the next wave of passengers could eat.

Micah's anger threatened to boil over. Many of the women looked ill, and throughout the dining hall, he heard round after round of coughs that ended with the distinct sound of a whooping crane. Whooping cough. Didn't these seamen recognize the danger of that highly contagious disease? Didn't they care?

Nothing improved on the third day; nor the fourth or fifth. The stench emitted by the men confined to their tight quarters paled compared to the putrid odor that originated from the inadequate and overcrowded cabins to which the crew relegated the women and children.

During the day, when the portholes were open, the cries of the children and the wailing of more than a few women, reached the hearing of their fathers, their husbands. Tempers flared among the confined men, and the cavalier and contemptuous scorn inflicted by the crew upon both the men and the women, festered like an open sore. Micah was so angry, so incensed, he wrestled to fasten his mind and his hope on the Lord. Where was God in this man-made hell?

Finally, the Puebla set out for California after six days at dock. As the motion of the ship signaled its retreat from the shores of Costa Rica, sorrow tightened its grip around Micah's chest. Images of Savannah's smile, and the echo of Alegría's soft cooing voice, nearly strangled him. He squeezed his eyes shut. *God, help her forgive me for leaving them behind.*

Savannah would be livid when she realized he made the decision for her. Yes, he could have discussed the idea of the three of them living together in a detention camp. Yes, she might have agreed with his recommendation that she and Alegría stay at the mission in Muy Bella instead of joining him. But he couldn't risk Savannah's tender heart speaking louder than the reality of the circumstances they might encounter. If this hideous nightmare was an introduction to his immediate future, he had no regrets. His was the right choice. The only choice.

~

After the midday meal, and after Savannah fed Alegría and Paloma, Benita abandoned her task of gathering ripe coffee beans, and relieved Savannah of her childcare duties.

"Take your time," Benita said.

If she dared reply, Savannah might release the sob that simmered just below the surface, something that was sure to wake the babies and scare Rolf and Brigitte. She swallowed her grief, nodded her head, and darted out the back door.

She ran up the hill, tearing between the coffee bushes, higher and higher, until the only part of the mission she could see was the roof of the chapel. After she lowered herself to the ground, she pulled her knees up to her chest and wrapped her arms around her legs. She rocked back and forth until her pent up tears ran their course.

Why didn't Micah ask her? He had no right to make the decision for her. For them. Things were bad enough while they detained him in San José, but at least she knew where he was, that he was safe. She and Alegría could visit. Now? Where was he? Where did they intend to take him? And for how long? How long did he expect her to live without him?

Although she couldn't explain it, the guard's comments to her as he escorted her out of the official's office kept Savannah's anger in check. Something in the man's message, as cryptic and brief as it was, assured her that Micah made what he thought was the best choice. And the guard agreed with him, or so it seemed. For an incomprehensible reason,

Savannah believed she should heed the guard's comments. She would not complete the paperwork, and she would not return to the camp in San José.

She needed to trust Micah. His decision to leave without her, and his deliberate concealment of the offer for her to accompany him, couldn't have been an easy choice. The mocking voice of the officer in charge echoed briefly in Savannah's memory. She would not second-guess Micah's decision, no matter the cost of their separation. But this was so hard, so unfair.

She leaned back on her elbows and inhaled the intoxicating fragrance of serenity. An array of tiny white blossoms dotted the row of coffee plants that extended in both directions. Their jasmine-like scent soothed her broken spirit. She loved this place, this country, this Misión de Cacao, and the man who answered her prayer. The prayer that she executed in the form of a letter, an advertisement for a husband.

The Good Lord knew her bidding was selfish, reckless, and immature. Yet, He blessed her with Micah Keller. The state of the world was madness right now, but in this place at this moment in time, all was well in Savannah Keller's world. She stood, dusted off her skirt, ran her fingers through her tangled hair, and started back down the hill.

When she walked back into the main house, the aroma of onions, peppers, and cumin met her at the doorway. She heard Simón chatting away, as usual, but his tone seemed more excited than normal.

In Micah's absence, God gifted her the family that awaited at the kitchen table. So preoccupied was she with her newfound peace, that it wasn't until she sat at the table, put her napkin on her lap, and looked up, that her eyes rested on an unfamiliar face with wide, expectant eyes and a tentative, hopeful smile.

"Señora Savannah," Simón exclaimed, "I got another hermana while you were gone."

Savannah couldn't help herself. She laughed, got back up, and wrapped her arms around the girl's shoulders. "Bienvenida, Simón's new sister. Welcome."

Chapter Fourteen

Carmita was painfully thin and looked twelve or thirteen years old, but when she spoke, her maturity surpassed that of some of the adults Savannah knew. She was quiet and polite. Savannah wondered at her story, her circumstances.

As soon as dinner ended, Carmita gravitated to the three youngest mission residents and kept Rolf and Alegría entertained while she soothed a colicky Paloma.

Benita and Simón carried out their evening chores, tending to the cow, securing the chickens in the chicken coop, and putting out food scraps and water for the pair of dogs that pretended to guard the property.

Pablo helped in the kitchen, a signal to Savannah that he needed to speak with her again. Savannah wanted nothing more than to finish putting away the dishes and to get Carmita settled into a place where she would feel safe, welcome, and loved. Trouble was, they'd run out of beds. They'd make do, Savannah knew, but the bigger concern was that they'd run out of food. She pushed that worry aside for another day.

"Why don't you have a cup of tea with me later?" Savannah asked Pablo. "I heard the man running the Shuler plantation earns a better profit on his crop than we do. I'd like to know what he does to make his beans more valuable than ours. Maybe we need to introduce some new varieties of coffee plants."

Roberto snorted at Savannah's suggestion. Everyone knew that the mission got next to nothing for their coffee and cocoa beans. The secret didn't lie in the quality of their competitors' crops, but the notoriety Micah earned when they added his name to the Black List. Nobody wanted to buy beans from Misión de Cacao.

"If you'd like some company," Roberto said, "just ask the boy to join you for some tea." He shook his head as he hung a dishtowel over the back of a chair. "Long day. I'm turning in early. Good night you two."

"Good night, Roberto," Savannah said. She turned to Pablo. "I need some time with Carmita. Join me on the veranda later."

Pablo didn't say anything, but he followed his father out of the kitchen and crossed the courtyard to the caretaker's quarters.

"Carmita, let me take Paloma from you. I need to feed her before she goes to bed."

The girl compressed her forehead into rows of tiny lines. "I thought Paloma was Benita's daughter."

"She is. Benita didn't have any milk. I nurse both of the little ones."

The lines fell away, but Carmita's expression remained troubled.

"Come talk to me while I feed her. Come sit." Savannah took the rocking chair in the bedroom and glanced at the shrinking space. The bed that she used to share with Micah rested against one wall. Alegría's crib took up a corner, and the mattress Rolf and Brigitte shared filled all but a small aisle that separated the beds from one another.

"Can I help you put Rolf and Brigitte to bed?" Carmita asked.

"Their nightclothes are in that dresser, in the bottom drawer. You don't need to do that, but I thank you."

Savannah watched as capable hands made easy work of getting the two youngsters properly dressed and tucked into their bed. When it looked as if they'd fallen asleep, Savannah cleared her throat.

"Tell me. How did you find your way to Misión de Cacao?"

Carmita lifted her long hair, twisted it, and released the locks down the center of her back. The sheen of her dark hair matched the glimmer of her mahogany brown eyes. Her skin was clear, the color of almonds; her fingers, long and delicate. In spite of her scrawny build, she was beautiful.

"I never knew my father. My mother had me when she was very young. Fourteen, I think. Her parents were very strict and when she shamed them, they made her leave."

"Where did she go?" Savannah asked.

"She had a sister who lived in Cartago, and we moved in with her family. The year I turned five, my mother met a man and she ran away with him."

"I'm sorry. I know how you feel."

Carmita knitted her brow again. She looked puzzled. "How could you know?" she asked.

"My mother left me too."

Savannah's confession seemed to give Carmita the courage to continue her story.

"I never understood how she did it. Leave me. I love children. I took care of my aunt's little ones. She has six. And these?" Carmita lifted her hand toward the toddlers and the two babies. "How could anyone leave a child?" Carmita's dark eyes brimmed with tears.

"How old are you, Carmita?"

"I just turned fifteen. I know I look younger, but I think it's because I'm little."

"What happened at your aunt's home?"

"I couldn't stay any longer. My uncle. He . . . he started giving me too much attention."

"Your aunt made you leave because she was jealous?" Savannah asked.

Carmita looked down and twisted her fingers around each other. "She helped me leave because she loved me."

Now it was Savannah's turn to look away. She regarded the face of the innocent babe she held in her arms, and then gazed at the solemn eyes of one who was just as innocent. Only not so young. Why was this life so hard? So hurtful?

"My aunt heard about this place. She arranged for one of the farmers to bring me here. Please. I don't have anywhere else to go. I can help tend the children. I can cook and clean, and I can tend to the animals and the crops. Whatever you need. Please."

"Come here," Savannah said.

When the girl stood in front of her, Savannah moved to the edge of her bed and motioned for her to sit down. While she held Paloma in one arm, she took her free hand and brushed a strand of hair away from Carmita's face.

"It's very good that you can do all those things, but you cannot earn a place at Misión de Cacao."

The girl's shoulders slumped and a shiver ran across her shoulders.

"No, no. I don't mean to make you cry," Savannah said. "You are welcome here, child, not because you can earn your keep, but because you need a family. You may stay because you need a home. When we welcomed you at dinnertime, we expected you to stay. Simón has already made you his big sister."

The overwhelmed girl wrapped her arms around Savannah, and Paloma too. She buried her face in the crook of Savannah's arm, and wept. Savannah hoped Carmita was unaware of the tremor that coursed through her own frame. This girl's pain was too much. Finally, Carmita sat up straight, wiped her nose with the back of her hand, and sniffled.

Savannah walked to the dresser, retrieved a handkerchief, which she gave to Carmita, and asked, "Did you bring clothes with you?"

"I'm sorry. I have nothing."

"It's all right." Savannah pulled one of her nightshirts out of the dresser and handed it to Carmita. "Get changed and ready for bed. I'll put a towel out for you. I have to take the baby to Benita, but I'll be right back."

"Thank you."

Savannah leaned forward until Paloma's cheek rested near Camita's face. "Your youngest sister likes good night kisses."

Carmita's eyes teared again, but this time a smile accompanied her emotions. She tipped her head forward and brushed her lips against Paloma's cheek. "Good night, little sister," she said.

Carmita had just enough momentum left in her slender body to whisper a word of thanks to Savannah. She dropped off to sleep before Savannah finished heating the water for tea.

~

"Tell me about San José's coffee business," Savannah said to Pablo. She handed him a cup of tea and leaned back against her chair. Exhaustion bore down on her eyes, her shoulders, her arms, her heart.

Pablo nodded toward the house. "How's the girl?"

"She'll be all right. Just needs a proper family."

Pablo chuckled. "She thought she'd find one here?"

"We've plenty of love to go around."

"Love doesn't fill hungry bellies. I'd like to find a job that pays more, but too many men are looking for work. Much as I hate working at Shuler's old place, I think I need to mind my business and earn a day's wages where I can."

"We're grateful for your income."

"I know you brought the subject up in jest, but let me talk with you about the coffee business. We may be in trouble," Pablo said.

"What have you heard?"

"It's not so much what I hear as what I see. It looks as if Randall has established a lucrative business. He brings suspicious activities—false or otherwise—to the attention of the authorities, and when the government absconds with the offenders' properties, it looks as if Randall gets a percentage of the transaction."

"Like he did with Shuler."

Pablo put his mug on top of the table. He leaned forward, put his elbows on his knees, and folded his hands together.

"He wants the mission. This place is his next target. I heard him talking to one of the overseers."

"But this place has nothing of value," Savannah said.

"That's not true. You've got land, maturing coffee bushes, buildings."

"Compared to the other farms and the plantations, this

place is rubbish."

"Not to Randall. Compared to the 'nothing' he owns, this place is a palace."

Savannah compressed her lips and set her jaw. This plan of Randall's had more to do with getting even for her choosing Micah than owning hectares and some tired buildings. Were all men—all of humanity, for that matter—driven by pride? Were they? If not for pride and all its self-serving accoutrements, the world wouldn't be at war. Perhaps the thought was too simple an explanation, but it was all Savannah could muster right then.

"Do you remember our conversation about a chess game?" Savannah asked.

"I do. Have you practiced since then?"

"No, but now that Randall has lined up his plan and declared his intention, I'm ready to make the first move."

Pablo shook his head and said, "I'd like to see what good that might do. I don't know how you can stop him."

Savannah stood, picked up the two mugs, and said, "Watch me."

Before Pablo could respond, she walked into the house. In the dark, she went into the kitchen and put the cups on the counter. She crept into the bedroom, gathered her bedclothes, and changed in the shadowy room. After she washed her face and combed her hair, she slipped into her bed, the one she used to share with Micah.

Savannah lay on her back and listened to the children's rhythmic breathing: Alegría in her crib, Rolf and Brigitte asleep on their mattress on the floor, and Carmita, who was fast asleep next to Savannah.

No one could earn a place at Misión de Cacao, but Savannah Keller meant to welcome and love those who looked for a place to call home, a place where they would find love. If she were smart, and if she had the Good Lord on her side, she'd only have to make one move to eliminate her foe.

Chapter Fifteen

February 1943. This was not the Texas that framed Micah's youth, nor was it similar to the demographics that shaped his years at divinity school. Neither did Crystal City, which was located just over 100 miles south of San Antonio and within 35 miles of the Mexican border, resemble the place of his birth.

Unlike Costa Rica, with its moderate climate and idyllic scenes at every turn, the place in which the U.S. government erected this internment camp offered either suffocating dust or mud. Nothing remotely between the two extremes existed in this forsaken, barren place.

Before the U.S. State Department reared its power and threatened to boycott all products produced in Costa Rica by German-owned companies; before Costa Rican authorities caved to the will of their dominating neighbor to their north; and before these same Costa Rican authorities seized the businesses and land of the potential conspirators—which conveniently allowed them to reduce their national debts and employ land reforms—Crystal City, Texas was a place where men grew spinach.

A migrant labor force once resided at the camp. Now, German men, most with wives and children in tow, inhabited the area of the camp designated for those of German ancestry. Those of Japanese heritage lived within their own assigned boundaries.

What a joke the legal process was. Micah, like the others, arrived in California where authorities arrested him for attempting to enter the U.S. illegally. No, he didn't have a visa, as the agents in San Pedro denied one to each deportee who disembarked from the ship. In fact, he had no legal documents whatsoever because the authorities confiscated everything before he departed Costa Rica.

Micah, unlike most of those ejected from Costa Rica, held U.S. citizenship. Of course, that didn't lend any credence to his protest of the situation, as his father was of German descent. Distrust carried greater weight than justice did.

So here he was, separated from his wife, his daughter—now one year old—his vocation, and his calling. If Savannah protested his leaving without her, he'd forbid her from joining him—assuming he had access to pen and paper, as well as the right to correspond with his wife so that he could reiterate his previous position.

By the time those who travelled on the Puebla arrived in Texas, their new keepers had to isolate some forty passengers who had whooping cough or impetigo. Had they known of the conditions onboard ship and the condition of the camp at Crystal City, no doubt more than a few of those women who volunteered to join their husbands might have refused the government's offer. They, like Micah, were in this mess for the time being.

This place they called a family internment camp was a sham. Buildings and facilities were still under construction. Individuals employed at the camp, whether in military or civilian positions, looked to be the bottom of the heap in terms of skill and personality. Not that any thinking person would find that situation a surprise.

Crystal City had nothing in the way of amenities, although those in charge promised improvements would come. Aside from having access to the grounds on the other side of the security fence, the employees and guards had about the same level of freedom as the detainees. With nothing located remotely near the camp, conditions rendered their freedom at about the same level as that of the prisoners.

Micah held out for justice, for surely a country such as the United States, one that fiercely defended the rights of its citizens, would reverse these nonsensical actions. Soon. These circumstances had to change.

~

Savannah rocked her torso back and forth and patted Paloma's back, hoping for a burp and not a spit-up mess. Roberto stood just behind her right shoulder, bouncing Alegría in his arms. Three young clerks sat at the front of the warm room. One paltry fan, situated on the floor behind the three, lifted the edges of the papers on the desks with the bored enthusiasm of a child listening to a politician's speech.

The closest thing to a politician in the crowded office was the young man sitting at the center desk. Jorge Diaz was the youngest son of the Municipal Executive, and although he held a college degree, he looked to be about seventeen or eighteen years old.

As the clerk at the desk to the right returned paperwork to his customer, Savannah leaned backwards and dug her elbow into Roberto's ribs.

"I don't think this is necessary," she said between

clenched teeth. Her voice was low, but the seething quality caught the attention of the man who waited behind Roberto. The man stepped back, bumped into the person behind him, and scowled at Savannah.

"We talked about this. Don't start now." Roberto's frown spoke louder than his whisper.

"But—"

"Next," the clerk called out.

"Roberto," Savannah said.

Roberto raised his gaze to the ceiling and shook his head. He turned to the man next in line and said, "Please. Go ahead."

"Let's just leave," Savannah said.

"You don't have a choice." Roberto tilted his head toward the clerks. "Quit stalling."

When the customer finished his business with Jorge Diaz, the young man looked up and waved his hand at Savannah and Roberto.

This time Roberto elbowed Savannah. "Now."

Savannah pulled her lower lip between her teeth, extended her papers toward the clerk, and tapped her foot in protest.

"This is highly irregular," the clerk said while he scratched his chin and read the paperwork again. He looked up at Savannah and said, "I don't think you have the authority to conduct this transaction."

"Why not?"

The young clerk studied the activities of the other two office workers who assisted their customers. While his nametag identified him as the son of one of San José's most influential politicians, his inexperience at his post, as well as an apparent fear of failing to fulfil his duties properly, expressed themselves in the form of a sweaty brow, damp circles under his arms, and a nervous twitch that pulled up one side of his mouth at the same time it forced him to blink.

He opened a folder that he retrieved from the corner of his desk and lifted a worn document. The paper had numerous creases, dirty finger marks, and notations penned within the margins.

"No one on this list is permitted to buy or sell property," he said as he pulled the collar of his shirt away from his neck.

"My name is not on that list," Savannah said.

"No, Señora Keller, but your husband is on this list."

Savannah shuffled six-month-old Paloma from one hip to the other. "He doesn't own the property. I do. Look," she said as she shoved her document in the young man's face. "This is my name and my signature. This legal document says I own the property. Where do you see the name Micah Keller?"

"It's not so simple," the clerk replied.

Roberto, who stood next to Savannah, wore a rather impatient frown, although it was anyone's guess whether the cause was Alegría, who he held in his arms, or the clerk's response to Savannah's request.

Alegría, fussy from the long drive and her need for a nap, reached her arms toward her mother and wailed. Roberto shook his head, traded babies with Savannah, and released an exasperated sigh.

Savannah bounced Alegría in her arms and leaned over the man's desk when she pointed to the bottom of the deed. "Everything is in order. Do you need to seek the advice of one of your superiors? We can wait if you like."

As if on cue, Alegría curled her lower lip and sucked in a silent sob that shimmied across her chest and shoulders before she let loose with a howl.

When one of the co-workers narrowed his eyes at Jorge, and jutted his chin toward Savannah and the wailing baby, Jorge lifted his shoulders and said, "I can handle your request."

He filled out his official forms, all the while Paloma fussed and Alegría cried. Roberto cast apologetic glances to everyone in the room. Savannah cooed to Alegría and patted the child's back. "Shh."

"Sign here and here," the clerk said. He pointed with one hand while his other hand offered his pen. "You understand, of course, that you will be asked to leave the country once you relinquish the property."

Savannah exchanged an angry glance with Roberto.

"What do you mean? I don't want to leave. I can't leave."

The young man shook his head. "It's not up to me. Sorry."

"Wait a minute," Roberto said. "It's one thing for Señora Keller to give me what's rightfully due me, but she owes me and my family much more than the value of the land. Have you ever seen Misión de Cacao? Have you?" Roberto towered over the clerk and made little effort to hide his opinion of the man's edict.

"No sir. I've heard of it, though."

"If you'd seen the property, you'd understand. The buildings are falling apart, the ruts in the drive are deep enough to swallow a truck, and the crops are worthless."

"Then why are you willing to take the property in exchange for the wages Señora Keller failed to pay you?"

"Because she has nothing else. My family intends to make improvements to the property." Roberto glared at Savannah with an expression that made her step backwards. He pointed a finger at the clerk. "If you send her out of the country, I'll never get what's owed me."

"That's not my problem," the clerk said.

"What about the orphans? What will you do with them?"

"The orphans, Señor?"

"The mission serves discarded children. You knew that, didn't you?"

"I did not."

"I have no intention of taking care of those abandoned children. If you deport Señora Keller, you need to make arrangements to collect the children." He turned aside and spoke, as if to himself, "And I'll have to find a wet nurse for my daughter. My wife will be grieved."

Roberto's huff enveloped everyone in the room. Some of the Ticos stared at the bewildered clerk. One young woman, visibly pregnant, tsk'd and turned her face to the wall.

In spite of Alegría working out the last of her tantrum, the sudden lull in activity heightened Jorge's distress. His damp brow now contained a profuse amount of sweat and his co-workers looked at him with disapproval.

"I do not have a place for your orphans," he said. "Perhaps I can make a notation that states Señora Keller is to remain at Misión de Cacao in her present capacity as caretaker of the children."

"Would such a statement carry any legal weight or could it be contested?" Roberto asked.

"I have authority to attest to the need for Señora Keller to remain at the mission. No one will question my signature. I promise you that." Jorge lifted his chin as he sent a threatening glare to the other two clerks.

Jorge scribbled his impromptu declaration at the bottom of the form and turned it around for Roberto to sign.

"I don't mean to impose, Señor Diaz," Roberto said, "but I can't risk anyone attempting to undermine your authority. Should anyone contest this statement, I'd be at a loss to fix things." He leaned forward, as if he had to share a confidence, but did not lower his volume when he gestured to Savannah and said, "I have enough to worry about already. You understand?" Roberto lifted his eyebrows.

Savannah clenched her jaw, turned away, and tapped her foot again. When someone standing in line discharged a tired sigh, it was all she could do to stay in place and keep her mouth closed.

"What more do you want?" Jorge asked.

"Would you be so kind as to ask your two subordinates to sign the paper as witnesses?"

Both clerks tendered wide-eyed stares at Roberto, but glanced back at their desks when Jorge looked in their directions.

The clerks interrupted their work, affixed their signatures, and made a show of the contempt they held for Savannah as they resumed their own tasks.

After Roberto executed the document, he grabbed Savannah's arm, tugged at her until she stood directly in front of the clerk, and handed the pen to her. "Sign."

Savannah tossed her long hair over her shoulder, glowered at Roberto, and frowned at the clerk.

"Fine."

After Jorge pressed his official seal on the paper and handed it to Roberto, Roberto pulled his lips into a thin line, his smile an obvious chore, and said, "Gracias, Señor."

"Good day," the clerk said. "Next."

Savannah kept her head bowed and pulled Alegría tightly to her bosom as they exited the offices and hurried down the sidewalk. She didn't wait for Roberto to open the truck's passenger door. She climbed inside, closed the door, and squeezed her eyes shut.

Roberto opened the driver's door and when he took his place behind the steering wheel, the truck's suspension jostled.

"Can you take Paloma?" he asked. His voice was smooth, matter-of-fact.

"Anything you want," Savannah said.

When Roberto put the truck in gear and pulled away from the curb, Savannah blew out a long breath. After travelling well beyond the boundaries of San José, Roberto pulled the truck to the side of the road and parked the vehicle.

"I didn't know you could be so cruel," Savannah said.

"I didn't know you could be so ignorant," Roberto said.

"Did you get what you wanted?" she asked.

"No. Did you?"

"No. Did we get what we needed?" Savannah asked as her lips hitched upward.

"Yes. I think we did."

Savannah hung her head and let it loose. She and Roberto laughed so hard they both wore tears. She wiped her wet cheeks and said, "If Costa Rica had their version of the Academy Awards, you would have won an Oscar. Picking a fight so we'd get Jorge Diaz? Have his *subordinates* sign?"

"Those two clerks loved that one," Roberto said. "Our little props were better than I imagined."

"They were better than props. Alegría and Paloma, the little dears, would have tied for best supporting actresses."

"What about me?" Roberto asked. Do I win best actor, or best supporting actor?"

"Whichever you want, Roberto. You were marvelous."

Chapter Sixteen

March 1943. Micah sat on the side of his bed, elbows on his knees, and hands rubbing the back of his neck. He studied the sparse furnishings in his assigned one-room residence. Since Crystal City camp designers expected families to occupy the camp, they intended to house childless couples, or couples with an infant or small child, in the twelve by sixteen foot room. Micah was almost amused that he should consider this space something of a luxury.

After detainees took a bus from the dock in San Pedro and a train ride to Texas, they boarded the bus that took them to Crystal City, where they passed the town's acclaimed Popeye statue. Once they arrived at the famous "spinach camp," processors assigned families to one of six types of housing units, depending on the size of the family.

When the officer who admitted Micah learned that he was unaccompanied, the peeved man seemed to take it as a personal affront. The man relaxed his attitude when Micah promised that his correspondence to his wife would include the subject of her joining him at the camp. Micah planned to reiterate his unswerving position in the affair to Savannah. He would not let her join him. The intake officer didn't need to know that part.

In the meantime, if the number of internees increased to an unexpected number, Micah might have to share his quarters with another unattached male. On this, another humid spring morning, he had the spacious accommodations to himself. He washed his face at his kitchen sink, grabbed his towel, and headed to the bath facilities.

Today, like yesterday, a continuous supply of clouds promised to hide the sun as it wandered from the eastern horizon, rested overhead at midday, and paraded out of the camp as it made its way toward the western skies. Micah knew enough about the climate in Texas to savor these days. Summer heat, coupled with the ever-present humidity, was not a welcome outlook.

Like most of the internees, Micah had a job at the camp. The job was real; the money fake. For his work as a mailman, he earned the equivalent of ten cents an hour, with that income remitted in the form of camp tokens. The camp reminded Micah of a board game—play money, pretend houses, and a pretense of normal family life.

Micah waited for the censor to hand off the first bundle of mail destined for those who resided in the German section of the camp.

"Here's your mail. Get to it." The heavy-set woman, probably in her mid-twenties, was gruff and rude—as she was every morning. Whether Melinda Young hated her job or her life, Micah could only take a guess. Perhaps he should inquire. Nicely, of course.

"Are you angry with me this morning, Miss Young?"

"For crying out loud, just go do your job. If you don't want it, we can give it to another Nazi."

Micah cleared his throat, stretched his neck forward, as if he hadn't quite understood her remark, and asked, "Is that what you think? That I'm a Nazi?"

"That's why you're here," she said with disdain.

"It's an accusation, Miss Young. I've not been given an opportunity to prove my innocence."

"Right," Melinda replied. "You're all innocent, aren't you? I read the mail, you know. All of it. Incoming. Outgoing. You stand there and pretend to be innocent? You're all a bunch of Hitler lovers."

"That's not true."

"I'd like to see all of you in front of a firing squad."

When Micah balked and stepped back, he wanted to protest.

Instead, she underscored her proclamation with, "I would. Makes me sick the way the United States coddles all of you. They give you better food, better medical care, and better accommodations than most of the folks who live in town *earn*. We have ration cards. And where there ain't enough to ration, we get nothing."

Melinda's revelation left Micah without a rebuttal. This required some gentle stepping and deep thought.

"I'm sorry things are hard for you. I'll be going now."

Micah took the pile of mail to an empty table and set about resorting the haphazard and careless efforts of the censors. When he walked outside, the first person to catch his eye invoked Melinda's vehement diatribe. He could only imagine the tone of the letters Herr Bergen may have penned and received.

Shortly after Micah's arrival, the detainees elected a representative—one from the Japanese population; the other from the German population—to act as a spokesman for his group. While this method improved interaction between the camp administrators and the detainees, the Officer in Charge promised that any individual who needed to speak to him directly, could do so.

Herr Bergen nominated himself for the spokesman's post, and those who understood the candidate's native tongue—German—swept him into office without bothering to find a translator who could explain the purpose of the proceedings to the English and Spanish-speaking population. The affair incensed Micah further when he learned that Bergen spoke English—when it suited him. After that seemingly devious act, Micah determined he would find someone who would teach him German.

Micah couldn't get over how many of the internees, cast out of Latin American countries, didn't speak a lick of Spanish. It seemed rather pompous, in his opinion, that a businessman thought so much of himself that he couldn't bother to learn to speak to his neighbors. But it wasn't as if the well-heeled German plantation and landowners circulated among the general population in the countries where they amassed nice sums of monies and assets.

Some of the Germans at the camp, like Bergen, held to the politics of their fatherland. Because Bergen openly espoused and supported the Axis powers and activities, he managed to instigate animosity among his like-minded adherents and those detainees who held some degree of fondness or support of the United States and the Allies. Micah understood the source of Melinda Young's anger. Herr Bergen incited the same reaction in him.

~

As Micah finished his rounds within the German section of the camp, he studied the speed at which construction advanced on a myriad of buildings, both inside the wire fence and without. Administrators expected the clinic to open within two months, and the hospital by mid-summer.

A lot of good that did the first woman to give birth at Crystal City. Micah declined the celebratory cigar, purchased with tokens at the internees' German store, but he stopped to chat for a moment.

"¿Otro niño? Felicidades. ¿Cómo está tu esposa?" Micah asked. Another son? Did that make three or four? Micah wasn't certain. Regardless, how could he not offer his congratulations and inquire as to the wife's well-being?

"Gracias. Muy bien," the father replied. His grin hid any discomfort over his child claiming the title of first-born at the camp.

As Micah resumed his deliveries, Benjamin Rubenstein, the internee physician who delivered the boy, stepped away from the celebratory father, and matched Micah's strides. The sweet scent of the doctor's cigar trailed along with him.

"Have you picked up the mail on my street yet?" Benjamin asked.

"No. Do you have something to entertain the censors?"

"The censors? Such a troublesome situation. It keeps one from complaining too loudly over the conditions here. I intend to keep a low profile. This Jew has no desire to suffer repatriation to Germany. You've heard the rumors, I expect."

"About the death camps? The gas ovens? Inconceivable."

"Sometimes I think all of mankind is lost," Benjamin said.

"We are. Your Torah says as much," Micah said.

"Yes, it does. I understand your New Testament is just as explicit, except that you think your Redeemer has already made things right. Look around you. Does this look 'right' to you?"

"It takes the Second Coming to make things right, doctor."

"What do you know of Judaism?" Benjamin asked.

"Not as much as I'd like. Speaking of my ignorance, do you know anyone who might teach me some German? I'm supposed to be among my peers here, but I speak only English and Spanish."

"Perhaps we could barter. A little of your New Testament knowledge for some basic German vocabulary and phrases."

"And if we hit it off?" Micah asked. "Do we delve into theology and the translation of books from English to German?"

Benjamin held out his hand. "As long as they permit the two of us to remain."

"Deal," Micah said as he shook the man's hand.

Micah gathered the last of the resident's outgoing mail from his wagon and dropped the box on the counter in front of Melinda Young.

"I hear some of the letters are charming today. Especially those of the children."

Melinda rolled her eyes at his attempt to start a conversation. When he pointed to the window over her shoulder, one that looked over the front of the temporary headquarters building, she turned and followed his aim.

"What do you think they're doing?"

"For pity sake," Melinda said. "The telephone must be out again."

"*The* telephone? The camp has just one telephone?"

"That's privileged information, Keller, so don't repeat

that."

"You're serious. One telephone? What are they doing?"

"See the Del Rio Border Patrol car parked in front of the offices?"

"Yes."

"They borrowed it so they could use the radio car transmitter."

"I still don't understand," Micah said. He studied the line of personnel that started somewhere within the office and extended to the vehicle. Most unsettling was the fact that all of the individuals held each other's hands.

"The reception was lousy here, so someone installed a station receiver inside the building."

"And the line of people?"

"They are a human antenna between the receiver and the transmitter."

Micah's shoulders bounced up and down before he could control them. His low chuckle erupted into a full-blown laugh, and he dared think he made a friend when Melinda's guffaw erupted. She laughed long and hard, and had to wrap her arms around her ribs. When she managed to catch her breath, she looked at Micah with a feigned expression of contempt.

"You should do that more often," Micah said.

"What?" Melinda asked with a growl.

"Laugh. You have a pretty smile."

"Get out of here, Keller."

By the time Micah prepared a simple meal, cleaned up after himself, and made one last trek to the communal washroom, the stars and moon held their place in the dusky night sky. Or so he assumed. He squinted as he made his way back to his room, trying to catch sight of the celestial bodies orbiting above the earth. Much of the world covered their windows with black cloth as night fell, so as to conceal their buildings from enemy aircraft. Here, the interminable security lights glared into the darkness, obscuring the view of the heavens and stealing the body's natural rhythm, its reaction to day and night, light and dark.

In these quiet evenings, Micah's unintended solitude opened the door to discouragement and longing. Many of the younger children seemed unaware of their circumstances, and when he walked among them as he worked, their playful laughter and cheerful antics reminded him that his daughter was far away, beyond his reach and his influence. Like a furtive thief, each passing day robbed Micah, Savannah, and Alegría of an immeasurable amount of love. All he had to offer were letters and prayers.

In a movement that was both welcome and bittersweet, Micah pulled a letter from his pocket.

Lovesick ▬ ▬ ▬ *missionary seeks to send her affection to her dear darling husband. Child of said couple sends* ▬ ▬ ▬ ▬ *kisses to her papa. Proof of his daughter's authentic wishes is relayed by the dirty handprint affixed at the bottom of this letter—like a king's signet ring. However, the artwork is not to suggest that the child spends her days playing in the dirt. Although she might—on occasion.*

News from ▬ ▬ ▬ ▬ *includes a splendid report on the most recent sales of coffee and cocoa to the brokers in* ▬ ▬. *Carmita turned fifteen since you've been gone. Now that she's almost grown up, she dotes on the younger children and helps in the kitchen, leaving me more time to spend in the* ▬ ▬. *I'm so grateful. New additions include a dairy cow, and more laying hens. Unexpected ▬ ▬ ▬ of bread, fruits, and vegetables ▬ ▬ ▬ ▬ ▬ ▬ ▬ ▬ ▬ ▬ ▬*

Just as the Good Lord blessed this lovesick wife with a remarkable and much-loved husband, He has the power to hold this family together in any circumstances.

Until we hold you in our arms again, remember you are loved.

Savannah and Alegría.

Carmita? The mission took in another child? A teenager? A Tico? Better prices for the crops? A good thing. Unexpected . . . bread, fruits, and vegetables? It sounded as if people had donated food to the mission. All positive things, but what changed? After his arrest, the Ticos were rude to Savannah at best. This letter made it sound as if things at the mission were close to normal. How was that possible?

Micah traced his finger over the censored words. Savannah, if nothing else, was resourceful and determined. She sounded good. Upbeat. Just as his letters pretended he was good. Upbeat.

He ran his fingertip along the edges of Alegría's smudged handprint. So small. He turned his right hand palm up, and set the handprint next to his open hand. How much larger would his daughter's "authentic signature" grow before he held her little fingers in his hand?

How he wished he could form a human chain to send a transmission from Crystal City to Misión de Cacao. If he could be the last one in the chain—the one who reached the doorpost of the mission—that would be even better.

Chapter Seventeen

"You have to move into the main house." Savannah grabbed Alegría before she could run outside. "It's bath time, Jojo. Go fetch clean bedclothes." After she trusted her daughter to obey her, Savannah turned back to Benita, who shook her head.

"Roberto and I talked about it. We cannot trade houses with you."

"You must."

"This is your home. Ours is back there. We like it there."

"The mission property belongs to you and Roberto now. The local officials won't believe the transfer was valid if I stay in the main house. You must trade places with me." When Benita held fast to her stubborn frown, Savannah choked back her despair. "Please don't make me beg."

"It's not right," Benita replied.

"It's necessary."

"All right. I'll ask Pablo to start exchanging furniture."

"No. Use what is here. Just bring your clothes, your personal things."

When Benita opened her mouth to protest again, Savannah held up her hand. "This is the right thing to do."

"Fine. But Rolf, Brigitte, and Carmita will stay here,"

Benita said.

"No they won't. They need to stay with Alegría and me. I don't want to disturb their routines. No more changes for them."

"The bedroom is too small. No one will sleep well. No one."

"Benita," Savannah said as mischief seized her serious tone, "At night I can hear Roberto all the way across the courtyard."

Benita pulled her shoulders back and narrowed her eyes when she said, "What do you mean?" Her crimson blush suggested she needed clarification regarding the source of the noise. Which only increased Savannah's levity.

"He snores," she replied.

Benita cast her eyes downward, coughed at her momentary discomfort, and said, "I'll have Pablo transfer the children's belongings."

From behind the closed door, and while she tended to Alegría's bath, Savannah heard footsteps falling back and forth down the hallway. When she joined Roberto's family for supper, Benita pointed to Savannah's self-assigned chair.

"We will not make any changes to the seating arrangement. Do not argue with me."

Savannah chuckled as she walked behind Benita. She squeezed the woman on the shoulder and said, "Yes, ma'am. I love you. All of you."

Roberto passed a bowl to Savannah and said, "You're family. We love you too."

"You'll like my bedroom," Simón said. "The hummingbirds zip around the bush below the window." One by one, he pointed to Alegría, Rolf, and Brigitte. Pretending to whisper, he said, "You have to be very quiet. They have a nest. With eggs. I saw it." He pointed to his thumb. "It's this big."

"Birds? Show me birds," Alegría said.

"Me too," Brigitte said. "I want to see."

After dinner, the three little ones ran after Simón while Benita and Savannah washed and dried dishes. Carmita offered to organize their new space in the caretaker's house.

Savannah found the four youngsters standing on tiptoe on one of the two mattresses. All of their little bodies leaned out of the open window while they searched for birds.

Savannah tugged on Alegría's ankle and tickled her ribs. When her giggles grew into squeals, Simón put his fists on his hips.

"You scared the birds. They won't come back until dark." He huffed, drooped his shoulders and said, "I'm going home."

When he reached the doorway, Savannah called after him. "Wait. You forgot your quilt."

"It's Jojo's quilt now. She can share it with Brigitte and Rolf."

"Simón, you don't have to give her your quilt."

"It's a good dream quilt. It's their turn to have sweet dreams." He walked out of the room, only to stick his little face in the doorway long enough to say, "Don't scare the birds, Jojo."

After the children climbed into the bed, Savannah snugged the quilt up to their chins. Alegría reached up and wiped Savannah's cheek.

"Mamá cry?"

"Simón did a kind thing when he left this for all of you. Sometimes tears come when we are happy."

"Mamá happy?"

Savannah bent down and kissed Alegría's cheek. "I am very happy. You, my little Jojo, make me very happy. You all do. Now, it's time to close your eyes and have sweet dreams."

As dusk conceded its temporary dominion to nightfall, the soft, rhythmic breathing of the children filled the space. Carmita came into the room, smelling of toothpaste and wearing her nightgown. She gave Savannah a hug and a peck on her cheek before taking her place on the empty mattress.

Savannah walked to the veranda, sat in the darkness, and listened to the orchestral offerings rendered by the birds, insects, and animals that called the land around Misión de Cacao home.

When she advertised for a mate, she wanted nothing more than a means to remain in Costa Rica. She warmed to Micah Keller in the short weeks between the time of their less-than-dignified introduction and their marriage, but didn't have need for a spouse, per se. Savannah thrived on independence.

Perhaps she learned to fend for herself because her mother abandoned her. She'd been headstrong and determined for as long as she could remember, so she couldn't be objective in her self-examination. However, she could identify without hesitation, the day she realized she wanted—no, needed—Micah Keller to be her mate.

Her concession to Micah's matrimonial rights drew her affection, but not her heart. It was evident to Savannah that he cared for her more deeply than she did for him. He was tender, patient, and kind while he waited for her to return his love. Yes, she knew he loved her. But when did she determine she loved him back?

It wasn't when the Tico officials put his name on the Black List. It wasn't the day they arrested him and took him to the internment camp in San José, nor was it the day they moved him to Crystal City, Texas.

It was the doctor's confirmation of her pregnancy that opened Savannah's eyes . . . and her heart. While she held the secret, she regarded Micah from a different perspective. He was destined to be a father, and she had every reason to believe he would be the grandest papá in all of Costa Rica. His character, his faith, and his generous spirit reflected the man's love. Micah Keller loved deeply. Suddenly, she wanted to return that love, not just as a dutiful wife, but as a woman who chose to lavish her love on the one who owned her heart. Micah didn't steal her heart from her; she gave it to him willingly.

Savannah dressed for bed, but instead of climbing into the bed that Roberto and Benita used to share, she slipped into the narrow space beside the newest gift God brought to the mission.

Carmita slept on her side with her legs and arms curled in a loose fetal position. Her dark hair and long eyelashes glistened in the moonlight. In spite of the cramped quarters, the caretaker cottage managed to accommodate one more. The bigger obstacle was the future, the unknown. Would Micah ever take his rightful place beside Savannah again?

~

Micah's feet hurt and his brain was weary. He'd been out of the classroom for a long time, and unlike having to remember Spanish, every word of German was new to him. When he considered the rules of grammar, proper pronunciation, and conjugation of verbs, it made for a case of gray-matter overload. What he did learn, in short order, was that his tutor,

Benjamin Rubenstein, was patient. Equally valuable were his sense of humor and the friendships he and his wife extended to Micah. Right now, though, Micah wanted to direct his attention to the English language.

My dearest Savannah and my Jojo sunshine,

A flutter of melancholy gripped Micah before he penned his first sentence. He was already a stranger to Alegría. She'd never heard him call her Jojo, the nickname derived from the word joy, which was the English translation of alegría. To some of the Ticos, those who pronounced a *j* with a *y*, her nickname would sound like Yoyo. Either way, it was clever. Cute. No, not cute. The single photograph Savannah sent so far, depicted a beautiful child. His child.

Your letters remind me that many things have changed since I left home. I sometimes think I won't recognize everyone once I return. Please tell Carmita I'm sorry I missed her birthday. Fifteen years old? I'm stunned. When did that happen?

Micah sat back in his seat and re-read his paragraph. He dared the censors to find a reason to black out his "stunned" reaction to Savannah's read-between-my-words message regarding the mission's newest refugee. He could play that tell/don't tell game with the censors.

I like my job delivering mail to the German internees, and I've found a routine that keeps me busy. It's the nights that are hard. Second most difficult is my inability to speak German, as many internees speak nothing else. My new friend, an internee physician, offered to teach me German. Benjamin and his wife, Ella, invited me to their home for dinner tonight. I think I enjoyed their company far more than I did the meal.

I've been here long enough to give you a fair description of life in Crystal City. In many respects it is an ordinary town where ordinary things happen. The administrators make an effort to accommodate the residents. Rumor has it that the Japanese obtained permission to produce their own tofu. If I had three wishes to present to those in charge, none of them would include tofu. Sounds awful, doesn't it?

The camp has a hobby shop, barbershop, beauty salon, and German and Japanese groceries. At the sewing shop, women weave things like rugs and curtains. Other endeavors are rather large in scale. Internees produce furniture, mattresses, crops, meat products, clothing and other goods. I guess we should be grateful. The jobs are a source of "income," and the products help furnish and feed households, but I suspect the activities save the government huge sums of money.

Children attend school and play on internee-constructed playground equipment. Schools have typical extracurricular activities, although rounding up a second team for some sports events is something of a challenge.

The most popular amenity, I think, is the swimming pool. It's enormous. It used to be a reservoir that irrigated spinach crops. When summer's scorching sun glares on this place, I hope to spend my share of time there.

I'll end my summary of "Life at Crystal City" with the following observation. If not for the fences and towers staffed by armed guards, one might manage to convince oneself that this was a normal place. In reality, only the youngest—those who have no prior reference point—could call this place home.

Like you, I pray that I find my way back to you in short time. Although I can't hold you in my arms, you fill my heart, and you are in my prayers.

Give my love to the others, but take an extra portion first.

With all my love,
Micah

He read the letter from start to finish, folded it, and inserted it into an envelope. The correspondence sounded more like a report than a love letter, but he couldn't share his innermost thoughts and feelings with Savannah. It wasn't that he might show too much of himself to the censors, it was Micah's reluctance to place his burdens of loneliness and helplessness on his wife. God knew it weighed down his soul.

At the start of each day, when the fencing and barbed wire beyond his window reminded Micah that he couldn't carry the load by himself, he handed his weariness over to Him. Once clad in the "Armor of God,"—including the belt of truth, breastplate of righteousness, and the shield of faith—Micah set out to do the tasks demanded of him, and kept an eye out for morsels of joy in the dismal place.

Chapter Eighteen

August 1943. Savannah tossed a pair of pants over the clothesline and leaned over to pick up another pair. As she stood up, she followed Carmita's gaze until she detected the source of the girl's attention.

Carmita didn't resemble the scrawny form who arrived at the mission just six months earlier. Whether a product of maturity or ample food to eat, she blossomed. Today, she looked more like a young woman than a gawky teenager, and when Savannah caught her ogling Pablo, Carmita's cheeks turned crimson.

"He's what American's call a looker," Savannah said.

"A looker?"

"Easy on the eyes?"

"What?"

"Someone attractive. Someone you want to watch because he's pleasing to the eye," Savannah answered.

"Oh," Carmita said. She turned her back to Pablo as he strode out of view, and pushed an errant lock of hair away from her face.

"He's not much older than you, you know."

"Really?" Carmita asked. Her voice sounded hopeful; her blush heightened. "I thought he was old. At least twenty, anyway."

"He's eighteen."

"Really?" Carmita asked again.

"He's a good boy. I hear he comes from a good family. Keeps good company," Savannah said.

"You can stop embarrassing me now," Carmita said.

The sound of an approaching vehicle interrupted Savannah's clever retort. An unfamiliar and dilapidated two-door sedan crept toward the courtyard. The sun reflected off the windshield, obscuring the identity of the occupants. When the driver exited the vehicle, Savannah squinted. The man looked familiar, but she couldn't place him.

He rounded the car, opened the passenger door, and held out his hand to another somewhat-familiar face. Memory provided recognition, but the condition of the woman stunned her. Savannah motioned for Carmita to follow her as she rushed to the car.

"Señora Keller? Rita? Is that you?" Savannah turned to the driver. "Eduard?"

The driver nodded. "Yes. Here we are. We apologize we didn't call you first."

"Rita? Give me your arm. Come, let's go into the kitchen and get something to drink." Savannah tipped her head toward Carmita and said, "Would you please check on the littles ones? If they're still asleep, come join us. If they're awake, bring them with you."

When Savannah pulled Rita's spindly arm through her own, she fought to retain some measure of composure, and started walking to the house. Rita's color was wan, her bearing frail. Micah's mother wasn't here to make a social call. Had she come to say goodbye?

When they reached the kitchen, a fatigued Rita Keller

tottered to the table and eased herself into a chair.

"Eduard, please have a seat," Savannah said. "What can I get you? Water? Tea? Coffee?"

"Water for me," Eduard answered.

"Is it too much to ask for hot tea?" Rita asked.

"Not at all. I'll just be a minute."

Rapid, tiny feet padded into the house and into the kitchen. "Mamá," Alegría cried as she ran into the room. She held up her hands and waited for Savannah to pull her into her arms.

Brigitte, timid around strangers, leaned against the doorjamb. When Carmita caught up with her two charges, she nudged Brigitte's shoulder.

"Come on in. Climb into your seat and I'll get you a cup of juice." She addressed Savannah when she said, "Paloma and Rolf are still asleep."

"Thank you," Savannah replied. "Rita, Eduard, let me introduce you to Carmita. Carmita, this is Micah's mother, Rita Keller. Eduard is Rita's brother. They come from Alajuela."

"Mucho gusto," Eduard said.

"Good to meet you," Carmita said.

Savannah worked one-handed to prepare drinks while Carmita kept Brigitte occupied. Savannah pulled out a chair, stirred cloves and cinnamon into her tea, and waited for it to cool.

"She's beautiful," Rita said as she regarded Alegría. "I wish circumstances were different. I would like to have spent more time with my granddaughter."

Savannah's spine stiffened. Was this an introduction to Rita's bad news?

"She has Micah's cheekbones and his coloring, his full

lips. But," she said as she reached over and put her hand on top of Savannah's forearm, "she has your gorgeous eyes."

"Kind of you to say," Savannah replied. "I fear, however, she acquired my fiery personality."

"That's not a bad thing. Not at all. You two will keep Micah on his toes." Rita sipped her tea, used two hands to lower the cup to the saucer, and wiped her lips on a napkin. "In his letters, he tries to sound positive, but I sense sadness. We corresponded when he studied at the university in Austin. The letters coming out of the camp are hard for him to write and equally hard to read. Which makes it more difficult for me to add to your burdens."

Savannah waited for her to continue, but it was Eduard who filled the silence. He delayed his explanation by clearing his throat and focusing his attention on the tabletop. He clasped his hands together and lifted his eyes until they met Savannah's expectant gaze.

"My sister is not well. The doctors cannot help her and I cannot care for her while I work. No one will come to the house to help. Alajuela is not so far away from the capital. Everyone knows." Eduard didn't bother to finish the rest of his statement. No one would care for Micah's mother because her son bore the distinction of Enemy Alien.

Savannah sought to make eye contact with Rita, but the woman wouldn't lift her head. Rita managed to wipe the first tear from her cheek, but the second, and those that followed, fell to the table.

Savannah refused to give Eduard an opportunity to make his request. They shouldn't have to ask. "You'll stay here. We want you here. We'll help as best as we can. Whatever you need."

"Just like that? You don't even know what's wrong with

me."

"It doesn't matter. I should warn you, however, that the most effective treatment the mission offers is love. Before we try any other remedy, we will immerse you in it. Pure, unconditional, unadulterated love."

Savannah's heart swelled with affection and gratitude when Carmita stood, looked at Eduard, and said, "Let me help you bring Señora Keller's things into the house."

"Thank you," Rita whispered.

"You needn't thank any of us," Savannah said. "You must be tired. Why don't you come with me? Let's get you settled for a nap."

With as much effort as it took to walk from the car to the kitchen, Rita hung onto Savannah's arm while they crossed the courtyard and entered Benita and Roberto's old bedroom, the room Savannah had yet to call her own.

Savannah helped Rita out of her shoes, fluffed the pillows, and snugged a thin blanket around Rita's shoulders.

"Would you ask Eduard to come in before he leaves? I want to tell him goodbye."

"Of course."

Savannah's eyes were awash with tears when she pointed Eduard toward Rita's new room and watched him as he went to share what had to be a final encounter between the siblings. How could she tell Micah about his mother? How?

~

As Micah pulled the cart that held his daily mail deliveries over the uneven ground, he wiped his damp forehead with the soaked cloth he held in his free hand. The thermometer on the door leading to Melinda's desk read 103 degrees. If one considered the level of humidity and that curious measurement called a dew point, the temperature ought to read 125.

As he deposited mail at the homes of the German internees, he stopped and took a drink of water. He shaded his eyes from the sun and surveyed one of the internee's construction projects.

"Buenos días. ¿Cómo está?" Wolfgang Leffler asked.

"Muy bien. ¿Que tal? Te ves ocupado." *Very well. What's up? You look busy.* Micah congratulated himself on his rudimentary second-language skills. He threw in the obvious, "Muy caliente"—*very hot*—just to assure the former Peruvian resident that he could carry on a conversation.

"Hot? Yes. I need to rest," Wolfgang replied. He wiped his sweaty brow with a rag that he pulled out of his overalls.

"I need a cold shower," Micah said.

"The camp doesn't have cold water."

"True." The most Micah could hope in the way of relief was a trickle of ground-temperature water dripping out of the showerhead.

"You'll be lucky to have any water at all," Wolfgang said.

"True," Micah replied a second time. More than likely, he would encounter empty pipes altogether.

"Too many new people. Not enough water. Not enough houses."

"Also true."

"How many men in your room now?"

"Three," Micah said. Despite worsening living conditions that came with the transfer of more internees to the camp than the number for which it was constructed, no one celebrated earlier in the month when the government repatriated a substantial number of Japanese detainees.

"Are you trying to keep up with your neighbors?" Micah asked as he gestured to the row of nearby properties that housed the Japanese families. Even in the heat, the flowers planted in front of a porch constructed by the internee resident managed to hoard the summer rains long enough to bloom and spread their color over an otherwise brown canvas. If they had known their stay was so temporary, would so many of them have invested the effort and sacrificed camp tokens to beautify their surroundings?

Wolfgang pointed to the partially completed framework on his house. He smiled when he said, "Too many niños. Not enough room. This is a new bedroom."

His wife, Ingrid, opened the front door far enough to call to her husband, and far enough for Micah to see Wolfgang needed to pick up the pace on his project. His wife looked ready to deliver twins.

"Your food is ready. Come and eat. Señor Keller? Would you like some rice and beans?"

"Thank you, but no. I need to finish my work." He turned back to Wolfgang and asked, "Do you need some help with this?"

"No, no, no. My neighbor, the one who lives over there? He is a real carpenter, and he promised he could work very fast."

"Adíos then," Micah said as he picked up the next batch of mail out of his cart. He thumbed through the pile while he walked to the next section of houses, but halted midstride when he heard a serpent's distinctive warning.

The reptile, hiding in the shade of a pile of rocks, was about two feet away from Micah's feet. Micah's heavy leather boots, a necessity given the distance and duration of his mail deliveries, protected his feet and ankles. His bare legs, however, were within striking distance.

The coiled creature held his head up and continued to signal its displeasure. Micah didn't flinch, but he couldn't control the sweat that collected on his forehead and formed a droplet at the end of his nose. A silent prayer dashed out of his heart and sprinted toward the heavens. *Please, God.*

As the standoff continued, Micah blinked. The potential executioner did not. The approaching footsteps and laughter from a group of schoolchildren returning home stole what little air Micah held in his lungs. His chest screamed in protest. The intricate pattern on the creature's skin shifted when it contracted its coil and flicked its tongue. It opened its mouth wide, exposing needle-sharp fangs.

Blood sprayed against the dry earth at the same time the snake's severed head came to rest on the toe of Micah's boot. Micah pulled in a shallow breath of air and stood, stupefied and panting, while he stared at the carnage.

"Keep going. You don't need to see. Go on. Hurry up now."

Micah turned and studied his rescuer. As the Japanese internee waved the children away, his other hand gripped the handle of a shovel. The bloody tip rested on the ground. The man, slight in build, wore the uniform of a laborer. Around his head was a white band, meant to keep sweat out of his eyes. His skin, bronzed by the sun and wrinkled by its exposure, added years to his face, but when he smiled, decades of hard work disappeared.

"Are you all right?"

"Yes. Thank you." Micah looked behind the man. "I didn't see you. How . . . ?"

"I was down there." The man pointed to a crew working to repair a section of roadway. He turned and pointed to the pile of rocks. "I needed some of those to fill in a bad spot." He shrugged.

"How did you . . . ?"

"Before Crystal City, I was a Samurai warrior," he said with a grin. He stuck out his hand. "You can call me Sam."

"Micah. Micah Keller."

"Nice to meet you." Sam looked toward the German houses. "Would you like the pleasure of dining on the Japanese side of the camp?"

"Oh, no. I couldn't."

"You heard about the tofu," Sam said.

Micah's hesitation said too much. Before he could find a suitable reply, Sam said. "We will have something special tonight." He leaned over and started rearranging the rocks in a circle around the snake's body.

"What are you doing?"

"Staking a claim on my dinner. No touching the snake for at least an hour. Venom, you know?"

"This is your special dinner?" Micah asked. He knew his eyebrows reached his hairline, but he couldn't pull them back down.

"Sure. Tastes like chicken." Sam's laugh erupted again. He pointed to a row of houses. "Down there, the house with the porch. See you at seven."

Micah tugged on his cart and took another look at the reptile. *Thank you, Lord.* He finished his mail deliveries and collections with a protracted degree of attentiveness, and berated himself for letting down his guard. Other dangers—scorpions, red ants, tarantulas, and the like—lurked in the camp, inside and out. In the future, he'd be mindful of his vulnerability. Better to plan for the unexpected than to have it turn his life upside down.

As he retraced his steps toward the Japanese residences, Micah paused at the scene where reptile met warrior. Tastes like chicken?

Chapter Nineteen

Micah sat on the stoop and stretched his legs while he waited for Benjamin Rubenstein to come back outside. From the cajoling, whining, and crying originating from inside the house, Micah surmised that three exhausted little girls, who ranged in age from six to ten, stayed far too long at the swimming pool. Not that he blamed the parents for prolonging the activity. The sweltering heat held the camp in its grasp.

When Benjamin took a seat beside Micah, he held a book in his hand.

"Sorry to make you wait."

"It's no trouble. What do you have there?" Micah asked.

"Your German lesson."

Micah peered over Benjamin's shoulder. "A Bible?"

"What better way to learn a language and to honor God at the same time? As a pastor, you should be pleased."

"Pleased to read the Bible? Of course. In German? You think I'm ready?"

"We will start with the Book of Isaiah."

Isaiah? Really? When Micah held out his hand, Benjamin gave him the Bible.

"You're reading the Old Testament *and* the New

Testament?"

"What? You think they have Jewish texts in Crystal City?"

"No," Micah replied. "I just figured you had a family Bible. Most people do."

Benjamin returned his response with raised eyebrows.

"Authorities took it from you when they arrested you." Micah's comment wasn't a question.

Benjamin nodded. "I purchased this one here."

"Have you read any of the New Testament?" Micah asked.

Benjamin smiled when he said, "Let's turn to Isaiah, chapter forty."

"Why that chapter?"

"It's one of my favorites. It describes God's greatness and His creation. He 'has measured the waters in the hollow of His hand and marked off the heavens with a span.' In one place it says, 'the nations are like a drop from a bucket.' Considering the state of the nations, I take comfort in those words. In the midst of war, God is still who He says He is."

"I take fear in the level of vocabulary I need to read these passages," Micah said.

"But what an incredible picture these words paint. If the verses stir up your heart, you'll retain the vocabulary."

"You think so?" Micah asked.

"I guarantee it."

Micah scanned the familiar layout of the text, the columns, the numbered verses. It was the unfamiliar language that intimidated him.

"Before we start, can I ask you something?"

"Sure," Benjamin said.

"I don't mean to be rude, but you're the first Jew to teach me from the Bible."

"War brings about unexpected friendships," Benjamin replied.

"How is it that you—the Jews—didn't recognize Jesus as Messiah? So much of the Old Testament tells of His coming."

Benjamin sat without answering and rubbed his chin between his thumb and index finger.

"You'd have to ask my rabbi that question."

Micah struggled not to react. What an odd answer.

After a long pause, Benjamin said, "I realize my response is unacceptable, but no one ever asked me that before. Let me think a minute longer."

Micah lowered his eyes to the text while he waited. Judging from the strange words in verse one, he had ample opportunity to increase his vocabulary. He recognized *mein*, *euer*, and *Gott* as *my, your*, and *God*. The rest? Who knew?

"I have an answer for you," Benjamin said. "We didn't recognize Jesus because he did not come as the king we expected."

"May I make a request?" Micah asked.

"First a question; now a request? Are you procrastinating?"

"Not intentionally. After chapter forty, can we jump to fifty-three?"

"If we are still at war and in this place by the time you read all of chapter forty, we can skip to fifty-three."

"With that vote of confidence, I guess we need to begin." Micah cleared his throat and attempted to read.

~

"Why aren't you in school?" Rita asked Carmita as she

entered the kitchen.

A fair question, and a subject Savannah broached soon after Carmita arrived at the mission.

Roberto stood at the counter as he mixed the maize and other ingredients he needed to make tortillas. He wiped his hands on his apron and said, "I need to check the hens," before he scurried out of the kitchen. Did the man expect a confrontation?

Savannah diverted her attention from her current task—that of feeding breakfast to Rolf, Paloma, and Alegría—and awaited Carmita's explanation.

Instead of taking a defensive posture, Carmita grinned. Her smile seemed to awaken a degree of joy in anyone caught in its path. The almost-a-woman teenager, though fetching on the outside, owned a heart that was even more beautiful.

"I quit school when I turned twelve."

"But you need an education," Rita said. "Who gave you permission to leave school?"

"My aunt and uncle. I lived with them before I came here. They had five little children, and when my aunt became pregnant with the sixth one, she had complications. The doctor made her stay in bed. Someone had to take care of the children."

"Why don't you go to school now? The children here aren't your responsibility," Rita said.

"It's been almost four years since I sat in a classroom. I can't catch up with students who are my age, and I can't study until I'm in my twenties."

"Don't you worry about your future?" Rita asked.

"I am content to do what my education allows. I don't need to graduate in order to take care of children or to tend the crops. And just so you know, I am really good with numbers, and I still learn things. I read books. Books in Spanish and in English."

"What books?"

"The Bible, mostly." Carmita looked at Savannah and laughed. "We have a few copies in the chapel, but unless Pablo sneaks a copy of the local newspaper into the house, I don't have any other reading material."

Rita looked at Savannah and asked, "Are you satisfied with this arrangement?"

"A lot of people don't finish school, and they manage. I agreed with Carmita's request, though, because I didn't want to subject her to the local bullies. It doesn't matter to some of the Ticos that Carmita is one of them, and a few students in particular are known to be quite cruel."

"Well then," Rita said, "I'll enjoy your company without worrying about your future." She shared a woeful expression with Savannah and pressed her lips into a tight line. "I wish the future didn't scare me so much. I'm terrified, you know."

Carmita leaned over and wrapped her arms around Rita. "When you are in bed for the night, I'll come to your room. I will do two things. I will prove to you that I can read, and I will do that by sharing verses that remind you of God's hope and promises." She released her hug and walked to the other side of the table where she hefted Rolf up to one hip, Paloma to the other, and took Alegría by the hand. "I need these three to play a game with me right now. I'll help Roberto clean up the kitchen later."

Savannah inspected the plate sitting in front of Rita. When Rita declined a bland meal of rice and black beans, Savannah suggested eggs and bread. It looked as if Rita moved the eggs around her plate instead of eating them. The bread was untouched, as was the coffee, now cold.

"May I get you some tea?" Savannah asked.

"Would you mind? It settles my stomach."

"Can you tell me what's wrong?" Savannah asked as she took the seat across from Rita.

"Cancer."

An ugly disease, regardless of the form. No wonder Rita was terrified.

"What kind?"

"The doctor said it started in my uterus."

"Isn't a treatment available?"

"Maybe someday. The disease has spread. My hope is that your local doctor is willing to come here and tend to me. Enough to help with the pain. Will he do that?"

"I know he will. I'll ask Pablo to contact Dr. Gutierrez. He's a good man. You can trust him."

After Savannah prepared and poured tea for her mother-in-law, she pulled her hair into a ponytail and pulled her wide-brimmed hat from the peg hanging near the door to the veranda.

"Will you be all right for a couple of hours?"

"I'm fine. You go ahead with whatever you do each day."

"What if you need something?" Savannah asked.

"I won't."

"You can't promise that. Wait here. I have an idea."

Savannah went outside and tugged at the door to the ramshackle shed until its rusty creaking hinges gave way enough for her to enter. She pulled the wrecked bicycle outside, and went back into the main house where she located a screwdriver.

When she returned to the kitchen, Savannah extended her prize to Rita.

"Some people tinkle little bells when they need assistance.

Since most of us are outside during the day, we need a little more volume. If we're lucky, we will hear this thing." Savannah cupped her hand over the old metal bell in order to muffle the noise, and pulled the lever.

Rita clapped both hands over her ears. "That will work, but I hope I don't need it."

"If you need anything, anything at all, please ring."

Savannah went to the back of the property where she found Benita pulling weeds from the vegetable garden.

"Any improvement?" Savannah asked.

Discouragement and concern etched tiny creases around Benita's eyes and mouth. "I thought the new fencing would keep the animals out, but now I wonder if we might have a different kind of predator."

"What do you mean?" Where dark green leaves promised an abundance of crops just a few days ago, uprooted and discarded remnants of precious food lay scattered around Savannah's feet.

"Come. Look over here." Benita led Savannah to the back corner of the garden and pointed. "The rain collects here, leaving mud. What do you see?"

Micah warned of this. In times of hunger, people would steal the crops. But who, besides the residents of the mission, knew the garden existed? And why would a hungry person leave so much wasted produce behind?

"Do you think some of the laborers from Shuler's farm scouted out the property?"

Savannah squeezed her eyes closed and pinched her face into a painful grimace. "No. I don't."

"You don't?" Benita blinked at Savannah's terse remark.

"Do you see more than one set of footprints?"

"No," Benita answered.

141

"Our visitor," Savannah said as she spit out the last word, "is more inclined to destroy our food supply than to take it for himself. Look around you. The intruder damaged far more vegetables than he pinched."

Benita's eyes widened. She understood. "Randall."

"If I were a gambler, I'd wager a fair amount of funds—if I were the owner of any funds, which I'm not."

"What can we do?" Benita asked.

"We can't accuse him. We don't dare bring attention to ourselves."

"Randall knows that."

"He does," Savannah said.

"What if we put out a trap for him?" Benita asked.

"A trap. Like what?"

"I don't know. Let's ask Roberto and Pablo."

Savannah walked back to the house with the day's meager harvest. What would they do? The number in the household increased at every turn. Resources did not. Work, too, increased exponentially. If not for Carmita's presence and her willingness to share her generous nature and parenting skills, the adults at Misión de Cacao might fear stepping out of their beds in the morning. Indeed, everyone from baby Paloma to the ailing Rita welcomed sleep after a day's play, labor, or suffering. The weight of responsibility sometimes overwhelmed Savannah.

At dinner, she and Benita shared the sad news about the garden with the others.

"What can we do?" Benita asked.

"This also happened a week ago. The same night the workers received their pay. The others go to town to drink, but because they don't like Randall, they leave him behind. Since he can't take out his anger on the other men, he releases it here," Pablo said. "Next week, I will hide near the garden and when he trespasses, I will confront him," Pablo said.

"You'd jeopardize your job at Shuler's old place," Roberto said. "We'd be worse off without your wages than if we lost the food in the garden."

"I could hide," Carmita said. "I'll do it."

"No." Pablo's brusque reply left no room for disagreement.

"We could let the dogs stay outside overnight," Benita said.

"Too dangerous," Savannah replied. "If they hurt him, the police would arrest us."

"Guess what I learned at school today?" Simón asked.

"Not now," Benita said.

"Yes now, Mamá. Listen. Please."

Although Savannah's burden didn't disappear, she enjoyed a breath of possibilities as Simón devised the master plot.

Chapter Twenty

If it weren't for the dishonest act that precipitated the after-dinner project, the entire household might have celebrated. As it was, Savannah had a hard time keeping her self-satisfied amusement in check. While she tucked the youngest children into bed, the men employed Simón's plan. In spite of Benita's objection, the creative genius behind the act had permission from his father to participate in its implementation.

Carmita led Rita to the other bedroom where she would help Rita prepare for bed, and then read to her for half an hour or so. After Savannah delivered and received a welcome supply of hugs, kisses, and bedtime prayers, she walked into Rita's room and stopped in the doorway.

"Could we do something different tonight?" Carmita asked.

"What would you like to do?" Rita replied.

"Could I let Savannah read from the Bible while I draw your portrait?"

Rita raised her hand to her hair and fingered her dull and fragile tresses. The first time Savannah met Rita, the woman's hair was dark brown and shimmered in the sunlight. Rita pressed her fingers to her sunken cheeks, their rose hue absconded by disease.

"A drawing? Of me? Whatever for? I look wretched," Rita replied.

"When I look into your eyes I see kindness," Carmita said. "If you let me draw your picture, I promise the result will please you."

When Rita started to protest, Savannah leaned into the room and said, "You know the authorities took our camera at the same time they searched for radios and other tools that a Nazi sympathizer might use against the local government."

"I didn't know. That's absurd."

"Pablo borrowed a camera a few months ago and took a photo of Alegría, which we mailed to Micah. Since we can't do that again, why don't you let Carmita draw a picture we can send to him?"

Rita's expression revealed conflicting emotions.

"Just lean against your pillows," Carmita said, "listen to Savannah read, and let me capture your beauty. You're lovely, and the picture will be too."

When Rita started choking, Savannah rushed to the bed, but Rita raised her hand and managed to say, "I'm fine. I started to laugh." She coughed and said, "I will pose for the drawing on one condition."

"What?" Carmita asked.

"I need a tiny bit of beet juice. Less than a teaspoon. Do we have any left?"

"Why do you want beet juice?" Savannah asked. "Haven't you eaten enough beets during the past week to turn your skin crimson?"

"Not quite," Rita replied. "That's why I need a dab of juice. I need to apply it to my cheeks. After that, you may read and Carmita may draw."

Rita raised her shoulders, adjusted her head against the

pillows, and bestowed a regal nod upon her audience.

"Yes, your highness, I'll get you some juice," Savannah said as she delivered a curtsy and went to run her errand.

When she returned, Savannah held a hand mirror while Rita dabbed a hint of color onto her face. It didn't come as a surprise to Savannah when the color refused to blend into her skin. Instead, it sat as bright fuchsia dots. One on each cheekbone.

"It does add color," Carmita said. "May I wear some too?"

Savannah bit her lower lip, but the edges of her mouth curled up. When Carmita finished her primping, Savannah stuck out her hand and said, "My turn."

In less than half an hour, while Savannah read and Carmita recreated Rita's face on the drawing paper, Roberto tapped on the doorframe and stuck his head into the room.

"Is she asleep?" he whispered.

"No. I'm not," Rita said. "Please come in."

Roberto glanced from one woman to the next. They each looked as if the doll maker went a little too far when he kissed his porcelain creations with a daub of rouge. When Roberto couldn't find any words to express his surprise—or perhaps it was embarrassment—he shuffled his feet and inspected the flooring.

"Would you like a detailed description?" he asked.

"Is everything, um, situated?" Savannah asked.

"It is."

"We don't need to know any more than that. We'll wait for Pablo's report tomorrow."

Roberto's eyes flicked over the women again as he backed out of the room. "Good night, then." His rapid footsteps revealed the speed and determination of his escape.

~

"You look troubled," Micah said as Benjamin joined him at his usual spot on the stoop.

"I pray for freedom, for an end to this war." Benjamin scoured the perimeter of the camp, or at least what he and Micah could see from their resting spot, and shook his head. "When you walked through the front gate, did it ever occur to you that you might die here?"

Where did that question originate? This defeated attitude was atypical of Benjamin.

"What happened today?"

"A young man who worked at the hospital died today. His arrest prevented him from completing his medical studies, but he was a fine assistant. A good man with a kind heart and a promising future. He leaves behind a wife and young child." Benjamin rubbed the side of his face with his palm. "Everything about this place is cruel and inhumane."

"Was he in some sort of accident?"

"Tumbled down some stairs. Broke his neck." Benjamin tilted his head far enough to give Micah a glimpse of his pain. "How is it that you always keep up your spirits?"

"What do you mean?" Micah replied.

"I know you miss your family, but you project an attitude of joy. All the time. I watch you and listen to you when we have our German lessons, and I covet the attitude you hold."

Micah's brow fell into deep creases. "If I'm different than most, it's because of my faith. I don't mean to stand out, but God calls those of us who know Christ to shine His light in the midst of darkness. Perhaps my light stands out here because this is a dark, dark place. That's not to say I'm immune to sorrow—or self-deprecation. I don't believe I'm fulfilling my calling as a husband, a father, and a pastor."

"Not in the way you'd like, but don't you think you're taking care of those responsibilities as best you can?"

"I appreciate your trying to make me feel better," Micah said.

"On the contrary. Your presence fortifies me." Benjamin lifted his Bible from his lap and said, "I know the Lord God, King of the Universe. When I was a young boy, I chose to love Him with my heart, my mind, and my soul. I still do, even in this camp, but you seem to have something more."

"Let's get reading, shall we? We left off at Isaiah chapter forty-three, didn't we?"

Benjamin opened the Bible and handed it to Micah. "We did."

"If you'd like to read ahead to chapter fifty-three, you might find that 'something more.' It's quite all right for the teacher to read ahead."

"I've read the book of Isaiah before," Benjamin said.

"I know, but this time, ask for a different perspective before you begin."

∼

Savannah was first to see Pablo as he sauntered into the house. His smug bearing implied he had news. Self-congratulatory news.

"Well?" Savannah asked.

Simón's chair screeched when he shoved it away from the table and scraped it against the flooring. "Did it work?" he asked. "Did it?"

Alegría and Paloma, both terrified by the noise and the

excitement, wailed. Which induced mournful sniveling from a sympathetic Brigitte and a confused Rolf. With the deft motion of an adept quartet, Roberto calmed Paloma, Benita comforted Rolf, Carmita embraced Alegría, and Savannah soothed Brigitte. Rita, still unfamiliar with the routines at the mission, sat wide-eyed as the chaos unfolded and the adults defeated the disorder.

Pablo washed his hands, hung the towel, and sat down at the table. He rubbed his palms together and said, "I left early enough this morning to examine the vegetable garden before I started work at Shuler's place."

Savannah forbade anyone from going near the garden today. In the event Randall didn't show up when expected, she didn't want to ruin the trap they'd set.

"Did he come?" Simón asked. "Did you find footprints?"

"I found much more than footprints," Pablo said with a chuckle. "Much more. It looks as if the garden thief followed the exact same path as he took the last time. The fresh prints followed the old ones." He shook his head. "I wish I'd seen it, but if the moon had been too bright, it would have ruined everything."

"Tell me," Simón said.

"Patience, little brother. The new footprints went between the carrots and the lettuce. Randall pulled out more carrots, and took a lot of the lettuce."

"He took lettuce?" Benita asked.

"I think so," Pablo said.

"Those leaves hold lots of moisture, don't they?" she asked Roberto.

Roberto replied with a nonchalant shrug and a wide grin.

"Then he pulled up some cabbage—"

"Get to the important part," Savannah said.

"His escape?" Pablo asked.

"Quit teasing," Carmita said.

"In that place where he exited the garden last time, where mud and things like grease and leftover beet juice collect, I didn't see a single footprint." Pablo craned his neck toward Simón and whispered, "Not one."

Simón slumped in his seat. "But that was the best part of the plan."

Pablo leaned into Simón and bumped his arm. "It was the best part. I didn't see a footprint because he must have fallen face-first into the slippery mess. I saw a body print with arms stuck straight out, like this." Pablo extended both arms wide. "I think I even saw a nose print."

Simón's celebration created a second round of howling and crying among the little ones, which required a second series of comforting.

"What happened when you got to work?" Benita asked. Some of the merriment left her face as she knitted her brow.

"If he'd ended up with red hands from picking the lettuce and pulling out some of the vegetables, Randall might have hidden the evidence of his trespassing. But his red-stained face?"

"I can imagine," Savannah said.

"I don't think any of us anticipated what Randall endured when he faced the other workers and the foremen today. It looked as if he tried to rub the stain off, but by the time he managed to get back to his quarters last night . . . well, it was too late for that."

"Did he say anything to you?" Benita asked.

"He glared at me a lot, especially when I said, 'What happened Randall? Did you get into that new pesticide some of the locals bought to protect their cocoa crops? I heard it doesn't work very well. And it has bad side effects for the person who has to spray the plants.' "

"You did *not* say that," Benita replied.

Pablo waggled his eyebrows. "Yes, I did."

"How much trouble will we get from Randall now?" Savannah asked. A solemn air fell over the group.

"I think we saved the garden, and except for some red-stained crops, we'll eat better than we have over the last month or two," Pablo answered.

"I hear a 'but' coming," Savannah said.

"Our little caper may have increased Randall's determination to ruin the mission and everyone in it, a hundred-fold."

"I was afraid of that," Savannah said.

Chapter Twenty-One

November 1943. Melinda dangled the paper bag in front of Micah. "I borrowed my father's adding machine last night. By my estimation, your personal tab now exceeds ten thousand dollars. By the time you leave here, I'll own your future paychecks until you reach ninety-seven."

"I appreciate the discount. By my calculations, I owe you twenty-four grand."

"I plan to audit your account before your departure. I'll find the discrepancy."

"I'm sure you will," Micah said as he unfolded the top of the bag. When was the last time he inhaled the aroma of roasted turkey? He stomach didn't care about the number of years; it growled in anticipation.

"You're a peach," Micah said. "You're welcome to join us, you know."

Melinda may have scoffed her response, but something in her eyes said she longed to accept.

"That's just plain hooey. Even if I wanted to, which I don't, I'd lose my job. I can't mingle with the internees. And, don't tell anyone where you got the turkey; otherwise, I'd have to find a means to silence you."

"I'll tell everyone it's a rare species of rattlesnake. You've heard of it, haven't you? The pilgrim rattler?"

"I think you need to go now," Melinda said.

Micah couldn't believe his good fortune. More surprising was the friendship he won with the unrelenting and liberal kindness he lavished on one of the most difficult persons he'd met in his lifetime. Melinda Young, the pseudo-combative clerk, was his friend—whether she owned up to it or not. Little did he know his persistence might result in the savory reward he held in his hands, which was also his contribution to the meal.

As Micah entertained Benjamin and Ella's three girls, more than a few residents who lived nearby peered from behind their window curtains. After Benjamin and Sam removed the front door to the Rubenstein's house, they lugged the door to the small front yard and set it on top of the pair of borrowed sawhorses.

"What do you think, girls?" Micah asked.

"It's the biggest dinner table in Crystal City," the oldest said.

Ella, and Sam's wife, Kai, busied themselves putting out the collection of tableware each internee contributed to the occasion. Once everything was in place, the unlikely group took their seats and prepared to enjoy a belated Thanksgiving dinner.

Benjamin started his prayer, directing his words to the King of the Universe. He asked Micah to add his thanks, which Micah delivered to the ears of God, in Jesus' name. Sam finished the invocation with what Micah imagined was some sort of Buddhist's prayer.

"Have you heard from your son yet?" Micah asked Sam.

"You have a son?" Ella asked.

Kai nodded. "Grown up. He lived in San Francisco

before the war."

"Correspondence is impossible," Sam said. "We haven't received any news since he left the U.S."

Micah looked at Benjamin and said, "The government repatriated Naoko two months ago."

"I'm sorry," Benjamin said. "It's so . . ."

"Unfair?" Kai asked. "Yes, but Naoko volunteered to return."

"He volunteered?" Ella asked. When her gasp and alarmed expression garnered too much attention from her daughters, she dabbed her lips with a napkin and said nothing more.

Sam put his hand over Kai's delicate fingers. Where Sam spent time outdoors, his wife had the complexion of a woman who never saw the sun. Her skin was porcelain, white and smooth, and accentuated her brown almond-shaped eyes. Single strands of silver interspersed her straight black hair.

"He was angry," Sam said. "Furious that the U.S. detained him without pressing charges and without a hearing. Naoko hoped he could find transportation to Hiroshima."

"My brother's family lives there," Kai said.

"If they send us back, we'll go there too," Sam said.

"If we're here over New Year's, we'd like to host the party," Kai said. "Will you come?"

"It will be too cold to sit outside, and our quarters are very small, but we want you to come. New Year's Day is the happiest day for our people, and we want you to celebrate with us," Sam said.

"God willing, we will be there," Benjamin said.

"I'd love to join you. Thanks," Micah said. "Once it's warm again, I'll take a turn as the host." He leaned over to the youngest Rubenstein daughter and said, "I don't think my roommates will let me borrow the door. We may have to have my party at your house."

"Mama, can we?"

"Of course," Ella replied.

At the end of the evening, after they secured the door back on its hinges, Micah buttoned his jacket and returned to his room. Evenings promised to bring a damp chill to the camp, and the cloudy days lent an air of gloom. A New Year's party? Another round of holidays without his family.

Sometimes, on these rare occasions when he enjoyed the good company of the few people he befriended at Crystal City, Micah regretted his edict that Savannah and Jojo stay at Misión de Cacao. But whenever the conversation veered into repatriation and the disorder it promised, it reminded him that he held no control over his circumstances. Savannah had better control of her situation, and Alegría's too, than he did.

~

"Can you give me another one?" Savannah reached toward Alegría and waited for her to put a clothespin in her hand. Instead, Alegría gave one to Rolf, who handed it up to Savannah.

"Thank you. You make a good team. May I have one more?" Savannah snugged the clothespin in place and asked, "Who wants to help me eat tortillas?"

"Me," Alegría said.

Rolf's eyes got big as he wrestled to his feet, but before he could race toward the kitchen, a gust of wind caught the damp sheet and blew it over his head.

"Where did Rolf go?" Savannah asked. "Alegría, where did he go?"

Her beloved girl answered with a giggle. Innocence and delight bounced around Savannah's legs as she picked up the clothesbasket and started back toward the house. Their pleasant chatter almost made Savannah forget the reason for their laundry task. Rita's night sweats now encompassed daytime hours. Savannah choked back her frayed emotions and her fatigue, and gathered food for lunch.

"If your bellies are full, go hop into your bed for a siesta. Shh," Savannah reminded them. "You must be very quiet."

Rolf put his fingertip to his beautiful smile and said, "Shh," to Alegría.

Alegría responded with a whispered, "Shh."

Savannah checked the time and took a seat on the veranda. When Dr. Gutierrez arrived, she watched him exchange a conversation with someone in the passenger seat before he walked to the house.

"You have someone with you? Why don't you have them wait here? It's more comfortable than the car."

In spite of Rita's declining health, it was a glorious day, one of those picture-perfect postcard-worthy days. One of the reasons Savannah couldn't leave this beautiful country. That, and the people who lived here.

"They'll be fine in the car. Besides, after I check on your mother-in-law, I need to discuss something with you."

The doctor's demeanor gave nothing of a hint, and when he tended to Rita, he gave all of his attention and caring to her. He didn't seem to mind stepping around Carmita, who sat next to the bed, and who held Rita's boney fingers in her hand.

Savannah swallowed hard. Rita, stubborn like her son, refused to let Savannah write to Micah about her condition. As Savannah stood in the doorway during the doctor's examination, she determined she could not keep her end of the bargain. She would write a letter to Micah. Tonight.

"Do you need more for the pain?" Dr. Gutierrez asked Rita.

Rita, who no longer had the energy to speak, replied with a slight shake of her head.

"Are you sure? You don't need to suffer. I will give you as much as your body needs."

She lifted her free hand and put it on Dr. Gutierrez's wrist. "I'm fine," she mouthed. She drifted off to sleep while the physician gathered his instruments and his bag.

"Is she suffering?" Savannah asked as she escorted him back toward the main house.

"Not at the moment, but I'm sure waves of pain grip her. I will leave more medicine. Give it to her as she needs it. If you detect labored breathing or an elevated pulse, increase her dosage."

"Thank you for coming. I appreciate your kindness."

"I wish I could do more. But, in fact, I have something I need to ask you. I don't want to add to your burden, but I don't know where else to go."

"Would you like to talk over tea? Invite your passenger to join us? Savannah asked.

"Not just yet. And thank you, but I don't need tea."

Savannah gestured to a chair as she took her seat on the veranda.

"Two days ago a young couple brought a boy to my office. They said they saw the boy wandering near the road, alone and injured. He had a broken arm, which I set. While I tended to the boy, my wife—who works with me—directed the couple to the bank. They said they wanted to withdraw funds so they could pay me."

"Even though the boy was a stranger to them?" Savannah asked. "How odd."

"They seemed well-to-do. Drove a nice vehicle, wore nice clothes." Dr. Gutierrez wrung his hands before he rested his tired brown eyes on Savannah.

Savannah knew that look. It was the same one the doctor wore when he brought the infant to the mission.

"They didn't come back," she said.

"When they said they found him, I thought they lied to me because the boy looked a lot like the woman."

"Why would they do that?" Savannah asked.

Dr. Gutierrez lifted his hand and said, "At first I didn't understand."

"But then?"

"The boy was distraught and combative when they brought him into the office. Nothing irregular in that respect, given the pain of a broken arm. As soon as my wife and I could hold him still, I administered a sedative."

"And?"

"When the sedative wore off, the child's behavior didn't change. With more than a little effort, I examined the boy. He's deaf."

Dr. Gutierrez's chest rose when he pulled in a deep breath. The sigh that followed, as heavy as the planet itself, brought tears to Savannah's eyes.

"You want me to take him."

"I'm ashamed to ask. I've no right to ask, but I don't know what to do with him. As you know, the Sisters in Heredia took in a handful of orphans recently, but they refused me when I asked them to make room for this one. They said they were beyond capacity already." Dr. Gutierrez stole a glance toward the car. "My wife cannot help me with my patients if she has to watch the boy. I cannot keep him, but where else can he go?"

Savannah pushed her hair away from her face, along with trails of reluctance, fear, anger, and resignation. "How old is he?"

"Given his dental development, his size, and his weight, I'd say he's four. I know he's too young for school, but I prayed his parents looked for a means to communicate with him. I took a piece of paper and wrote the word *name* on it. He looked at me as if I were an idiot."

"You don't even know his name," Savannah said.

"I'm sorry." The doctor lowered his head.

"How *does* he communicate?"

"He's never learned. He screeches, mostly."

"What about Rita? He'll terrify her."

"Please. I know what I'm asking of you. Can you help me?" The man's voice pleaded; his countenance ripped Savannah to pieces.

"I cannot make that commitment without the agreement of the others. It wouldn't be right. Can you bring him back tomorrow afternoon?"

Dr. Gutierrez stood, wiped a few tears out of his eyes, and nodded.

As the car disappeared from view, Savannah lowered herself to her chair, ran both hands along the sides of her head, and rocked her body back and forth. More than once she'd imagined what it might be like to run away, to find transportation to take her back to the United States. Maybe dear old daddy would take her in until the governments released Micah. They could start over.

But then she'd be just like her mother, or Carmita's mother, or Rolf and Brigitte's parents. Selfish, cruel, heartless.

The doctor's request was more difficult than the one that left a newborn Paloma in the arms of strangers—strangers who chose to widen the scope of their love far enough to take in the babe. Would they be willing to do it again? The more immediate question: Was she?

Chapter Twenty-Two

December 1943. "We set a new record," Melinda said as she handed a box filled with envelopes to Micah.

"This is a new camp. Every event sets a record," Micah replied.

"Are you always so snippy around the holidays?"

"I don't mean to be. Sorry," Micah said. Levity seemed to stay just beyond his reach these days. How could the ache of emptiness—a void—exact such a heavy burden?

"Your banter hasn't changed, Keller, but your delivery has."

"Sorry. What's the new record?"

"One-thousand incoming pieces of mail in one day. A big uptick in parcels for the German residents. You should be grateful the Japanese celebrate the New Year instead of trading Christmas gifts."

"Those parcels are extravagant sacrifices for most of the senders." Micah said. "None of us here can reciprocate."

"You send letters, don't you?" Melinda asked.

"Of course."

"Look," Melinda said as she leaned forward and lowered her voice, "no one has anything extra these days. We're in the middle of a war. If your wife had to choose between a fancy handkerchief, nylon stockings, or a love letter, which would she choose? Hmm?"

Savannah with a dainty handkerchief? In stockings? The image of a cosmopolitan Savannah pushed through Micah's gloom, and a chuckle joined his answer when he said, "My wife has no need of the first two selections. I'll make sure she receives the third."

"Keller?"

"Yes?"

"I'm sorry about your Japanese friends."

Micah returned a tight-lipped grimace and headed out to make his daily deliveries. For the most part, delight and expectation filled the faces of the residents who received packages. A few, like Micah, seemed to ache at the reminder that too many miles separated the sender from the recipient.

When he reached the spot where he encountered the rattlesnake, Micah stopped, took off his hat, and ran his hand through his hair. He turned his gaze to the row of houses and rested his eyes on the one with the porch. Another couple lived in the place now.

Micah's sole source of comfort, if one could call it that, lay in the chance that Sam and Kai might join their son in Hiroshima. First they had to get there; then they'd have to find him. An unlikely possibility given their personal circumstances and the global disaster called war.

Was Micah snippy because of the upcoming holidays? How could he be otherwise? Benjamin understood when Micah's joyful attitude fell flat. Since Sam and Kai boarded the bus that marked the onset of their journey to Japan, Micah's joy failed to materialize. What was worse was Micah's realization that God hadn't turned his back on Micah Keller; it was Micah who turned his back on God. Micah ventured another look at the house before he continued his rounds. He needed to fix the mess that was his spiritual condition.

~

Savannah slid into the space beside Brigitte and drew Alegría to her lap. In spite of the mission's purported ties with an enemy alien, a few brave laborers who worked Shuler's old place sat in a row in front of them. When Benita began singing, the men's voices joined the others.

The sweet sound of worship filled the tiny chapel, a tender offering following a night of restlessness and uncertainty. No matter how she tried, Savannah couldn't rid her mind of the unseen face of a four-year-old boy. She was no nearer reaching a decision about the matter than when Dr. Gutierrez posed his request.

Roberto's message on this almost-Christmas Sabbath called the congregation to action. In addition to sharing the story of Jesus' birth and the hope He brought to the world, Roberto quoted verses from Jesus' Sermon on the Mount:

Blessed are the poor in spirit . . . those who mourn . . . the meek . . . those who hunger and thirst for righteousness . . . the merciful . . .

Savannah's concentration stalled. "Blessed are the merciful, for they shall receive mercy." The Good Lord showered Savannah with mercy, over and over again. His compassion and blessings, like a cleansing rain, supplied refreshment. How could she turn her back on an innocent child who needed—craved—mercy? Regardless of the others' reactions to the needs of the deaf child, Savannah's position was clear.

After the service ended, and while the four youngest children took their naps, the adults, and one confused but happy to be included Simón, gathered in the kitchen.

Savannah put the last damp dishtowel on the rod to dry, and danced around Roberto when he bent behind her to put a pot in the cupboard.

"You're getting to be pretty handy in the kitchen," Roberto said.

Savannah turned at the compliment. "I used to look for excuses so I could be outside."

"Used to?"

"Don't misunderstand. I don't like kitchen chores, cooking, cleaning, and the like."

"But?" Roberto asked.

"When I put a bowl of food in front of the children and see the delight in their eyes for something so simple, yet so important, as food, it makes the task more of a . . . I don't know what to call it."

"An undertaking of the heart?"

A smile spread across Savannah face. "Yes. Exactly. Something I want to do instead of something I have to do."

"Are you ready to start making the tortillas? Hmm?" Roberto asked.

"One small thing at a time," Savannah said.

Savannah and Roberto joined the others around the table.

"I need to discuss an important matter with each of you," Savannah said.

Simón looked up, wide-eyed, and said, "Do we need to put a trap in the garden again?"

"No, not this time."

The shrill clang of the bicycle bell resounded from the

caretaker's cottage.

Carmita stood and said, "I'll check on her. I'll ring the bell if I need help."

Sorrow tugged at Savannah's heart. Rita's health plummeted every day. As soon as the group made a decision regarding the deaf child, Savannah intended to write to Micah. A tough day, all around. In the lull, her countenance lifted when she replayed the words *Blessed are the merciful, for they shall receive mercy.*

Several minutes passed before Carmita returned.

"She needed more medication. The pills she took earlier didn't help very much." Carmita lowered her head and added, "I hate to see her suffer."

"Come sit down," Benita said. She patted the top of the table, warmed Carmita's tea with a helping of water from the teapot, and handed her a small pot of honey.

Savannah cleared her throat, all too aware that her request was costly. If all of these agreed, what about Rita? She, too, had a voice in the matter.

"Dr. Gutierrez asked us to take in another child, a boy."

Pablo winced when he asked, "Where will we put another one?"

Savannah liked that he used the word *we* instead of *you*.

"It's more complicated than finding a place for him to sleep. Or feeding him. Or clothing him."

"What?" asked Roberto. "Is the child a delinquent? How old is he?"

"Dr. Gutierrez thinks he's about four."

"He doesn't know? Was this one abandoned too?" Benita asked.

Savannah saw Carmita's body stiffen at the comment. If Carmita failed to grasp how her mother could leave her, how might she react to parents who discarded a disabled child?

"The boy broke his arm. A couple took him to the doctor for treatment. They said they found the boy. They left before Dr. Gutierrez learned anything else."

"Why does this boy require a family meeting?" Roberto asked. "Just set another place around the table and give us an introduction."

Now the hard part. "He wouldn't understand an introduction. He can't hear."

Deep lines marked Benita's forehead. She started to say something, but pursed her lips together.

Savannah watched Simón as his puzzlement grew to understanding.

"You mean he's deaf?" He shrugged. "So, he can point when he wants something. That's okay."

Roberto shifted in his seat and directed his comment to Simón when he said, "It's not so simple. He doesn't know words. He probably doesn't know how to tell you what he wants by pointing. Correct?"

"Dr. Gutierrez said the boy is difficult. He shrieks because he cannot tell anyone what he wants."

"Why does he shriek if he can't hear himself?" Simón asked.

"He must have learned that when he uses those muscles he gets attention," Pablo said.

"Oh my," Benita said. "Is there no one else? Someone who might know what to do for the boy?"

"Dr. Gutierrez already made inquiries. He can't find anyone." Savannah studied Carmita's serious expression. She seemed more sad than alarmed. "You haven't said anything."

"A family who lived near my aunt had a little girl who didn't hear well. She could hear a little. She couldn't speak.

Her mother taught her how to use her hands to tell her what she wanted. Maybe we could do that too."

"Until he learns, he might be horrible to have around," Savannah said.

Pablo scoffed, but not in a mean way, when he said, "I think that's an understatement. He could make everyone of us miserable."

"Does that mean you object to bringing him here?" Savannah asked.

"I didn't say that. The boy needs a home. If you need to take a vote, I say we make room for him."

Savannah saw tears brim in Carmita's eyes before the young woman looked down and wiped her hand across her cheeks. Benita sniffled.

"Are we in agreement with Pablo?" Roberto asked. After he observed the bobbing heads, he said, "It's settled, then."

"Not quite," Savannah said. "I need to speak with Rita. This affects her too. I'll be right back."

Savannah offered a prayer as she walked across the courtyard. None of them had the capacity or background required to care for the child. God had to provide a way. It wasn't the first time they'd had to rely on Him. Savannah's smile wasn't measurable, but it held a degree of expectation and hope.

Rita's long hair hung over her shoulders and framed her pale, ashen face. With her eyes closed, she looked at peace. At rest. It took a long moment for Savannah to realize the medication had nothing to do with Rita's relaxed posture. It was the absence of pain. Earthly pain. It had released its hold on her body and set her free.

Chapter Twenty-Three

January 1944. Following Christmas and New Year's, the number of parcels and pieces of mail received at the camp dwindled to a trickle. The decreased volume shortened Micah's work hours and minimized his exposure to the winter weather, but it left too much free time. Time to fret. Something that, in another lifetime, was foreign to him. But here? Emotions, irritation and impatience in particular, greeted Micah each morning at the same instant his feet hit the floor.

Maybe the culprit was recognition that the New Year marked the second anniversary of his arrest; or perhaps he should lay blame on another day spent without his wife and child. His confinement at Crystal City, with an internee's limited freedom to move about the camp, was nothing like the incarceration of a criminal. Still, this place rendered him claustrophobic. He could only hope that Savannah's letter—the one he tucked at the bottom of today's deliveries—would soothe his testy spirit.

A last-minute sensation of another person's presence gave Micah no more than a split-second to avoid a headlong collision. The near-victim walked with her head down, a means to shelter her face from the nippy wind.

"Excuse me. Sorry," Micah said. He had to grab the woman by the forearm to keep both of them from tumbling.

"So sorry," the woman replied.

"Ella?"

The woman lifted her face and adjusted her scarf. "Micah?"

"Why are you out in this? It's awful outside today."

She lifted a pillowcase, folded in half and protecting whatever she packed inside the cloth. "Benjamin forgot his change of clothes."

When Micah responded with a furrowed brow, she said. "It rained this morning. That means he had to walk in a foot of mud to reach the front door of the hospital. He always takes a change of clothes. Today, he forgot."

"I can run those up for you," Micah said.

"You have your own job to do. But thanks."

"You're sure?"

"I am. Wait. I have something to tell you. You unruffled Benjamin's religious feathers when you challenged him to study chapter fifty-three in Isaiah."

"He says he isn't prepared to debate the scripture with me yet," Micah said. His mouth widened and the edges hitched up at the reminder.

"The other night he asked my opinion," Ella said. "Nothing short of a miracle, you know. My Benjamin, the learned one, asking for my interpretation of scripture? Anyway, I wanted you to know. I'm convinced."

"Convinced?" Micah asked.

"Jesus is Messiah," Ella stated in a tone that left no room for misunderstanding.

Micah's eyebrows arched and his eyes widened at the revelation. "You . . . you believe? How—"

"How did that happen? I decided to close my memory to the opinions of certain men, religious leaders and such, and read the passages with an open mind."

"You already knew the prophecies," Micah said.

"Of course. What I didn't heed was Isaiah's description of the man who owned all of those attributes. I found Jesus in the process."

Before he gave it a second thought, Micah wrapped Ella in a bear hug. He released her just as quickly. "Sorry. But I'm so happy for you."

"It's wonderful. It is. Except where Benjamin's concerned."

"Uh, he didn't like your feedback."

"He wasn't angry. Not at all. More troubled, if anything."

"I'll have to keep praying that he finds the truth," Micah said. "In the meantime, I think you might see a little bit of a dance in my step. I'm overjoyed for you."

"I've never been happier. I must go now. See you soon."

"Shalom, Ella."

"Shalom, my friend."

Elation accompanied Micah as he finished his mail route. He'd give anything to shout out the news. Instead, he'd pen a letter to Savannah—answer her letter, share the good news, and celebrate with the only method available.

~

"Carmita, help me," Simón wailed.

Savannah and Benita, running from opposite directions, came to the boy's aid. The scene choked the air out of Savannah's chest. Benita's flailing arms earned nothing in the way of a response. Simón looked hysterical.

Savannah reached on either side of the newcomer's face and pushed hard enough to get the jaws to release their hold on Simón's wrist. Before Benita whisked her whimpering son away, Savannah saw the ugly teeth marks, the welt. Given a choice, she'd take the shrieking over the physical abuse.

They decided to call him Cedro, which meant strong gift. If they'd known the boy used his physical attributes to do harm to others, they might have called him Arrio, for war-like.

What had Roberto asked about the boy the day they elected to bring him into the mission family? "Is the child a delinquent?" At the time, Savannah thought the question was unimportant. Just an offhand comment. How could a four-year-old be a delinquent? If she'd only known . . . The boy was a heathen. Wild. Undisciplined. Untrained. The question she needed to address at the present: Was the boy trainable?

Dr. Gutierrez promised he'd share any information he gathered about a school somewhere in San José that taught deaf children. On this particular day, Savannah wondered if the school boarded its students. The terror Cedro invoked left everyone quite desperate.

Simón took the brunt of Cedro's tantrums, and judging from the angry sheen Benita still carried in her eyes when they sat for dinner, Savannah surmised Simón had instructions to keep his distance from the boy.

Even Carmita, whose gentle demeanor ought to have calmed Cedro to some degree, searched for some other task—any task—that might separate her from him. The bulk of the boy's parenting chores lay squarely on the shoulders of Savannah and Roberto. From their opposite sides of the table, they exchanged nervous glances. They'd not had a pleasant meal since Dr. Gutierrez dropped the child off and retreated from the premises. Although the doctor's arms were empty when he left, his shoulders wore the mark of an oppressed negotiator.

It was Roberto's turn to take Cedro for a very long walk around the perimeter of the property. If they couldn't reason with the boy, they decided, they'd wear him out. Anything to deplete his energy—and the volume and duration of his screaming. The good doctor understated the child's proficiency where that particular trait was concerned.

When Roberto and Cedro returned from their exercise, Savannah sat with the mission brood, all of whom wore pajamas. Rolf and Alegría snuggled with the dollies Carmita made from pieces of worn-out clothing. Although Savannah held a book in her hand, she made up her tale as she went along.

Roberto took a seat on the floor next to Savannah, and pulled Cedro onto his lap. Savannah breathed a sigh of relief when Cedro didn't wriggle in protest, but he grabbed at Rolf's dolly.

"No." Rolf drew back and shook his head. He squeezed his doll. "No," he repeated.

When Cedro kicked at Roberto and tried to snatch the toy again, Alegría wrenched out of Savannah's reach, and Cedro redirected his attention to Alegría's prize. Instead of pulling away, Alegría handed her doll—her favorite thing—to Cedro.

At first Cedro looked confused. He pulled the toy to his chest and held onto it for dear life. His eyes flashed challenges to everyone in the room, but when Alegría—her beautiful, sweet girl—smiled at Cedro, the combative, horrible, delinquent smiled back. He looked at Roberto, as if for conformation that he might keep the doll, and leaned his little-boy form against Roberto's chest. When he smiled again, Savannah choked back her tears and finished telling her bedtime story.

"And the little princess Alegría gave her favorite toy to the new prince and they became the best of friends forever and ever."

Savannah pulled her daughter up to her lap and snuggled into the sweet fragrance of her hair. That God would use a two-year-old to teach them how to love. Her heart wept with humility and gratitude.

~

The drawing of Savannah and Alegría stole Micah's breath, and as he traced Carmita's pencil strokes on the paper, his composure evaporated. When he heard one of his roommates at the door, he turned to face the wall and rubbed the evidence of loneliness out of his eyes.

While he saw traces of Savannah in his daughter's face, he saw more of himself. His cheekbones, his hair, his mouth. His little Jojo had her own charming smile. How could he thank Carmita for sharing her talent with him? What an incomparable gift.

The second drawing caught him by surprise. When did Carmita have an opportunity to draw his mother's portrait? Had she traveled to the mission over the holidays? He kept the letter in his lap while he gazed into the lovely eyes of his first love. His teacher, his cheerleader, his mother. Such a beautiful woman.

A shudder of emptiness shook his body. How he missed them. He unfolded the letter, but pushed his shoulders back when the first words that came into focus were those of an apology. Straightening his form, however, did not compensate for the blow that followed.

Micah took care to secure the drawings in a safe place before he tore out of the room, his letter fisted into a jumbled wad. He didn't stop running until he reached the swimming pool. Why his distraught body led him to this place, he couldn't say, but its isolation from the rest of the camp afforded the solitude he craved.

As the evening light waned, Micah smoothed out the creased letter and squinted to read the long message. He gathered some comfort in knowing Savannah cared for his mother during her illness, that Alegría brought small doses of sunshine to her grandmother. For that, he was grateful. But his own absence? It seemed so unforgiveable. It was too much.

The wind stung his skin as he folded the letter and slipped it inside his shoe. He snugged it in place with a sock. The wintry soil bit the soles of his feet with the same intensity as a scorched earth might sear his exposed skin.

By the time the water reached his knees, his feet recognized a fleeting, tingling sensation. When his shoulders met the surface of the pool, his feet felt nothing. Nothing at all.

Chapter Twenty-Four

He hadn't meant to wade into the water, but only to stick his toes in the frigid liquid, supposing the jolt to his body might re-engage his senses. Savannah's letter left him numb.

Rather than uncovering some level of reason, taunting words drove him forward: useless, impotent, bereft, robbed, miserable.

Disorientation.

With his next step, his face submerged and his hair lifted from his scalp in a mysterious awareness of weightlessness. He squeezed his eyes shut to protect them from the cold.

Darkness.

The perception of floating vanished. He sank, weighted down by heavy saturated clothing, fatigue, and remorse.

Fear.

He fought the urge to gulp air. It was too late for that.

Alarm.

He flailed his arms and urged his legs, now paralyzed by the cold, to push him out of danger.

Consequences.

He didn't mean to die. What of God's promises? Could Micah call upon his Creator at a time of self-inflicted folly? He wore God's words on his heart: called, redeemed, loved, forgiven.

Grace.

A prayer to the One who is mightier than the watery deep and stronger than Micah's floundering humanity; the Giver of Life.

Save me, Lord!

The surface, a gasp of air, his feet finding purchase in the shallow end of the pool. Micah's throat emitted a groan as oxygen replenished his airways.

A gift.

After God awarded him enough strength to heave his body out of the water, he lay on his back, his chest pitching as he gulped air. Far above, stars shimmered in the expansive night sky.

Order.

His heart throbbed at its temporary abuse, but as the thudding subsided, weeping—not the brisk wind—shook Micah's body. An anguished cry for forgiveness, for the reality of what he might have done, rang into the silence.

He half-expected an armed sentry to undo God's unwarranted blessings. Micah's presence beyond the confines of his quarters after curfew justified a lethal shot to his chest. Neither the guard nor the penalty materialized. Micah's respirations quieted. Finally . . .

Peace.

Micah forced his sodden, depleted mass of flesh and bones upright, shoved his bare feet into his shoes, and used his socks to cover his trembling hands. He ran with all he had left in him, back to his room, back to the life God gave him.

Called.

Micah was alive, confined at Crystal City, Texas, and still possessed the purpose for which God delivered him.

~

Carmita stood at the sink while she pressed a cool cloth to her lip. When she pulled it away and motioned for Savannah to dispense her diagnosis, Savannah winced.

Carmita's fat lower lip was just one of the marks left in Cedro's wake. The unruly and angry child dispensed his wrath on every member of the household. Cedro terrorized everyone—adult and child alike—with relentless kicks, pinches, pokes, and bites, all punctuated by his incessant screams.

His most recent victim tested her split lip with a brush of her fingertips.

"At least I still have all of my teeth," she said in a feeble attempt to downplay the seriousness of Cedro's rock throwing.

"He could have put out an eye," Savannah replied. "I don't know what to do. He acts like an animal, a boy who has lived in a cage, not a home. Didn't his parents *try* to love him?"

Roberto had abandoned his kitchen duty when Carmita dragged the boy, still kicking and shrieking, into the main house. With his strong arms, he encircled Cedro's arms and immobilized his legs, and carried the boy outside.

In what became a too-common remedy, Roberto walked with the boy in his arms. He walked until Cedro's shrill outburst stopped. Eventually, Roberto would lower Cedro to the ground, while still gripping his hand, and begin a long trek around the mission grounds. Somedays the number of laps around the property was too high to count.

Good exercise, perhaps, but nothing productive arose

from this too-frequent method meant to calm the boy and to protect the others.

Last night's exercise in futility was more protracted and later than most of the other incidents. While a brilliant moon lighted her path, Savannah took a turn at what they'd come to call the Cedro March.

"Why don't you rest for a while on the veranda? I'll bring you some fruit juice," Savannah said to Carmita.

Alone in the kitchen, Savannah inhaled; she expressed the air with a shudder. Exhaustion buried her today. She craved a moment of peace, quiet, and rest. Time for introspection, time to mourn.

When a tender hand pressed her shoulder, Savannah jumped.

"I'm sorry. I thought you heard me," Benita said.

"My ears are still ringing from Cedro's tantrum." Savannah tilted her head toward the door, beyond which she could still hear the boy wailing. "Poor Roberto."

"I don't know how to interact with that child," Benita said.

"Neither do I. Dr. Gutierrez planned to take a trip to the school for the disabled children. He thought they might have some books or some suggestions he could give to us."

"Did you see his face the last time he stopped by with the bread?"

"I did," Savannah said. "I know he feels responsible for turning this place upside down." Her mouth formed a pout when she turned to Benita and said, "We have to find a way. We can't discard him. We can't."

Savannah's resilience resembled a log fallen across a stream and blocking the waterway's path. Like the relentless power pushing at the tree trunk, her being confronted persistent fatigue, the emptiness of loss, and too little time for too many responsibilities. Like the surge that dislocated the log and released torrents of water, Savannah's fortitude crumpled and tears erupted in an unstoppable deluge.

She wore red-rimmed eyes when Carmita leaned into the doorway.

"I forgot your juice. I'm sorry," Savannah said.

"I'm fine." Carmita looked over her shoulder. "But you need to come here."

Benita, who held Paloma on her hip, followed Carmita and Savannah outside. Soon after the car doors slammed, Alegría, Rolf, and Brigitte, all rubbing naptime cobwebs out of their eyes, gathered behind the women. Rolf tugged at the hem of Savannah's skirt. She picked him up without looking at his sweet face, as she transfixed her attention on the men in uniform.

Movement at the corner of her eye earned a glance toward the Shuler property line where Randall, along with three other men, approached, as if to join the others. The two uniformed men arrived at the veranda at the same time as Randall and his co-laborers. Randall set his feet apart, folded his arms, and tilted his chin upward.

The younger of the two officers held a document, which he reviewed prior to speaking.

"Which of you is Savannah Keller?" the young man asked.

Savannah wanted to roll her eyes at the obvious. She was the only non-Tico among the group.

"Who's asking?" She mimicked Randall's stubborn pose when she crossed her arms and tipped up her nose.

"We have a complaint. About the noise."

"She doesn't own the mission any longer," Benita said.

Savannah shook her head as imperceptibly as she could, but Benita ignored her.

"According to the person who filed the complaint, the source of the noise isn't the mission, but Savannah Keller." The policeman adjusted his hat and appeared to wait for some sort of response.

Savannah raised her shoulders, turned her body so she faced Randall square in the face, and asked, "Who filed a complaint?"

"You know I did," Randall said. He spit on the ground. "Every man who lives at the Shuler place woulda' signed the thing if they thought it would help stop the disturbances. Ain't nobody sleeping at night because of the noise over here. Ain't much better during the day neither."

Roberto, with Cedro in tow, rounded the corner of the house and came to an abrupt stop.

"Trouble?" he asked.

"You're da—" Randall started to say.

The elder of the two policeman raised his hand. "We came to give Savannah Keller a warning about the noise."

"Are you serious?" Roberto asked. In his annoyance, his grip on Cedro tightened enough for Savannah to clench her jaw and hold her breath.

Cedro did not fail to react in the manner she feared. If the action hadn't decried the unhappy state of the child that was Cedro, it might have evoked genuine amusement when two policemen and three Shuler plantation laborers stepped back, each with their mouth hanging open and their hands clamped over their ears.

Benita reached for Cedro and whisked him away from the crowd. When it was possible to speak again, the older policeman looked at Randall.

"Is that what you mean?"

Randall raised his eyebrows and pulled his mouth into a tight line.

"What's wrong with the boy?" the younger officer asked.

"He's new here. Abandoned. We haven't learned how to communicate with him," Savannah said.

"Obviously," said Randall.

"But that's not normal. What's wrong with him? Is he an imbecile or something?" the policeman asked.

Savannah's hands curled into fists.

"He's deaf," Roberto said, his voice harsh.

Savannah peered at Randall when he backed up another few feet. He looked as if someone had slapped him. He unclenched a fist and pointed a finger at Savannah.

"J-j-just make him stop screaming. Else we'll report you again."

The policeman handed his paperwork to Savannah and said, "Next time we'll have to arrest you. This was a favor, a warning. It'd be best for everyone if you could find a way to handle the boy."

Pablo, who approached the mission from Shuler's place, reached the courtyard as Randall and the others retreated to their jobs. Pablo shoved Randall's shoulder and said, "Leave my family and this place alone. You're not welcome here."

"Pablo," Savannah said, "everyone is welcome at the mission."

Pablo glowered at Randall, shoved him again, and said, "Fine. You're welcome here when you come to sort out your life and decide you want to be the man God intended you to be. Otherwise, keep your miserable self elsewhere."

Savannah closed her eyes so no one could see them rolling in their sockets. That wasn't exactly what she had in mind for Pablo's apology. Although she tended to agree with him.

Chapter Twenty-Five

"Come in, come in," Benjamin said as he held the door open. "I'm relieved to see you."

Relieved? What an unusual greeting. Micah stepped into the small room, shook off a layer of cold along with his coat, and followed his host to the small table. Spirals of steam from the three bowls sitting on the tabletop curled into the air. Ella, who faced the sink when Micah walked in, turned around and smiled.

"Welcome, Micah. Please take a seat. Tea will be ready in just a minute."

"Where are your girls?"

"Next door," Benjamin said. "You're left with adult company this evening."

Micah took the chair across from Benjamin and inhaled. "Smells wonderful."

"It's just soup," Ella said.

"Ah, yes, but it's your soup, not mine."

Ella set three cups of tea on the table, along with a loaf of bread. She removed her apron and hung it over the back of her chair before she sat down.

"I'm the one who's relieved to see you," Ella said.

Micah was thankful to find himself among the living today as well, but he hadn't decided whether he ought to disclose his incident at the pool. His behavior horrified him. He feared it might undermine his testimony, as his actions defied those of a faithful follower of Christ.

"Let's bless the food and then Ella can explain," Benjamin said as he extended his hands toward the others. With their prayer circle formed and words of gratitude spoken, Benjamin looked up at Ella and asked, "Can you wait until the soup and bread are gone before you quiz our guest?"

"Seeing how he is in one piece, I can wait. Please, both of you . . . eat."

Aside from the unnerving expectation of an inquisition, the meal and companionship satisfied Micah on many levels: physical, spiritual, emotional. He wondered at the circles under Ella's eyes. They seemed to match the ones his reflection threw back at him this morning. In spite of the strain of a near drowning on his body, sleep eluded Micah.

After Ella cleared the table, she joined the men again, clasped her hands together and said, "Since I began my thorough study of the Book of Isaiah, it didn't come as a surprise to me when God nudged me awake last night. It was still early, really, but I'd drifted off to sleep already. When I awoke, I was compelled to open the scriptures, but instead of falling open to the fiftieth chapter, where I'd left off, the pages opened to chapter sixty-two."

Ella tilted her head and rested her gaze on Micah when she said, "My eyes focused on one verse: 'On your walls, O Jerusalem, I have set watchmen.' At the same time I read this, your face came to mind."

Micah shifted in his seat and forced himself to swallow the tea he'd just sipped.

"Several times I started to turn the pages back a few chapters, but my eyes held to that verse. Your image didn't leave me. I surmised that God had awakened me so that I, like a dutiful watchman, would ask for your protection. And so I prayed for you."

"And here I am—in one piece, as you said," Micah replied.

"Did something happen to you last night?" Benjamin asked.

"Let me not surmise, but state that your prayers and my pleading brought me back to a safe place, and to your home tonight." Micah bit his quivering lower lip and squeezed back the tears that welled in his eyes. "God heard your petition and mine. Thank you for your faithfulness, your obedience to God's prompting."

"Do you want to talk about it?" Benjamin asked. Such a gentle man, a man who loved the Lord, yet didn't recognize that he'd missed a necessary piece of the gift of life.

"I think I need to," Micah replied.

"Let me heat more water for tea while you gather your thoughts," Ella said.

As the story spilled out of his mouth, Micah recognized the kind gift of friendship and fellowship he enjoyed with Benjamin and Ella. Micah loved this man, this couple.

"When God first put you in my path," Micah said to Benjamin, "I thought it was because He knew I needed a German language instructor."

"And now?" Benjamin asked.

"Now?" Ella repeated. "I believe that God sent you to us so you could tell us about Yeshua, Jesus. That, and He knew you weren't a perfect man and that you might be in need of prayer from time to time."

"Thank you," Micah said as he lowered his head.

"He also wants to surround you with people who will mourn with you," Benjamin said. "We share in the sorrow of your mother's passing."

"I thank you again," Micah said. "You're both very dear to me. I don't know what I'd do without you."

"You'd manage," Ella said. "God sees to your needs whether we're here or not."

At the end of the evening, Micah stood and pushed his arms into his coat sleeves. "I'll see you Wednesday for dinner and a lesson. I hope you don't have high expectations, but I promise my rendition of soup will be edible."

"I'm sure it will be fine," Ella said.

Benjamin glanced sideways at his wife before he murmured, "Not if he cooks like I do."

"Not to worry. I'll have plenty of bread and some jam," Ella said. "No one ever leaves the Rubenstein house with a hungry belly. I see to that."

~

The warning dispensed by the local police department instigated bouts of anger and fear. How could Randall be so selfish and so determined with his quest to bully Savannah and the others who called the mission home? What would make the man stop? Anything?

Didn't he recognize that the adults at the mission sacrificed in order to help the castaway children? Wasn't it obvious that life at Misión de Cacao was already hard enough? Was the jerk blind or just an idiot?

"You know," Pablo said as he looked up from his seat on the veranda, "Randall had a point."

Savannah increased the intensity of her stomping as she paced from one end of the narrow porch to the other. With her arms already crossing her chest, she squeezed her hands around each bicep and dug her fingernails into the skin instead of releasing the pent-up scream she held down her throat—one certain to rival the intensity of Cedro's outbursts.

Savannah paused her theatrical march when she stepped in front of Pablo, blew a wisp of hair away from her face, and huffed into the night air—just for good measure. The inhale that followed carried the sweet scent of wood burning nearby. Any other time, the fragrance had the power to quiet a person's senses.

"What point?" Savannah asked.

"The screaming. Cedro's screeching is unnerving, to say the least, and it's something none of the men expect to hear while they're working the coffee crop. It's creepy. Like a banshee wailing."

"You're joking," Savannah said, although Pablo's detached expression begged to differ with her assessment. True, Cedro's verbal expression was awful, but creepy?

"Am I?"

Savannah dropped into the chair next to Pablo and slumped in the seat. "Banshee is a little strong."

Pablo arched his eyebrows.

"Let's soften the comparison to that of the vermiculated screech owl."

"You remember that bird?"

"How can I forget? Those beady yellow eyes and those eerie red feathers?"

"That's not why you remember the screech owl," Pablo said. "It was the eerie interruption by the bird calling out to its mate. Not freaky, but still creepy."

"Okay. Fine. You win. Cedro's tone and volume are enough to disturb anyone living within thirty kilometers of the mission. What do we do?"

"I thought Dr. Gutierrez planned to bring you some help. Reading material, or something of the sort."

"He's visited only a few times since he brought Cedro here. I think he's afraid we'll hide the boy in the back of his car in the hopes that he takes him back to town. Or maybe he hasn't found anything useful. Wouldn't surprise me," Savannah said.

She got up to go to the caretaker's cottage. "Please thank your father for wearing Cedro out tonight. Let's pray the boy sleeps soundly."

~

Savannah stood just inside the door of the chapel, swaying to Benita's song and rocking a squirming Paloma. At eighteen months, the girl, normally so easy-going and pleasant, weighed enough to test Savannah's stamina.

The sun barely skimmed the surface of the horizon before Paloma began her protests. Mornings were hard enough after a night of Cedro nightmares, but readying everyone for the Sabbath created more activity than normal. If she were lucky, Savannah might catch a nap with the children. That Central American siesta sounded heavenly, which was not to say that Benita's voice didn't evoke a scene as fine as heaven itself, but it was hard for Savannah to manufacture the image with little fists pounding against her shoulders.

After Benita took her seat between a yawning Alegría and

a fidgety Rolf, Roberto delivered an opening prayer. The heavy footsteps on the porch decreased to a light tiptoe as the latecomer slipped into the sanctuary. Savannah snuck a peek, but had to slam her hand over her mouth to silence her astonishment. What nerve. Did he carry salt in his pockets so that he could rub it into his verbally inflicted wounds?

Savannah berated herself for letting him distract her during prayer time, and then had to offer a silent plea for forgiveness for her untoward and unloving—yes, un-Christ-like—response. That man tested every fiber of her faith.

Randall ducked into the first empty seat he found, probably unaware he'd walked right past his designated nemesis. When Roberto spied the latest arrival, he stumbled over the first few lines of his sermon, but managed to gather his composure and press onward.

At the end of his message, Roberto hitched up one side of his mouth and said, "You know, life's pretty hard for everyone right now. No one can escape the effects of a world war. It's at these times we need to stand up and be a light in the dark world. Hard as it may seem, it's what Jesus called us to do. I think, too, we can hold each other up when we're honest about our needs or our weaknesses. I intend to share some of mine. When I'm done, anyone who has something to say can just stand up and get it off their chest."

Savannah, who slunk into a chair when Paloma nodded off, craned her neck so she could see better from her spot near the door. Randall shifted in his seat, but she couldn't tell whether he wanted to get comfortable or to hide from some of the words Roberto delivered.

"Every now and then I worry about food." Roberto patted his stomach, which was flat as a board. "Although I've never gone hungry, I worry we might not have enough to go around here."

Randall wriggled at that remark. The man was probably too proud to leave, though. Wouldn't want to draw attention to himself in front of the few men from Shuler's place who sat a few rows in front of him. Savannah bit the inside of her mouth. When did she get to be so hateful? She needed some quiet time before the Lord. Lots of confession time.

"It makes sense to wonder how the resources we have here can feed more and more mouths. But just when it seems we don't have enough to go around, someone leaves food. Sometimes at the gate, sometimes on the veranda. Once I came into the kitchen from doing chores outside, and I found two loaves of bread on the table. No note, no explanation, just the blessing of food.

"So, I need to repent, folks, for those times when I doubt the Lord intends to take care of me and all the others who live here. Even if we have to get creative with what we call a meal, He provides enough. I'm grateful."

Roberto tapped the top of the dais and took a seat next to Benita. Simón got up, walked to the place his father just vacated, and tried to peer over the lectern.

"Wait a minute," he mumbled. He went back to his chair, scooted it behind the dais, and climbed onto the seat. He teetered a little when he stood, but when he got his balance, he waved to Savannah.

"Papá's right. We have too many people here. And they keep coming. But when God brought Carmita, He gave us a niño helper. And when Señora Rita was here, Carmita was an abuela helper, a grandmother helper. So that's the thanks part. But we still have problems, don't we, Mamá?"

Benita turned her head to either side, looking for Roberto or Carmita to translate her son's comments. They both shrugged.

"We need God to send us a Cedro helper. And He could hurry up about it because I'm going crazy." Simón looked at his father and said, "Is this when I'm supposed to say 'amen'?"

"Yes," Roberto replied. "And then you're supposed to come back here with your chair."

Randall's chair scuffed the floor when he stood. Everyone turned around to see who'd made the noise. He looked down, squared his shoulders, and walked to the front of the chapel.

Savannah braced herself for . . . well, she didn't know what. Randall wasn't so awful that he'd ruin a church service. Was he?

"Uh, I guess I should thank you for not running me out of town. Or maybe lynching me. I've been a poor neighbor." He grimaced while he ran his hand through the back of his hair and lifted his gaze to Savannah. "No, I've been worse than a poor neighbor. So first thing I need to say is I'm sorry."

Savannah blinked back a tear. She expected animosity and unkindness. An apology? The thought pricked at her conscience and exposed her own hostility and spitefulness. The cloak of conviction gained weight as Randall continued speaking.

"I'm the one who complained to the police about the noise." He nodded toward Cedro. "About the boy. I didn't understand—not that ignorance is an excuse. It ain't. But now that I see how awful I've been, I want to change my ways. If you'll let me, I'll start by working with the boy. Maybe I'm that Cedro helper."

Savannah scratched at her neck. Now what?

"I know how to speak to someone who can't hear." He

lifted his arms. "I know how to speak with my hands. If you'll let me give it a try, I might be able to help the boy. If he can talk with his hands, maybe he'll quit protesting with that awful howling."

Randall lifted both shoulders again, but this time in something more akin to surrender than a combative posture. "That's it. That's all I got to say." He took a few steps toward his seat, but when his gaze fell on Simón, he said, "Sorry. I forgot. Amen."

Chapter Twenty-Six

February 1944. The demarcation between the Japanese and German housing units ebbed and flowed like the ocean tide. After the deportation of so many Japanese in August, the German population surpassed that of their Asian counterparts. With the subsequent influx of new internees, the Japanese contingency gained substantial ground— literally—which seemed to necessitate the relocation of some of the German residents.

Most times, Micah couldn't make sense of the reorganization efforts, but every such occasion unraveled parts of his organized mail route. Today, mail destined to members of seven families ended up in an undeliverable pile. When he returned to the administration building, he pulled the correspondence out of his cart and strode to Melinda's desk.

When she flicked her eyes upward, Micah said, "I need some help with forwarding addresses. If you have a minute to help me, I'll run these to the recipients before I go back to my room."

Melinda didn't say anything, and as she returned her attention to the task resting on top of a pile of papers, she stuck her hand out, palm up.

Micah straightened the stack of letters and lowered them to the outstretched hand. When Melinda continued to ignore him, he cleared his throat.

"Benjamin Rubenstein's quarters look empty. Did his family finally move to better accommodations?"

Melinda dropped her pen to the table and removed her glasses. She squeezed the bridge of her nose and winced. "You'll need international postage if you want to forward correspondence to the Rubensteins. They boarded the bus about an hour ago."

The words stalled Micah's heartbeat as effectively as a deft and merciless punch to the ribcage. On this rare occasion, Melinda's voice failed to transmit her sarcastic tone. Discomfort and sadness took the place of her habitual scowl.

"I'm sorry," she said.

"Did you know? I mean . . . did you know his name was on the list?"

"I am not permitted to discuss things of that nature." Melinda turned away from her post and kept her back to Micah while she looked out of the window located on the far side of the room. The scene, though dull, reflected freedom. With a 180-degree turn, her view was that of a human cage.

"But they're Jews. How can anyone deport them? That's a death sentence for a trumped-up charge and an arrest that, by all things decent and lawful, was illegal."

Micah's voice picked up volume as he made his declaration. A few clerks lifted eyebrows; most sunk their heads into their shoulders and studied the tops of their desks. Didn't anyone have the decency—the courage—to stand up to these immoral rulings?

"You have a lot to lose, Micah Keller. Don't draw attention to yourself." Melinda's eyes begged his focus, but all things fair and humane distorted Micah's perception.

Melinda Young wasn't responsible for the Rubensteins' departure. Micah knew that. But her attempt to appease him was just the tail end of a long trail of illogical justifications sent down the line from one official to the next, until the last person to mouth the "Sorry, it's just the way things are" stood to collect the brunt of Micah's wrath.

Instead of answering, Micah gritted his teeth until a muscle in his jaw protested. The pain won the few seconds he needed to defuse his response.

"The wife brought this to me while they waited for processing. This is for you." Melinda handed him an envelope. Her fingers brushed his hand and lingered long enough to declare her sympathy. "I'm sorry," she said again.

"What about the other families? The other six?"

Melinda shook her head. "I'll take care of their mail."

Micah cringed as images of Benjamin and Ella frolicking at the swimming pool with their daughters came to mind. Nothing in Micah's person could remove the sorrow that rose in his throat, entombed his heart, and formed tears in his eyes. Maybe one day he would manage to push aside the pain, but Micah knew the emotion waiting to take its place was unadulterated rage.

From Micah's perspective, the outlook for those detainees who faced repatriation was grim. When he first learned that a number of those who left the camp did so willingly, it escaped logic. Two things became apparent, regardless of the catalyst for a family's exodus from Crystal City.

Like Sam and Kai's son, some individuals were so angry

over their incarceration without due legal process that they were eager to leave the United States. Micah had to wonder whether the volunteers' anger clouded their decision to overlook the dangers of repatriation—the unknown situations that awaited them in their fatherland—or if they didn't recognize the risk. Nonetheless, it was common knowledge that some of those who left the camp did so unwillingly. This tended to quiet the population that remained, and to soften the tone of complaints made to those in charge.

Just as effective in modifying internee behavior was the departure of Herr Bergen, the spokesperson for the German detainees. It seemed that along with his incessant need to manage every grievance uttered by a detainee, Herr Bergen took with him much of the antagonism that he nurtured among the German population. In his absence, the camp seemed to release a collective sigh of relief.

But Benjamin, Ella, and their daughters? Micah couldn't reconcile their innocence with the penalty the family faced when they reached Germany. On his way to his room, he passed the hospital where Benjamin gifted fellow internees with his skills and medical knowledge. The wind carried the faint remnants of children's chatter and laughter, a sound now void of the contributions made by Benjamin and Ella's girls.

Micah's legs and footsteps seemed as heavy and numb as lead. He'd never been in battle—not a physical one anyway—but had to wonder if the sensation that suffocated him was similar to the shell shock that befell a wounded and traumatized soldier.

He found one of his roommates in their quarters, hunched over their small table, penning a letter. Pieter glanced up, pointed to a bag sitting on the corner of the table, and resumed writing as he said, "Brought you some chicken. Rice and beans too."

One of the benefits of working in the community mess was Pieter's frequent offering of leftovers. As its name implied, the community mess didn't produce quality meals, but no one who dined there dared complain about the quantity.

"Thanks," Micah replied. "Are you writing to Cynthia?"

"Yeah." Pieter didn't talk much in the first place, but after his fiancée's letters dried up, he quit communicating altogether. For some reason—maybe for the need to have a post-Crystal City future in sight—he mailed the maximum number of weekly outgoing letters to Cynthia: four letters, each three or four pages long.

If this evening progressed like the others, Pieter's frenetic pretense of an engagement would render him exhausted, and he'd be asleep by eight-thirty.

Micah wanted to read Ella's letter, but once he reached the line where she penned her signature, that would be the end of it. He wasn't ready for his relationship with the Rubensteins to end. Not now. Not ever.

The overcooked chicken was tough and dry, and the undercooked rice crunched between Micah's molars. He didn't care. It was a meal he didn't have to prepare. It wasn't as if he had an appetite; he ate because he needed sustenance. As he picked at his food, Pieter discharged a pitiful huff, folded his letter, and stuffed it into an envelope.

After Pieter left for the community bathing facility, Micah removed his letter, but before he started reading, he offered a prayer for the Rubenstein's safe travel and for God's mercy at its outcome. Micah's shaking hands induced another petition:

Please, Lord, help me walk through this.

Dearest Micah,

We received such short notice regarding our departure that we cannot arrange to see you before we leave. Benjamin and I offer our deepest apologies and regrets. It seemed fitting that we share a last hug, but it's not meant to be.

We thank you for your friendship and kindness, and the gift of your sense of humor. The light you illuminated in this dark place managed to ignite a few new beams of truth, and it is my prayer that we carry that brilliant gift with us on our journey.

It is no secret that we will disembark at a dangerous place, but this Jewess, the one you call a Messianic Jew, does not fear for her own life, her future. I ask that you keep Benjamin in your prayers, and the girls too, as they need to know where to place their hope.

Like the watchman in Jerusalem, please intercede to Yeshua on behalf of my family, so that when we reach Germany—a place that no longer resembles our homeland—we find ourselves equipped for the battle.

We suspect the authorities will confiscate everything of value, so I've enclosed an heirloom that once belonged to Benjamin's mother. Please take this home with you and ask your Savannah to wear it. It gives me great comfort to know that she will cherish this for its sentimental value.

If you like, we can consider this a temporary custodial arrangement. Should Benjamin and I ever have the opportunity to return to Costa Rica, we will talk about returning the item to the Rubenstein family. Until then, every time you see this on your wife's hand, please know that we love you.

We won't forget you, Micah Keller, for your imprint is firmly etched in our hearts.

Shalom,
Ella Rubenstein

Micah picked up the small package, its contents wrapped in a piece of cotton fabric and tied with white string—the customary wartime giftwrapping. Before he untied the bow, he knew it was Ella's wedding ring. Although he'd eyed the precious stone and fine gold setting many times, he could fathom the emotional attachment Ella and Benjamin had to the piece.

While it lay in the palm of his hand, the brilliant stone gleamed. The facets caught the glimmer of the waning sun as it cast its beam into the window, and multiplied the reflection in tiny dots of light.

Micah covered the ring and retied the string, and found a safe hiding place for it amongst his belongings. He nodded to Pieter when he returned, but neither spoke while the roommate climbed into his bed and turned his face to the wall.

Micah leaned his elbows on his knees, bowed his head, and started praying. Once the tears fell, he had no means to stop them.

Chapter Twenty-Seven

Brigitte bounced on her toes when she saw Dr. Gutierrez and his wife step out of their sedan. The blond-haired five-year-old clapped when she saw the basket in Luz Gutierrez's hands.

"Did you bring us a treat?" Brigitte asked.

"Of course I did. I know you have a sweet tooth." Luz lifted the corner of the cloth.

Savannah stretched her neck and said, "Sweet corn bread? How kind. Thank you."

"My husband wants a word with you," Luz said. "May I take the children inside and give them a bite?"

"Yes. Please make yourself at home," Savannah replied.

Luz called to Alegría, Rolf, and Brigitte, and gestured to Cedro to follow. The anticipation of food kept the older boy quiet—for now.

Luz lifted one-and-a-half-year-old Paloma with her free arm, and hoisted the girl up to her hip. When the olive-skinned toddler grabbed at the basket, sunlight reflected against her dark curls and chased her giggle into the house.

Savannah paused at the sight. What a haphazard collection they were. Rolf and Brigitte, both fair and lean, were tall for their ages, and on most occasions the siblings deferred to their rowdy contemporaries. The brother and sister liked books, enjoyed solitude—being alone with each other—and they minded Savannah the first time she asked them to do something. In that respect, and most others, the traits Rolf and Brigitte displayed were quite distinct from those portrayed by Alegría.

Miss Independent, at two, challenged Savannah's patience more often than she cared to admit, but how could she complain? Alegría's mettle mirrored her mother's features. Better to encourage Alegría's feisty independence and endearing inquisitiveness than to enjoy a lump of a child who'd rather nap than contend for attention.

And Cedro? Well, they had a lot to work out in that respect. Savannah doubted the boy knew who he was. They'd have to help him sort that out before they could identify his unique nature.

A smile tugged at Savannah's mouth in spite of the vast sums of work those youngsters required. If she added Simón and Carmita to the list of dependents, the tally was higher than she cared to calculate.

In reality, Carmita's rank belonged with that of the adults. Except for those spells when the young woman needed mothering, she was a capable, willing, and loving contributor and influence where all of those little children were concerned. Where Pablo was involved, Carmita's traits might require a different sort of assessment. The shy glimpses they took of each other didn't escape Savannah's notice.

What might Micah think when he returned to the mission, to not just a wife and a child, but a ready-made clan of quite distinct pieces and parts? How might she prepare her beloved for that daunting but splendid reception?

Savannah's buoyant imaginings floundered at another

intimidating prospect. What of the changes the war and incarceration inflicted on Micah? Had his circumstances sown seeds of bitterness? Anger? Depression? Would she recognize him?

Dr. Gutierrez cleared his throat, which garnered Savannah's attention again. He held a tattered and dog-eared book in his hand. He started to sit down, but when he spied Randall walking across the mission property, he bolted upright.

"What's that man want now? I heard about the trouble he stirred up with the police. What ilk of wretchedness would induce a man to complain about a child crying?" Dr. Gutierrez ended his opinion by spitting—wholly uncharacteristic of the courteous and easy-going professional. His voice resembled a mountain cat's warning growl.

Savannah decided not to remind the doctor that crying wasn't an appropriate description of the sound Cedro articulated. She didn't need to defend Randall. He'd explain himself well enough if the doctor would give him a chance.

Dr. Gutierrez stepped off the porch and wagged his finger at Randall.

"Go on back to Shuler's plantation. You don't have any business here."

Randall's eyes widened and his mouth dropped open. He bent forward and grabbed for the book. The good doctor pulled his arm back and hugged the book to his chest.

"Where'd you get that?" Randall asked.

"It's none of your concern. Go away."

"Wait," Savannah said. She walked toward the two men and stopped when she stood next to Dr. Gutierrez's elbow. "I invited him here."

When he turned to gawk at Savannah, Dr. Gutierrez's

head spun fast enough that she thought she might have to put him in a neck brace.

"I'm the boy's teacher," Randall said.

"You? Teach the boy?" Dr. Gutierrez finished his opinion with a "Pfft. Ridiculous."

Randall's frame stiffened but he resisted a verbal scrimmage. "Where'd you get that?" he asked again. He pointed to the book and then held out both of his hands. "Please. May I see it?"

When Dr. Gutierrez hesitated, Savannah nudged his arm and said, "Go on."

With the book resting on the palm of one hand, Randall opened the cover and pried through the first few pages. He feasted his eyes on each page, his excitement growing with each turn of the paper. He acted as if he were looking for the dark red X on a treasure map, the mark that revealed the location of a chest of gold.

"May I keep this?" Randall asked. His salivating mouth left a speck of spittle on his lower lip.

"Of course not. I brought it for Savannah."

"Well, what is it?" Savannah asked.

"The director at the school for disabled children gave it to me. It's a dictionary of French sign language," Dr. Gutierrez replied.

"French what? I don't know what that means," Savannah said. "Both of you, come sit down. Have some coffee."

"I have to get back to work. I came by to tell you I will start my lessons this evening," Randall said. "But this book? I never reckoned you'd find a copy. Not here. It's is a treasure."

Savannah's image of the treasure map surfaced. "Well, there you go," she said. "Would you explain it to me though?"

"People have used their hands to communicate for centuries," Dr. Gutierrez said. "The French assembled a 'hand language' so to speak, which is used in parts of Europe. Parts of Africa, too, according to the director. Costa Rica doesn't have a standard sign language, but he thought this might help you interact with Cedro."

"I know this book," Randall said. "That's why I volunteered to be the boy's teacher."

Savannah peered over Randall's shoulder and studied the book, but neither man's comments explained its usefulness. She pointed to the cover. "The book is in French. How will that help?"

Dr. Gutierrez ignored Savannah's question. Instead, he rested an intent gaze on Randall and asked, "Where did you see the book before?" Judging by the doctor's tense posture, Randall remained on his list of degenerates. Probably figured Randall stole a copy.

"Had one growing up. My mother taught all of us. Well, except my father. He thought he was too high and mighty to use his hands to speak. Thought it might dirty himself like eating dinner with his fingers."

Savannah leaned back in her chair and chewed on the little snippets of personality and upbringing Randall declared in his terse dialogue. If Randall didn't get along with his daddy, would he be a suitable teacher for Cedro?

"That's a common attitude in the United States," Dr. Gutierrez said. "Most folks up there think people who can't hear are more animal-like than human. They have a few special schools for the deaf and dumb. It sounds like the educators don't expect any of them to advance very much."

As Dr. Gutierrez spoke, Randall's jaw twitched and anger

flickered in his eyes. Savannah wanted to reach out, pat his hand, and assure him that the good doctor was simply answering her question. Randall's hand, however, formed a fist, which looked ready to connect with its target.

"What a horrible attitude," Savannah said. Not once did she consider Cedro dumb. He just lacked language skills. What did the educators expect?

"My sister," Randall said between clenched teeth, "wasn't dumb. She was just like every other five-year-old, only smarter. Wasn't her fault she got sick. Almost died. Meningitis stole her hearing. Didn't damage her brain or her sweet spirit. My father worried more about what society thought than he cared about his broken daughter. He broke the family. Not deafness."

Sometimes clarity came at a cost, a recognition that one's personal opinion grew not from empathy, but from outward and untoward biases. After Savannah's declination of his marriage proposal and his subsequent expulsion from Misión de Cacao, Randall did not turn into a despicable man. The anger he spewed was deep-seated, and a suitable reaction for someone who harbored animosity.

Savannah lowered her gaze to her empty hands. The cost of her clarity was the knowing. She wasn't to blame for Randall's rancor, but her aloof treatment toward him probably fostered more ill will. Had she known his history, would she have treated him more kindly? Why hadn't she treated him well in the first place?

"Someone gave my mother a copy of the dictionary," Randall said as he handed the book back to Dr. Gutierrez. "When I work with Cedro, will you let me use the book?"

"I will," Savannah said. "But if you use a French sign language, does that mean Cedro will 'speak' French?"

"Some of the signs are gestures, not letters. My mother kind of mixed the French and the English."

"We are adept at mixing languages here. Shouldn't be a problem," Savannah said. "After Cedro understands that you mean to give him lessons, will you let me sit with you?"

"That's the plan," Randall said. A warm smile—the first honest expression of pleasure Savannah had witnessed on the man's face—materialized.

"My goodness, can you picture Micah when he returns? We've gone from speaking English here—well primarily anyway—to English, Spanish, Spanglish, and bits of German. French sign language too? The poor man will think he's returned to a foreign country."

Savannah's words, meant to be an exclamation of enjoyment, wiped every shred of contentment off Randall's face. She spoke without thinking ... again. Mention of Micah's place in her life served an unpleasant reminder to Randall that she hadn't chosen him.

As he nodded toward Dr. Gutierrez, Randall kept his face from Savannah's line of vision. He stepped off the veranda and said, "I'll be back to work with the boy."

~

Until Micah learned the nature of his unexpected summons to the administration building, he held his breath. He hoped for a hint from Melinda, and he tried to catch her attention as he passed her desk. She acted as if she'd never seen him before. What could Micah do if his name found its way to the next deportation list?

"Keller," the guard snapped.

Micah followed the man into one of the offices in the

sprawling administrative building. An officer sat behind stacks of files that encroached on his workspace. Without looking up from his paperwork, pointed to the chair resting in front of his desk. A small fan stuck atop the files nearest the man's elbow, wobbled as it whirred.

"Sit."

Uncertainty and turmoil contended with each other while Micah grappled for some element of composure. Was it his turn to go? Would they send him back to Germany, the place the U.S. considered his homeland?—that, in spite of the fact that he had never set foot there. The value of those unlucky enough to exit the camp—whether voluntarily or not—was in their use as a commodity, a pawn in a prisoner swap. His life for an American.

The loud but useless fan didn't prevent a ring of sweat from forming under the administrator's arms. The room was austere, the walls bare with the exception of a clock, the minute hand of which advanced ten increments before the officer gave Micah his attention.

"Keller." It was a statement, not a question.

"Yes, sir."

"You have a wife and child. Why haven't they joined you here?"

Why? The man needed to ask? If Savannah and Alegría came to this place, the wretched accommodations inherent with detention aside, the family of three would make a better bargaining chip in a prisoner exchange.

"They are not considered a risk. They have every right to remain at the mission. My wife and the local caretakers have continued to serve the community in spite of my absence."

The officer didn't appear to be particularly interested in Micah's response. He dropped a pencil on top of his notebook, propped his elbows on the table, and leaned his torso forward.

"Do you speak German?"

If Micah knew the motivation behind the question, it might help him form the most self-serving response. The officer did not tender a hint.

"Limited."

"You know enough to carry on a conversation with a child?"

"If I can use my hands along with my incomplete vocabulary." Micah lifted his hands, but dropped them back into his lap when the crevices framing the administrator's sour expression deepened.

"What about Japanese?"

"What about the Japanese?"

"Not *the* Japanese," the official said with a huff. "The language. Do you speak any Japanese?"

"Me?" Was the man serious?

"Yes or no?" Annoyance took a giant step toward irritation when the administrator set his jaw.

"No, I don't speak Japanese."

"Then I suppose you'll have to place more reliance on hand gestures."

For what? Was Micah's mail route now to include the Japanese residences as well as the German? How? He'd have to begin his route at four in the morning in order to finish by midnight.

"You know the Mueller family?"

"Of course." Micah knew all of the German detainees, their ages, their birthdays, their favorite foods.

"The family is on their way to Germany."

Along with the memory of the Mueller household, the

Rubenstein family, his dear friends, came to mind. Bile crept up Micah's throat. The authorities enacted this process repeatedly, but with each deportation, as he put faces with names on the lists, his heart earned a scar. How it kept beating was beyond his imagination. He inhaled through his nose; he wanted to vomit.

"Fraü Meuller's departure creates a void in the classroom. At the Federal High School."

The student body at the Federal High School was a complicated collection. Students from both sides of the camp who hoped to remain in the United States after the war, chose to study there—as opposed to the German or Japanese language schools intended for those children who were most likely destined to return to their homelands. But what did that have to do with Micah?

"Since you are a learned man, with some experience in the classroom, you are to take her place. Aside from utilizing your college education to further the children's studies, your religious background will serve the children of these residents—whose loyalties may be in doubt—quite well. Don't you agree?"

He was here to receive a new assignment? The relief that coursed through Micah's body was as genuine as if the officer had just announced his decision to postpone Micah's execution.

"I will give it my best. When do I start?"

The bored officer looked at the clock and said, "School began eight minutes ago. You're late."

Once outside, Micah drew dusty air into his lungs and gagged on the conflicting emotions that grew from the news of the Meullers predicament and his own good fortune. Micah was not destined for Germany—not today.

Chapter Twenty-Eight

Savannah sat next to Roberto on the veranda, where they kept a distant watch over the activity in the yard. Now she understood the reason for Simón's presence in Cedro's first language class. Roberto seemed rather smug about his younger son's assignment as an assistant educator.

A balmy breeze toyed with Savannah's hair, and carried faint scraps of conversation and giggles from the caretaker's quarters where Carmita shared bedtime stories with Alegría, Brigitte, and Rolf. Somewhere inside the main house, Paloma's bare feet ran across the tile floor. She'd already streaked past the kitchen doorway twice, wearing nothing but a bow in her hair, and ignoring Benita's pleas for bath-time cooperation.

"Do you need to go help your wife?" Savannah asked.

Roberto's grin grew wide enough to reveal a pair of dimples, a rarity. "She's fine. Just fine."

Paloma did possess a wild trait, which she most often shared in the evening when all of the adults at the mission were beyond exhausted. It was Roberto upon whom the task of bathing Paloma generally fell. Benita's evening chore, as far as Savannah could tell, was long past due.

"Plantain?" Savannah asked as she passed a bowl to

Roberto.

"Sí. Or should I answer 'oui'?"

"Let's stick with an English 'yes' for now. I think I can empathize with the people of Babel. You know, the people whose language God confounded when they tried to construct a temple that would reflect their self-acclaimed notoriety."

"I miss my native Spanish, you know," Roberto said. He plopped a thin slice of fried plantain into his mouth, chewed the crunchy morsel, and asked, "Do you intend to bribe the boy with sweets every time he has a lesson?"

Savannah shrugged. "Maybe." She loved the plantain fruit. So similar to a banana—except for the fact that it was inedible in its raw state—but sweeter.

"What's Randall doing?" Roberto asked.

"I don't know, but he has Cedro's attention, and I don't hear screaming."

"The quiet is quite refreshing," Roberto said as he snagged another sweet.

More than once Savannah watched Cedro grab for a plantain out of the bowl Randall held in his lap. Randall shook his head and wagged his finger and, from her distant perspective, he appeared to mouth the word no. He also gestured with his hand. It looked as if Randall taught a sign or some sort of gesture to Simón, and then duplicated his effort with Cedro.

When Cedro's attention wandered to Simón, Randall earned it back when he leaned sideways and nudged Cedro on the shoulder. Every now and then Randall rewarded one of the boys with a plantain chip.

Savannah smelled Benita and Paloma before she saw them step onto the veranda. Sweet almond seeped from the pair.

"Did she spill a bottle of shampoo?" Savannah asked as she crinkled her nose.

"Again," Benita said with tired exasperation in her voice. She gave a bit of plantain to Paloma, who held it between two pudgy fingers. She licked it until it was soft, then let the fruit fall to the ground. One of the dogs, accustomed to Paloma's finicky eating and habitual food dropping, snatched the treat with greed.

When Paloma reached her sticky fingers toward her clean hair, Benita grabbed both of her daughter's hands and marched back into the house. While Benita ran water from the faucet, Savannah heard the woman tsk.

Randall looked toward Savannah and Roberto and gestured for them to join the language class.

"We have something to show you," Simón said. He pointed to Randall, held out his empty hands, and raised his eyebrows at Cedro.

Cedro looked at Randall, and when his teacher nodded, he made a motion with his fingers.

"He did it," Simón exclaimed. Then he pointed to himself. Again, Cedro gestured with his fingers.

Cedro's uncertainty, visible in the form of a tightly wrinkled brow and pursed lips, disappeared when Simón clapped his hands and spun in a circle. When Simón finished his celebration with a hand sign, Cedro's little face lit up.

Ah, what Savannah might have given for a camera to capture a memory. Not that she had the faintest idea what had just transpired. The details didn't matter. Randall had just gifted Cedro a voice, and that achievement was très magnifique!

WHILE I COUNT THE STARS

~

"Keller. You got my message." Melinda pushed her chair away from her desk, ran her hand through her hair, and offered a this-is-the-best-I-can-offer scowl.

"The note said you had a package for me. Something the mailman couldn't leave at my residence." The need for an in-person pick-up escaped Micah. He never left notes for the internees to collect mail at the administration building. Ever.

Melinda spun around in her chair, grabbed a large envelope, and handed it to Micah.

"Why did you need to hold this for me? I don't understand."

"I just wanted to see your charming face."

"What?" Micah stammered.

"Your mail route replacement is as dull as my co-workers. My brain and my surly personality needed a challenge. And here you are." She upgraded her scowl to a smirk.

Micah hefted the envelope and said, "This correspondence isn't some sort of emergency then?" The anxiety Melinda's note raised when one of the other teachers handed it to him hours earlier, started to subside. Micah enjoyed his first relaxed breath of the afternoon.

"How's the teacher?"

"Me?"

"You're teaching now." Melinda's new expression mimicked impatience, but Micah knew better.

"This teacher? He's fine. Loves the classroom."

"But does he love his students?"

"Unfair question. I haven't been in my new position long enough to make a diplomatic assessment."

"So," Melinda said, "diplomacy aside, how's the overall experience?"

Micah rested his elbow on the counter beside Melinda's desk and said, "Truth? The story thus far is something I could only imagine in a nightmare. You know how, in the average school, students typically join some sort of peer group."

"Yeah, yeah, yeah. The brains, the jocks, the artsy-smartsy ones, the misfits, the musicians. Yeah, I know," Melinda said. Before she gave up her position in the conversation she asked, "Which were you?"

"I played a little sports but wasn't any good. I guess most of my friends were of the genius sort," Micah said.

"It's cute that you think you're so cute," Melinda said. She never flirted with Micah. She was either starved for a good debate, or hungry to exchange a few words of friendship.

"What about you? Which group?" Micah asked.

"Me? Juvenile delinquents. You know: unteachable; incorrigible; rude; the members of the student body with the longest list of detentions served."

Somehow, Micah didn't find that surprising. He probably wore his assessment on his face. He cleared his throat.

"I pictured you more in the home-economics echelon."

"You're not cute any longer," Melinda said.

"Well then, let me describe the groups I've encountered at the Federal High School. Picture the child who transfers to a school in the middle of the year. He knows no one. He's behind on every class because the coursework in his previous school system differed from the Texas education requirements. Or so the administrators assume. Do you have any idea how few students possess transcripts from their previous schools? How hard they are to acquire? Do you?"

"Uh, no," Melinda said as she scooted back.

"Not only is the student angry that his parents forced this relocation on him—involuntary internment or not, it's always the parent's fault—he finds himself in a community framed by fences and armed guards, and fellow students who are as thoroughly traumatized, hateful, depressed, and spiteful as he is."

"Do I dare ask what you're teaching?"

He didn't mean to balk, but she couldn't have hit a nerve more sensitive than that one. "What am I teaching, or what is it my goal to teach?"

"Uh, I guess you can answer that however you like."

"I'm assigned to teach math. I like math. I do. But do you have any idea how many school systems don't require any math for students who are . . . say . . . in vocational training?"

"Uh, no."

"Neither do I. But, suffice it to say, I have seniors—*seniors*—who have to try to finish coursework taught during the freshman year in high school. And let me tell you, those children are as unhappy about the rules as I am."

"Many of them signed up for vocational studies just to avoid math. I did," Melinda said.

"I rest my case."

"I take exception to that."

"No, no, no. That's not what I meant," Micah said.

"Isn't it?" Melinda asked with her accusing eyebrows, the caterpillar-like features that, at this moment, resembled the letter *s*, laid sideways.

"I didn't mean to say you couldn't do my coursework," Micah said.

"You sure about that?"

Micah clicked his tongue against the roof of his mouth. "I know how to settle this heated exchange. You game?"

Melinda lowered her chin, which forced her to peer at Micah over the rims of her glasses while she listened to his proposition.

"I'll bring one of my geometry tests. You can take it, throw it back in my face, and revel in your brilliance when I have to give you an excellent grade."

The eyebrows flattened into a thin line, as did Melinda's mouth when she replied. "I got nothing to prove to you, Keller. Go home and read your mail."

He didn't try to silence the, "Uh huh, I thought so," that escaped from his mouth as he made haste toward the exit.

~

When he walked into his quarters, Pieter looked up from the table and nodded.

"Leftover beef, cabbage, and potatoes in the pot. Help yourself."

"Sounds great. Thanks." It did. A warm meal, the effort expended by someone else. Sounded marvelous.

While the little burner heated up the saucepan, Micah slid his fingernail under the clasp on his envelope and tugged out a small stack of paper.

"Whatca' got there, Keller?" Pieter asked.

"I don't know."

"Looks like some secret code. How'd it get past the censors?"

"I don't know," Micah replied again.

"What's with the French at the bottom of the picture? You speak French too?"

"Um . . . no."

"Dinner's burning," Pieter said as he waved his hand through a billow of smoke.

Micah grabbed the pan, shoved it under the faucet, and turned the handle. Nothing happened.

"No water pressure tonight," Pieter announced. He lifted a water glass to Micah. "Here, use this."

"Thanks," Micah replied as he poured a stingy amount of water into the pan. It sizzled for a moment, and as Micah stirred the contents, the cookware released its hold on his meal. He spooned the concoction onto his plate, grabbed a fork, and took his seat.

"Carmita—"

"The teenager your wife took in?" Pieter asked.

"Yes. Carmita drew these. She copied them from—I'll quote the letter—'a very old copy of a French sign language dictionary.'"

"What's sign language?"

Micah coughed when a piece of cabbage lodged in his throat. Another child? A child who couldn't hear? Couldn't speak? How could Savannah and the others care for any more children? What number did Cedro make? If he counted all of the mission residents under the age of eighteen, the number was seven. Seven? How in the world could Savannah, Roberto, Benita, and Pablo clothe, feed, and parent the tribe? An equally serious consideration: How did they retain their sanity?

Micah peered at of the sketches. He raised both hands, spread his fingers apart, and flicked his hands from front to back.

"I think this gesture means 'how.' See? Take a look at this drawing."

Pieter turned the page around so he could study the drawing, and mimicked Micah's interpretation of the sign.

"Why would anyone use their hands to talk?" Pieter asked.

"It's a language for folks who can't hear."

"You mean to tell me your wife took in a deaf child? What's she thinking? They don't think like other children. Something's wrong with their brains."

"Not true," said Micah, dismissing Pieter's opinion as he scoured the rest of his letter.

"Why is Carmita sending these to you? Does she think you have a deaf student to teach?"

"Savannah wants me to be able to speak to the boy when I come home. I'll learn sign language here at the same time they teach it to the boy. They call him Cedro. The doctor thinks he's four."

"The boy doesn't know how old he is?" Pieter asked.

"He can't talk," Micah said as he raised the stack of drawings. "That's why they're teaching him to sign. Poor boy couldn't even tell them his name. Might not even know what his parents named him." Micah sat back in his seat and pondered that remark for a while. The situation was unimaginable. How hard this must be for everyone at the mission.

Poor Cedro. The boy had to feel more unsettled and confused than most of Micah's students at the Federal High School. Savannah's last comment, the one above her signature and Alegría's handprint, wove its way to Micah's soul:

I don't know how much we might teach Cedro, but I suspect that for the first time in his life, he feels some sense of belonging. We've a long road ahead of us in terms of language skills and behavior challenges (the details of which I will spare you), but what we do have in endless supply is love. If only our bodies had such a stock of energy, I'd be ecstatic. We work hard here, but our sleep is sweet.

Micah rustled through Carmita's drawings until he found the page he knew she'd included. The one depicting the hand with the ring and middle fingers bent downward, the thumb stretched outward, and the index and little fingers extended straight up. The sign for the French *je t'aime*. I love you.

Chapter Twenty-Nine

December 1944. Micah stood in front of his classroom and counted the empty seats. The school year started on good footing, what with the introduction of amenities so common to American high schools: a student council and honor society, the organization of sports teams, a drum and bugle corps, and a pep squad. The camp administrator went so far as to support a class yearbook and parties. Nevertheless, the real world—that place that existed beyond the fence bordering Crystal City Internment Camp—gave no heed to such frivolities.

War didn't take note of holidays, nor did political and military dignitaries. With no apparent thought as to the upheaval, faceless officials compiled a list that sent more than 600 Germans to their homeland. In light of reports regarding the condition of the country, the expectations of the deportees could be nothing less than horrific.

Europe was a mess. News passed through the camp of Allied troops engaging in combat in Italy and France, of conflict in Poland, Russia, Belgium, and the Netherlands. Greece, Albania, Yugoslavia, and more. Allied troops and Axis countries played a deadly game as they advanced and retreated in skirmishes throughout the globe. Would this madness never end?

The empty seats sobered the students still under Micah's tutelage. He heard their murmurings, saw their defeated faces. How was he to teach if they believed they lacked a future? He couldn't blame them for the attitude that lingered in the hallways. Why study if, in the end, their destiny was menial labor, incarceration, or near-certain death?

Micah turned his back on his students, picked up a piece of chalk, and raised his hand to the chalkboard. He spoke as he wrote two word problems on the board. "It is not my place, nor is it the objective of a public school to teach you about spiritual things."

Micah turned around, shoved his hands into his pockets, and said, "Some of you know I am a pastor, and I am aware that many of the things you've experienced in coming to Crystal City have proven difficult to handle. I'm in the same boat as you, but I have some things that hold my life and my heart together."

He pointed to the two lines he wrote on the chalkboard. "If any of you need help with these equations, or just want someone to talk to, after school you can find me over by the field where the football team practices. All of you are welcome."

When the bell rang, signaling the end of the school day, Micah said, "Don't forget to do your regular class assignment."

After the last student left the room, Micah studied the impromptu equations he wrote on the board:

Sin + disobedience = death - Romans 3:23
Faith + obedience = life - John 11:25

He erased the board, picked up the Bible he brought with him each day, and turned out the light. He didn't know how the students might receive his invitation, but he knew he had to tender it. God tugged at him to do so, and Micah aimed to be obedient.

~

Randall insisted that Savannah-the-student take on the new role of Savannah-the-teacher. She chose an outdoor venue for her first French sign language class, and as the others made themselves comfortable in their place in the group's circle, she slipped out of her shoes and tucked her bare feet under her skirt.

A cloudless blue expanse and a timid breeze bathed the mission property in serenity. If she closed her eyes, Savannah expected she might hear the honeybees buzzing as they darted among a clump of delicate orchids. Given other circumstances for the outdoor retreat, she might spread out a blanket and take a nap.

Brigitte sat on one side of Savannah, Rolf on the other. She handed a small bowl to each of them.

"No snacking. Those are prizes."

Brigitte, whose blue eyes rivaled the sky, wagged her head up and down. Rolf, already poised to grab a fistful of plantain chips, pulled back his hand and wrapped his fingers around the rim of the bowl.

"The first thing Cedro will teach you is your name," Savannah said.

"I thought you were the teacher. How is Cedro going to teach? He can't talk," Brigitte said.

"Did you learn some letters at school this year?"

Savannah asked.

"Yes."

"What is the first letter in Brigitte?"

"That's easy," Brigitte said. "*B*."

"That's right. Now look at Cedro. When I point to you, he will show you the letter *B* in sign language. Ready?"

"Simón, have Cedro watch me," Savannah said.

When Cedro looked up, Savannah pointed to Brigitte, and Cedro signed the letter *B*.

"See? That's your name in sign language."

"No, it's not. My name isn't *B*. It's Brigitte."

"That's true, but we will use just one letter for our names so that it's easy and fast. Otherwise, I'd have to sign your name like this." Savannah went through the series of eight signs that spelled Brigitte's name.

"That's too hard," Brigitte said.

"So one letter is better?" Savannah asked.

"Yes."

"When I point to Brigitte again, I want everyone to sign the letter *B*."

Alegría, who sat on Roberto's lap, got caught up in the game and did her best imitation of four fingers straight up and her thumb pointing to the base of her little finger. When Roberto applauded her work, Alegría gave him a smile worth its weight in precious gems. Savannah held back an all-out celebration. If only Cedro could be so well behaved during the remaining hours in the day. One day? Maybe?

"Wonderful," Savannah said. When she earned Cedro's attention again, she pointed to him and raised her eyebrows.

Cedro pointed to himself, and when Savannah nodded, he signed the letter *C*.

"Everyone show me how we sign Cedro."

223

When her students—from the youngest, Paloma, to the oldest, Roberto—accomplished their hand spelling, Savannah turned to Rolf.

"Fantastic," she said. "I think everyone earned a plantain. Would you walk around the circle and let everyone take a chip out of your bowl?"

Savannah repeated the naming process for Alegría, Rolf, Paloma, and Simón.

"What about me?" Carmita asked. "You already gave the letter *C* to Cedro."

"Yes, we did. And we already used *R, B,* and *S* for Rolf, Brigitte, and Simón. So we need to use two letters for the rest. Watch while I show you." Savannah signed while she said, "Carmita will be *CA;* Roberto will be *RO;* Benita will be *BE,* Pablo will be *PA;* and I will be *SA.*"

What turned out to be a pleasant pastime and family-building effort, rather than a burden, ended when the group grabbed the last plantains out of the bowls.

"Let's practice using our hands whenever we say each other's names," Savannah said. "Pretty soon, we'll learn how to speak with our manos," Savannah raised her hands and wiggled her fingers, "as fast as we speak with our mouths."

As the mission residents stood and the circle dispersed, Simón slapped Pablo on the back. While he formed two letters with his fingers, he said, "Big brother, your new name is Pa. Almost like Papá. You must be really old."

Simón laughed at his cleverness, but Carmita, who stood next to Pablo during the exchange, blushed. Savannah turned her face away so that the self-conscious young woman couldn't see her pleasure. It appeared as if Carmita were mulling over the number of Pablo's years. Recalculating, perhaps, whether the number was too many or—possibly—

just right.

~

"Savannah? May I speak with you?" Pablo asked. He poked his attractive face into the doorway. He had a scruff of day-old beard on his chin and his silky black hair waved over his forehead. He was handsome like his daddy, and possessed warm, probing eyes like his mother. His posture was relaxed but when his eyes retreated from Savannah's gaze, he betrayed an anonymous undercurrent. "Mother fixed tea. Can you join me on the veranda?"

She took the seat on the opposite side of the barrel table, the place where she and Pablo engaged in chess matches, exchanged worries over Randall and the vegetable garden, and shared idle chatter. It was also the place to sit and do nothing more than sip tea and stare into the countryside.

"You had your mother make tea?"

"I started to heat the water, but she shooed me away. Said it was the one thing she knew how to prepare in the kitchen."

"If the rest of creation owned your mother's other talents, as well as her endurance, the world would be tidy, in good repair, and prepared for unexpected catastrophes." Savannah sipped her tea and watched Pablo from the corner of her eye. "We do have a rather random and unpredictable way of operating around here, in case you hadn't noticed."

"Every unexpected thing hasn't been a catastrophe," Pablo said as his mood slipped down a gear, from casual to solemn.

"Far from it," Savannah said. "Sometimes, though, the hurt overshadows an abundance of good things. When I get to feeling low about Micah, and about the war, I need you to point to all of the blessings we have running underfoot here."

"Do you think it's wrong to celebrate in wartime?"

The question didn't seem to fit the verbal puzzle the two of them sat down to piece together tonight. The turn in conversation shouldn't have surprised Savannah, but the peculiar question found her unprepared.

"I think certain times call for sackcloth and ashes, while others demand a joyful and thankful observance. In Biblical times, when the Jews lived in captivity in Babylon for seventy years, the prophet Jeremiah advised the people to lead normal lives, to build houses, plant gardens, marry, and bear children. Those are joyful things, and if we can find them during this upheaval, don't you think we ought to embrace them?"

"I want to, but part of me feels guilty, as if my happiness is an offense to those who hurt," Pablo said.

"People shouldn't be resentful of others' situations. You can't base your life on other people's opinions—which is not to be confused with wise counsel. Those two things are not the same." Savannah leaned across the barrel and whispered, "Tell me. What have you got to celebrate?"

Even in the dusky light she could see Pablo's face color. He leaned back in his seat, took a long sip of tea, and put the cup down with an exaggerated flourish.

"I want to marry."

Tears sprang into Savannah's eyes as she deciphered his words, and with a hasty flick of her hair off her face, she brushed the moisture away.

"Marry?" She held her fingers in front of her mouth, lest he see her lips tremble. Biting her lower lip was wholly ineffective. Her mind spun at the pronouncement. What about the affection he and Carmita had for each other? Was she still a child in Pablo's eyes? When did he find time to court anyone? How? Who?

A wide grin spread across Pablo's face when he said, "With your permission, I want to build a small cottage over there." He pointed to a small patch of land beside the caretaker's residence, which was now Savannah's home. "It wouldn't be big, but it would offer privacy, and since we'd still be here at the mission, we'd be around to help keep things—as you said—tidy, in good repair, and prepared for unexpected catastrophes. What do you think? Would you allow it?"

The skin on Savannah's forehead fell into a mass of deep furrows. She pinched every muscle in her face so hard that she had to worry if she'd ever wear a normal expression again. Did she miss something?

"What do you mean when you say, 'we'd still be here'?"

Now it was Pablo's turn to look confused. "We. Carmita and I want to stay here after we marry."

Savannah's gaping mouth effectively ironed out every worry line on her face. She took the back of her hand and tapped her lower jaw back into place.

"You and Carmita?"

"Of course. Who else?" Pablo asked.

"I-I-I didn't know you and she spent time together. I'm surprised, but I want you to know how happy this makes me. I'm thrilled." That, she was. She had no reservations. None.

"So may I build a cottage?"

"You don't need my permission. This property belongs to your family," Savannah said.

Pablo pressed his lips together and wagged his head back and forth. "You know that's on paper only."

When Savannah opened her mouth to protest, Pablo held up his hand and said, "If you want to pretend that this property belongs to my parents, then give me your blessing to build a structure near yours. I don't want you to think we're encroaching on your living quarters."

"Pablo Vargas, the construction of a new cottage will bring me much pleasure. In fact, you can count on me to help with the building, because I suspect one charming young woman is counting the days until you carry her over the threshold."

"One thing, though. I haven't asked her yet. You have to pretend we didn't have this conversation."

"I'll do my best to keep quiet."

Later, after she readied for bed, Savannah checked on each of the children and took a long look at the beauty who would soon be a bride. While Savannah rested her hand on the doorframe, she gauged the effect of the marriage on her household. The construction of a cottage next door wouldn't encroach on her in the least. In fact, Carmita's move to the proposed homestead would give Savannah more space in this tiny dwelling.

The thought left Savannah wanting. As the moon disappeared behind the clouds, cloaking the mission in heavy darkness, her delight in the news flagged. It wasn't jealousy. She wasn't one of those people who resented another person's joy. The image of the joyful bride and groom induced the pang of emptiness and reminded Savannah of the cost of her separation from Micah.

The weight of the nothingness in her empty arms pressed against her heart. At times, such as this night, the void suffocated her.

Chapter Thirty

February 1945. For the first time since his arrest three years earlier, news of the war told of measurable accomplishments in the fight against the aggressors. Not only did the German army fail to recapture Belgium in what news reports dubbed The Battle of the Bulge, they retreated in face of the Allied forces. More good news came to the internment camp when the Soviets managed to expel the Germans and their conspirators from Warsaw. Unlike other skirmishes, when land holdings changed back and forth, German forces failed to recoup and recover. Or so it seemed. Micah could only hold onto the hope that this marked a turning point.

"Mr. Keller, if the war ends and they send us home before the school year is over, will I still graduate?" Daryl, the designated leader of the Federal High School's drum and bugle corps, pinched his forehead into tight furrows. "I mean, I want to be out of here and go to college, but if I don't graduate, I'll probably have to do my senior year over again. That wouldn't be fair."

Fair? Did anyone in this place remember the meaning of the word? Sure, administrators bent over backwards to help the students excel, in spite of adhering to State regulations regarding minimum credits in the various subjects. Exacting the same standards for these detained students seemed ridiculous, but more than once Micah had successfully lobbied on behalf of students as they fought for accreditation for subjects studied elsewhere. He found himself standing in front of the Officer in Charge on enough occasions that the man knew Micah by name. Well, by his last name, anyway.

"Even if the last battle were fought today, I don't think any of our situations will be resolved before the end of the school term," Micah said.

"Four months? Once this crappy war is over, you think it will take more than four months to get out of here?"

Micah bent his head toward Daryl. "Think about it."

Richard, one of the other drummers who sat on the grass near the football team's practice area, dislodged a stone with the tip of his shoe, and kicked it away. "He's right."

"I lose a year no matter what," Daryl said. "If they let us out of here too early, I won't graduate. If they keep us too long, I won't get to enroll in college. So much for my plans."

"You think God's plans can fix this mess?" Richard directed his question to Micah. "Like that proverb said?"

"Are you referring to, 'Many are the plans in the mind of a man, but it is the purpose of the Lord that will stand'?" Micah asked.

"Yeah, that one will do. You think God will put our lives back together?" Richard asked.

They wanted his opinion? Micah smiled at the irony. He shared their angst, their impatience, their self-righteous anger, their loathing of a life absconded. But if one were to believe the scripture, one must take the words as truth.

"Our lives are 'together' while we're in this place."

Daryl picked up a stone and tossed it away from the group of eight students who still assembled on a regular basis for Bible study. At times the occasion turned into a peer group ministry rather than a study. These teenagers had tough questions, ugly circumstances, and uncertain futures.

"You call this 'together'?" Daryl asked.

"If you let the Lord lead, you're always in the right place," Micah said. "Jesus said 'Come. Follow me.' He didn't say, 'Where do you want to go? I'll tag along and make sure it turns out the way you want.'"

"That's cute, Mr. Keller. I like that," Brenda, one of the girls on the pep team, said. When her friend, Amy, started giggling, Brenda punched her arm.

Micah tried to ignore the girls' exchange. Brenda's crush on her teacher had the capacity to make Micah blush. With great care, he kept the girl at a proper distance.

At the sound of footsteps, Micah and the students craned their necks to see who approached. One of the camp guards had his eye on Micah. His expression was grim enough to cause Brenda and Amy to scoot backwards.

"Keller?"

"Yes?"

"What are you doing all the way out here?" The guard glanced at the students, paused at the sight of their Bibles, and scowled.

"Studying," Daryl said.

"You're to come with me," the guard said as he pointed to Micah. "Hurry up."

Micah stood, brushed dust off his pants, and nodded to his students. "Richard, why don't you take the lead and start with that proverb."

"I don't know which—"

"Chapter twenty, verse eighteen," Micah said as he turned away.

"Do you have any idea how long it took me to find you?" the guard asked.

"No. Is something wrong?"

"How should I know? I just take orders, and since I've been gone too long, it probably looks like I don't know how to follow an order. Hurry up."

The guard's legs were longer than Micah's, and it looked as if Micah might have to sprint to keep up. Never mind the ghastly scenarios spinning in his mind. What was the problem, anyway?

The two men rounded the side of the administration building and collided with another pair of guards.

"Where have you been, Morgan?" one of the guards hissed as he looked over Micah and his escort.

"Don't ask. He couldn't have been farther away if he'd been trying to escape."

Micah stiffened. "I wasn't trying—"

"I was kidding, Keller. Take it easy, will you?" The guard's labored breathing interrupted the flow of his retort. "He's all yours, boys."

Micah wrenched his head in an excruciating turn as the guard named Morgan abandoned him and the other two armed officers led him into the building. When they exited the door that delineated freedom, Micah gasped. He froze long enough that both guards stepped away from him.

Not for long. Both backtracked three paces, grabbed an arm, and led Micah to a waiting pickup truck. Not a military or official vehicle. Just an ordinary, used-to-be-white, dented and tired pickup truck.

"What's going on?" Micah asked for the third time since the driver pulled away from the camp.

The guard to his right grunted. The driver did likewise.

Micah reminded himself to breathe. He filled his lungs with the dusty air that swept into the truck's cab as it traveled along a lonely two-lane highway. The scenery lacked anything resembling human habitation, with the exception of an occasional discarded tire or bits of paper that accumulated in an empty ditch.

He expelled the spent oxygen in a slow, deliberate exhale. For some reason, this situation reminded Micah of the prison break he imagined every time he grew weary of his detention. In his dream state, he slipped out of the administration building, snuck into a pickup truck—although he hid in the truck bed; not the cab—and he dragged the pleasant air of freedom into his body as the vehicle jostled over the bumps in the road.

He didn't think this was the normal method used to begin the deportation process, but after three years of imprisonment, who knew if rules existed anymore?

A small sign and then a larger billboard hinted that civilization lay somewhere in the vicinity. A house. A barn. A couple of scrawny cows. Cows! He hadn't seen one since he left Misión de Cacao. When the sight warmed Micah's heart, a lump lodged in his throat. If cows had the capacity to move him, how might he control his emotions when he saw people? Free people.

Indeed, inhabitants came into view, and Micah choked back his emotions. A little girl sat on a swing, her brown hair billowing as she swung to and fro. The mother hung clothing on a line behind the swing set. Micah winced. It hurt to inhale.

"Lighten up, will ya?" the driver said.

"Would you just tell me what's going on?" Micah asked.

Neither man acknowledged the question as they entered

the city limits. The real Crystal City. The driver slowed, took a couple of turns while Micah gaped at the normalcy surrounding him, and stopped the vehicle.

"Get out," the guard to his right said as he climbed out of the truck. "Put this on."

Micah held out his hand, but couldn't bring himself to follow the order to don the article.

"Would you just tell me? Please?"

"You've got ten seconds to put that on." The driver twisted his torso just enough to remind Micah that he was armed.

Micah extended his arms in surrender. He murmured to himself, "It is the purpose of the Lord that will stand . . . it is the purpose of the Lord that will stand . . ."

~

"If Pablo doesn't quit hammering soon, I'll scream," Carmita said. The teenager wiped a tear from her cheek as she knelt on the kitchen floor. Cedro stood inches away from her face, screeching. Each time she bathed the raw skin on his leg with her warm cloth, the decibel level in the house rivaled the squeal of the old truck's brakes when it traveled down a steep road.

Neither Carmita nor Savannah had the luxury of cupping their hands over their ears to curtail Cedro's response to a relatively minor injury. The boy saw blood; therefore, the boy had to scream.

The gash on Alegría's arm, on the other hand, worried Savannah. Each time she released the fingers she pressed against Alegría's wound, it seeped blood. Driving the rattletrap of a truck to town after dusk was not a pleasant expectation any more than Alegría having to deal with stitches.

Alegría sat in her chair, uncharacteristically quiet and quite pale. She sobbed, without sound, as heavy droplets fell from her eyes, dribbled to her chin, and dampened the front of her dress. Her eyes, so sorrowful, so identical to her mommy's, begged for comfort. Her bottom lip quivered, and each time Cedro wailed, a shudder ran over the little girl's shoulders.

Still holding a cloth over the wound, Savannah hung her head. Where was Micah? Why wasn't he here? A woman needed her husband to be present. The title of wife afforded nothing. Nothing! She needed a helpmate, her other half. She was so, so tired of the responsibility. All of it.

Of late, the hard days outnumbered the pleasant. Cedro's progress was measurable, but its impact on his behavior was sporadic and unpredictable; hence, the current catastrophe.

"How long will it take for Pablo to build that room of his? He's driving me crazy," Carmita said between clenched teeth.

"More than a few days," Savannah replied. "He can only work when he finds materials and he has the time."

"Well, why does he have to build something now, while this place is already so loud?"

"Are you blaming your patient for the frenzy?" Savannah asked as she nodded toward Cedro.

"Him too."

It seemed to Savannah that the same day Pablo told her of his plans to ask Carmita to marry him that Carmita decided to prove she was too immature to be an adult. From the first day Pablo lugged boards and bags of cement to the area where he intended to build a new residence, Carmita complained.

First it was the sight of the materials that ruined the ambiance. Then it was the disturbance Pablo created when he took to hammering and sawing boards. Just yesterday, Carmita's complaints expanded to include Pablo's inconsiderate schedule, which meant additional clean up time in the kitchen.

Maybe Pablo might sense the need to wait a few more years—or maybe a decade—before he wed. From the fervor with which he attacked his task, however, it appeared the young man was in a hurry to announce his intentions to the piqued Carmita. She was as oblivious of his plans as he was of her angst. At least the pair would have a life together, which was more than Savannah enjoyed. Good for them.

Savannah squeezed her eyes shut at her sarcasm, her fatigue, and her overwhelming circumstances. She ignored the chair as it toppled over when Carmita released Cedro and let him run back outside. Savannah pretended to ignore Carmita's murmuring as she shoved the chair back under the table and walked to the courtyard, but when Alegría's tears fell onto her hands, Savannah's shoulders heaved as she let her guard down far enough to weep.

A gentle hand touched her shoulder.

"Savannah?" Benita knelt on the floor and took the cloth from Savannah's hand. "Here, let me see." Savannah heard Benita catch her breath.

"I can't make it stop," Savannah said.

"You need to take her to Dr. Gutierrez. I'll get Pablo. He can drive you."

When Benita returned, she relieved Savannah of the task of tending to Alegría's wound until Pablo pulled the truck in front of the door nearest the kitchen.

"You look a wreck," Benita said.

"I'm sorry, I just—"

"Don't Savannah. You blame yourself for everything that isn't perfect, and expect to be able to fix everything. Let me go with Pablo. You need to lie down."

"I have to take my daughter. She's scared."

"Savannah Keller, I am second mamá to your daughter. She trusts me. I'll take care of her just the way you would. You need a rest. Go on. We'll be back in a couple of hours."

Roberto stood at the truck as Savannah escorted Benita and Alegría outside. He opened the door and helped Benita inside the cab. As soon as the door closed again, Alegría rested her head against Benita's bosom and closed her eyes.

"See," Benita whispered. "I can do this."

As the truck pulled away, Roberto said, "You heard mi esposa. I'll manage the troops for a while. Do you want me to call you for supper?"

"No, but please fetch me as soon as Benita and Pablo return with my girl."

Savannah retreated to her bed and closed her eyes, and at the sound of someone knocking on the doorframe, opened them to evening's waning light. How long had she slept?

"Um," she said as she raised herself to her elbow. "Is Alegría back? Is she all right?"

Pablo's pleasant voice was quiet and tender when he answered, "She's fine. Dr. Gutierrez fixed her up with six stitches."

"My poor darling. I need to get my feet under me and give her some love."

"She's fast asleep. Mamá suggested you let her stay with them tonight. Alegría and Paloma are down for the night."

"I still need to kiss her good night, and I imagine Carmita

would like some help getting the others ready for bed."

"Where is Carmita, by the way?" Pablo asked.

"What do you mean?"

"She didn't come to supper. We thought she might be napping, like you."

"Carmita missed supper?" That meant Roberto fixed the meal and managed the brood of children by himself. Savannah stood and wiped the sleep out of her eyes.

"Why didn't your father come get me? How in the world did he handle all of the children on his own?"

Pablo lifted both shoulders. "I don't know. But where do you think I might find Carmita?"

"She didn't have an easy day. Maybe she took a walk among the coffee plants. I do that, you know, when I need quiet and solitude," Savannah said, although at the time she couldn't recall the last time she enjoyed quiet and solitude— with the exception of the past few hours, anyway.

"I'll go look," Pablo said.

More than an hour later, as the sun hung so low on the horizon that only a slender line of pink remained, Savannah sat on the veranda with Benita and Roberto. With every child asleep somewhere within the confines of the mission, an uncanny stillness rested over the place.

Benita leaned over and patted the top of Savannah's hand. "Are you all right now?"

"Yes. Sorry for the drama."

"No need to apologize. None of this is easy."

Pablo's hasty footsteps announced his return. He gulped air, rested his arm against the porch railing, and said, "Has she come back?"

"You didn't find her?" Savannah asked.

"I looked everywhere. She's not here."

Chapter Thirty-One

The guards directed Micah up a narrow walk that led to the side door of a white building. The place looked like a church. Or maybe a funeral parlor. Once inside, the men paused while their eyes adjusted to the dim lighting. One of the guards pointed to a narrow stairway to their right.

The stairs opened into the lower level of the building where the tile floor had enough layers of wax that it shimmered when a light glanced over the surface. When a deep sound reverberated from overhead, one of the guards looked at his watch. Micah gulped. This game wasn't funny.

"Here's the deal, Keller," the driver said. "We three are going upstairs where we will take seats in the bench closest to the front door. We will not speak to each other. We will not physically restrain you."

"Unless you force us to," the other guard said. "The suit jackets help us blend in with the crowd. They do not prevent us from reaching our guns and shooting you, although that'd probably make the hostess mad as a hornet."

"Yeah," the driver said with a chuckle. "You don't want to mess with your hostess. No sir. No way."

"You ready?"

Ready for what? Micah ran his fingers over the lapel on

the navy blue jacket. Nice jacket. Would look better with a tie, but it wasn't part of the package. Apparently. And who was the hostess? Only one way to find out.

"I'm game," Micah said. "Let's go."

The guards continued to sandwich Micah between them as they walked down the hallway and climbed stairs that opened into a small foyer. Sunlight gleamed through tall windows that encircled the space. Heavy wooden double doors that opened to the front of the building stood wide open, exposing a long sidewalk and a manicured spread of grass.

When the three men slipped into their assigned bench, every person sitting in front of them turned and stared. Most looked disappointed. A few voiced their displeasure at the appearance of the newcomers as they ran their gaze up and down.

Yeah, they were underdressed. The sanctuary, a pleasant chapel with several small stained-glass windows near the front, housed about twenty-five or thirty people, all dressed for a special occasion. Like a wedding.

Which is what the organist announced when she began to play the traditional wedding march. When Micah glanced at his guards, both stared straight ahead, but the edge of his driver's mouth lifted enough for Micah to see his amusement.

A sweet little girl of about five skipped down the aisle, followed by two women who had to be bridesmaids. Micah studied both women. Never saw them before in his life. Why was he here? Did the regular pastor get sick? Was he supposed to run to the front of the chapel after the bride arrived and help her and her groom exchange vows? Micah had no reason to complain about this unexpected burst of freedom, but it would be better to know why he was here.

The veil didn't hide the answer. He'd know the bride anywhere. Micah hung his head and shook it back and forth. He had to bite his lip so that his snicker didn't echo throughout the sanctuary. How did she pull this off?

The bride paused at the entryway to the chapel, with her hand around her father's arm. Micah's shoulders smacked the back of the pew when he saw Melinda's escort. The Officer in Charge? Melinda's father? No way.

Micah's response caught the bride's attention, and when she turned her head, she tripped. Her father prevented her stumble from taking her to the floor, but he lacked a means to close the woman's gaping mouth or stuff her bulging eyes back into their sockets.

She didn't expect him? Micah slid down in his seat. What he wanted to do was slither onto the floor and out the front door. Who was the brilliant person who invited Micah without consulting the bride? He sucked in his breath. Oh boy.

Melinda and Micah stared at each other long enough to induce a few coughs among the guests, which encouraged the bride to continue her march up the aisle. More than once Micah saw her start to turn her head around. More than once her father stuck an elbow in her ribs.

Micah wanted to bolt. Ruin Melinda's wedding? She'd pulverize him if she ever got the chance. He squirmed as he pictured the guards pulling their weapons out of their jackets and chasing him across the church lawn. They'd shoot him before he made it to the pickup truck.

The guard who drove the wedding-crashers to town leaned into Micah, muted his comment with his hand, and said, "Sit still, will ya?"

Once positioned next to her groom, Melinda focused on

her soon-to-be-mate, but when her father made his way to his seat, her eyes wandered beyond the guests seated in the front pews long enough to glance at the three men situated in the back. The groom leaned over and whispered something in her ear, and even from his distant view, Micah saw her squeeze the groom's hand.

After the service the guards waited until the chapel emptied before they stood.

"What do you want to do, Langston?" the guard who drove asked his fellow officer.

"OIC said we could go to the reception if we thought we could keep Keller in line, and his identity hidden."

"Yeah, but this guy has a big mouth. Did you see how he got everybody's attention when the bride caught sight of him? I thought I might have to shoot him, just to let everybody know they were safe."

Were they joking? Micah's head turned from one man to the other while they acted as if he wasn't in hearing range.

"Don't know, Cooper. What do you want to do?"

Micah finally knew their names. The driver was Cooper; the sidekick, Langston.

"You think they have cake?" Cooper asked.

"Naw. Where would they get sugar? And eggs? Huh?"

"Maybe the OIC has connections. Or maybe he grabbed some from the mess at the camp. The *detainees*," Cooper said with some derision in his voice, "always get enough sugar and eggs." When he glared at Micah, his sincerity, or lack of, was not apparent.

"Guys," Micah said, "I don't think the bride expected us here. She probably doesn't want us at her reception. Brides want their wedding day to be perfect." Micah jabbed his thumb against his chest when he added, "I don't make the day perfect. Let's just go."

Cooper looked at Langston, eyeballed Micah, and said, "You think we should go? Fine." Cooper turned toward Langston and said, "We're staying. Keller? One bad move out of you and you're history. Understand?"

"Yeah. Sure." Micah hadn't intended to use reverse psychology on these two. Yeah, he wanted to go to the reception, but only if he was welcome there. He didn't want to mess up Melinda's day. Since she didn't make arrangements to have him attend, she might not be too happy to see his face downstairs where the celebration was underway.

"Here's the story we need to tell," Langston said. "You work at the camp."

"That's not a story. I do work at the camp," Micah said.

"Just listen," Cooper said.

"You're there on a temporary basis. Assigned to the mailroom. That's how you know Melinda. You didn't bring your family to Crystal City because you couldn't find a place in town for them to live. You keep a room at the camp. Anything else, Langston?"

"Uh, yeah. Don't tell anybody we're here on official business. We're guests just like you," Langston said.

"Nobody hears about our being armed. Got it?"

"Sure. Got it," Micah said.

They took the stairs to the lower level and followed the sound of laughter and music. Just before they stepped inside the large room, Cooper leaned over to Micah and said, "Stay away from this door. You hang out on the other side of the room."

"Got it," Micah said.

As soon as the three stepped inside, the groom looked

up, excused himself from a conversation, and strode over to them. Micah braced himself for the invitation to leave.

"Which one of you is Keller?" he asked.

Both of the guards looked as if the groom had just insulted them. The groom was supposed to pick out the "criminal" among the three? Really?

"I am," Micah said.

The groom stuck his hand in Micah's direction so fast that Micah stepped backwards. The groom grabbed Micah's hand and pumped a welcome that was as hearty as his voice.

"Good to finally meet you. So glad they made a way for you to join us today. You're my wedding present to the bride."

Gerald Carter wore a smile worthy of a face on a magazine cover. He was average height and had broad shoulders, but no one would ever guess the man was a Texan. His pasty-white skin looked as if he never ventured outside. He looked like he belonged in a suit in a boardroom somewhere in New York City.

Wartime weddings often came during rushed courtships and too-short furloughs, as men hustled from stateside to foreign soil. Gerald's glasses, with lenses thick as a soda bottle, hinted that he was unfit to serve in the military.

"Listen, I need to get back to Melinda, but I wanted to thank you for everything," Gerald said.

Everything? What everything? Who was this man who acted like he and Micah were pals? The guards exchanged a series of expressions that were as perplexed as Micah felt.

Gerald reached into his jacket, pulled out an envelope, and handed it to Micah.

"This explains everything." He shook Micah's hand again, and grinned like a six-year-old who just caught his first catfish. When Gerald looked up and saw Melinda watching the conversation, he said, "Help yourself to some food. I gotta go dance with my girl."

Micah stared at the groom, who whisked his bride to the center of the room. Someone put a new record on the gramophone and the pair began to dance. One of the guards, probably the amiable Cooper, slapped Micah on the back.

"Let's get some cake, boys."

Roberto motioned to Pablo to take a seat. "Benita, would you get the boy a glass of water?"

Savannah watched a reluctant Pablo lower himself to a chair. His panting filled the uncomfortable silence on the veranda while Savannah replayed the scene in the kitchen with Carmita. Did she give a hint that escaped Savannah's notice? At the time, Alegría held Savannah's attention. Carmita's griping, while heard, seemed nothing out of the ordinary.

Waves of nausea and guilt clawed at Savannah. That wasn't true. The complaints weren't typical, and she hadn't bothered to probe into Carmita's moods to see that the young woman needed a mother's love. The pain that coursed through Savannah's being was fraught with guilt and regret. She'd taken Carmita for granted, demanding the teenager take the role of a parent, all the while she needed someone to fill that role in her life.

Savannah crossed her arms and hugged her chest. What a terrible injustice. Now? Where was that beautiful child? She wiped tears away from her face, and stifled a moan. Savannah didn't mean to feed Pablo's fears.

When Benita returned, Pablo gulped from the glass she handed to him.

Roberto leaned forward in his chair and said, "Before everyone get's worked up—"

"Too late for that, Papá," Pablo said.

"I know, Son, but we need to be practical. We can't drive around in the dark, looking along every centimeter of the road. Whatever we do, it will have to wait until morning."

Pablo, with his elbows on his knees, covered his face with his hands. When he sat back up he said, "You're right, but I wish someone could tell me why she ran off. What happened today?" He turned toward Savannah. "You said she didn't have a good day."

"You probably didn't hear Cedro howling while she cleaned him up after he fell."

"Oh, I heard him. I just decided to keep working. The hammering helped drown out the noise. Did she say anything?"

"She complained about the noise your construction project made." Savannah sat up and looked at Pablo. She parted her lips, but didn't know how to form the question.

"What?" Pablo asked.

"Does Carmita know why you're building the new house?"

Pablo shrugged. "I said I needed a place of my own, and that it was time I got out from underneath the care of my parents. It was time to start a new life, get ready for a family."

"How did she react to that news?"

"She seemed peeved, to tell you the truth."

Savannah turned her head far enough to catch Benita's widened eyes.

"Does Carmita know how you feel about her?" Savannah

asked.

"How could she not? Isn't it obvious?"

When Benita tsk'd, Roberto threw her a look that suggested he was as clueless as Pablo was.

"Son," Benita said, "have you and Carmita ever talked about marriage or about having a family?"

"We don't need to. I already know she wants to be married. She wants seven children. She told me as much."

"Oh dear," Savannah said, more to herself than to the others.

"Oh dear?" This, from Roberto.

"What?" Pablo's voice earned a degree of impatience.

"Have you kissed the girl?" Roberto asked.

Lack of light notwithstanding, Savannah knew Pablo blushed. She could feel the heat from where she sat.

"What? No. I mean, she's too . . . too innocent."

"Pablo, my sweet boy," Benita said, "just as men cannot read the mind of a woman, we females cannot read the heart of a man."

"That sounds really poetic, but would you explain? Would someone please explain?" Pablo asked.

"Perhaps she does not know that you are building the new house for her. Perhaps she thinks you have fallen in love with someone else." Benita sat back in her chair. Her head swung side to side. "Oh, Pablo."

"You think she doesn't know?" Pablo grabbed his head with both hands and gripped his hair. "This is my fault? What did I do?"

"Well, let's look at the bright side," Savannah said. "She wouldn't have acted this way if she didn't want to be the one who held your heart. Her actions, although not wise, reveal the way she feels about you."

"Little good that will do me if she's run away. What if I can't find her? What if someone else finds her and—"

"Stop," Roberto said. "Take each other's hands. Let's pray the girl back home. And let's be fervent about it. You and Carmita will give us beautiful grandchildren. We all have much at stake here."

Chapter Thirty-Two

Micah's feet weighed a thousand pounds apiece as he walked the few steps that separated liberty from confinement. The two guards were as chatty on the return trip as they'd been on the drive to town. It seemed the only difference in the atmosphere was the hint of garlic that drifted into the truck cab when Cooper the driver burped. After the first outburst, the man patted his stomach and said, "Haven't seen food like that since what? 1941? Ate too much. Sorry." He didn't bother to apologize for the subsequent eruptions.

For a wartime wedding, the bride's family managed to lay a spread of sandwiches and a tiered cake that satisfied the appetites and sweet tooth of every guest. The reception was calm, comfortable in spite of Micah's awkward presence, and marked one of the most pleasant occasions he experienced since his arrest.

Those other instances flitted through his mind, and for a brief moment, the recollection of lost relationships—Benjamin, Ella, and their girls; Sam and Kai—stole a piece of the present gaiety. How could a wedding fail to bring a bittersweet ache to Micah's heart? The last wedding he attended was his own. The memory kindled a pang he hadn't allowed to emerge for a very long time.

Now on the internee side of the fence, and having returned the borrowed jacket to Cooper and Langston, Micah looked and felt the part of a detainee. Once again he faced the tedium of the unknown. Were the Allied troops making headway that would hold, leave room for advancement, and finally end this war? How much longer could he stand living this way?

Jealousy threatened to bury Micah's happiness for Melinda. The world outside the fence, though still breathing and beating under the shadow of war, had choices. They could live in the place of their choosing, walk along a riverbank, travel to visit loved ones, write letters without a censor reading their private thoughts.

Letters . . . Micah reached into his trouser pocket and pulled out the letter Gerald Carter shoved into his hand before the euphoric new husband wrapped his arms around his wife and spun her around the dance floor. Melinda's laughter echoed in Micah's mind as he took a seat outside one of the canteens, now closed for the day, and pulled two sheets of paper from their holder.

Dear Mr. Keller,

I didn't expect I'd have much time to visit with you today. In fact, at the time of this writing, I don't know if you have permission to leave the camp. That decision is still in the hands of my future father-in-law. But I feel compelled to tell you how grateful I am that you befriended Melinda.

We grew up in Crystal City, and all through high school the two of us dated. I thought we were a serious couple, in spite of her reminding me on a regular basis that her future was somewhere far away from this place. She wanted to go where things were bigger, better, and brighter.

She went to Dallas to go to college and sent a few obligatory letters the first two years she was gone, but then the letters stopped. Sometime during her junior year at school, she showed up back in Crystal City. She hid at her folk's place for probably two months before I got a chance to talk to her. Almost had to tie her up to get her to stay in the same room with me.

I don't know what happened to Melinda while she was away at school, but the defiant, out-to-change-the-world coed that left, returned in the form of something shattered. She withdrew from friends, refused to go to church, quit taking care of herself, and put on about fifty pounds just to underscore her point. She wanted nothing more than to be left to her misery.

Persistent person that I am, however, I wrangled my way into her presence every so often, mostly to remind her I still loved the girl who went away. I knew that girl still lived deep inside Melinda. Somewhere.

She started talking to me again about a year and a half ago. I showed up at her front door and instead of having to pry my way into the house, she invited me. She didn't talk about herself. She yakked about some man at the detention camp named Micah Keller. Told me about all your awful traits and how you kept after her to smile a little more, or laugh at herself.

Somewhere along the line, when you befriended her, Melinda found her self-worth again. I know you have to have seen the results. She lost that weight, started taking care of that pretty hair, and even started wearing lipstick.

She still talks about her friend, Micah Keller, but her tone is softer, gentler. Something more like admiration and thankfulness than dismissive and judgmental. Melinda might never tell me what happened to her in Dallas, but what she tells me now is all I need to hear. My girl still loves me. She's found her tender heart again. I think you had a lot to do with that.

On this special occasion, I wanted to thank you, and more than anything, I wanted Melinda to share this day with a friend she treasures, so it is with a heart full of thanks that I welcome you to our wedding today.

I'm real sorry about the fix you're in, what with your detention and your wife and daughter being so far away. I wish I could do more. But whether it was the Good Lord's intention to send you here, or whether He just made the best of your circumstances, He used you to change Melinda's life, and mine, and a whole lot of other folks who love that gal—almost as much as I do.

You're a good man, Micah Keller. I wish you all the best.

Sincerely,

Gerald Carter

Micah folded the letter, stood, and brushed the dust off the seat of his pants. The line, *I wish I could do more* puzzled him, but he lacked the means to request an explanation. At the moment, more pronounced emotions, both stirred by the wedding, pushed his curiosity aside. Jealously and gratitude were not compatible bedfellows. He had a choice. The latter lifted a collective two-thousand pounds from his feet as he made his way to his room.

~

Savannah picked up her mug, which held as much steamed milk as it held coffee, and took a sip. None of the adults at the mission slept during the night, and now, as a dozen child-sized feet ran around the kitchen, the previous night's calamity threatened to wrest any order from the unfolding day.

Benita began a search of the grounds again, starting at the chicken coop and working her way up the hillside. From her view at the kitchen window, Savannah watched Benita climb.

The early morning sunlight shimmered against the dew that collected overnight. Tiny specks of light danced on the expanse of greenery, reminding Savannah of the fiery stars she saw the day she met Micah after her tumble down the same hill. A spasm assailed her chest as Carmita came to mind. Oh, that she and Pablo might come together and find the love that she and Micah shared. Savannah lifted up another prayer.

Where are you, girl?

Pablo and Roberto, gone since before dawn, searched the area from the pickup truck. Before they departed, they said a prayer over the hulk of metal and mechanical parts, too.

Hours later, after Simón and Brigitte set off for school, and Paloma and Alegría went down for naps, Savannah and Cedro sat on the veranda while they practiced sign language.

She pulled Cedro into a hug when she recalled the boy's interaction with Alegría first thing this morning. Alegría took a step behind Savannah and put a protective hand over her bandaged stitches. Cedro pouted, hung his head, and signed, "Sorry." Savannah leaned down and whispered to Alegría, "He said he's sorry." Alegría responded with a tentative smile and took a few steps until she reached Cedro and pulled him into a hug.

Somehow, they would manage. No, they'd do better than manage. They were family, albeit one with more than its share of challenges.

Suddenly Cedro looked up. He pointed to the yard behind Savannah's back. Randall and Carmita walked, arm in arm, down the hill, not as friends, but as one person leaning on the other for support.

"Carmita?" Savannah yelled. She grabbed Cedro's hand and started running. When Cedro strained to keep up with her, she picked him up, and by the time they met Randall and Carmita, Savannah couldn't catch her breath, let alone speak.

"Are you all right?" she wheezed.

Carmita's face was as white as one of the wild orchids that grew near the courtyard. Her distressed expression looked as fragile as the flowers' delicate petals. She put her fingers to her lips and started crying.

"I'm sorry. I didn't mean to scare you. I just . . ."

"Shh. It's all right. Let's just get you to the house. Where are you hurt?"

"I twisted my ankle."

"Don't think it's broken," Randall said.

Carmita looked traumatized, and so very sorry. An explanation could wait, although Savannah suspected none was necessary. Relief engulfed Savannah, but her contribution to the ordeal in the way of neglect, scraped against her heart like a scab that wouldn't heal.

After they reached the veranda, Savannah and Cedro pulled two chairs out of the kitchen and sat down with Carmita and Randall. With his hands now free, Randall engaged Cedro in a lively conversation while Savannah pulled an empty crate out of the kitchen and used it to elevate Carmita's foot.

"Coffee should be ready. I'll be right back," Savannah said. Before she made it back inside, the pickup truck's noisy muffler drew her attention to the driveway. Benita rounded the house at the same time, and when she saw Carmita, she raced up to her and buried her in a hug.

"Goodness, girl, what have you done to yourself? You scared us. I'm so glad to see you."

Pablo didn't give Carmita a second to answer his mother's question. He bounded out of the truck, leapt onto the veranda, and wrapped his arms around Carmita, whose face turned the deepest shade of scarlet Savannah had ever seen.

Embarrassed, she leaned away from Pablo, wiped tears from her cheeks, and squeaked out a feeble, "I'm s-s-sorry."

Pablo stepped back long enough to let Roberto hug Carmita, but he didn't step far away.

"What happened? How did you get hurt?" Roberto asked.

Randall quit his exchange with Cedro and turned his ear to the adult conversation.

"I needed to get away from the mission for a while. It was . . ." she looked at Savannah. "Yesterday was a hard day. I walked through the garden, and the coffee plants, and the cocoa plants, but I couldn't shake off my mood. I kept walking, but didn't pay much attention to where I went."

When Carmita paused, as if she were deciding what to tell and what to keep to herself, Benita asked, "Do you need a glass of water?"

Carmita shook her head. "I ended up in another coffee plantation, and when I found a little outbuilding, I went inside. It smelled nice. Like hay. Or straw. I sat down and leaned against the wall that faced the sun. It was warm. I was tired. I fell asleep. When I woke up, it was dark. I tried to find my way back, but I couldn't catch my bearings. I decided to stay in the building, but when I turned to go back inside, I tripped over a rock or something, and I hurt my ankle."

"While I checked some of the coffee crop this morning," Randall said, "I found her in one of the fields, limping. Sorry I didn't have a truck to borrow. We had to walk back here."

"Do we need to take you to the doctor?" Roberto asked.

"I don't think so. I just . . . I just want to say I'm sorry."

Tears streamed down Carmita's face, breaking Savannah's heart. If only it were in her power to prevent pain and misunderstanding.

"Carmita," Pablo said, "did your long walk have anything to do with my construction project?"

Carmita's resolve, what was left of it, flitted away like wisps of dandelion seeds caught in the breeze.

Pablo shifted in his discomfort, but trudged forward. "You think I have a woman in mind that I want to move into that place once it's done, don't you?"

Carmita looked at Savannah. Her eyes pleaded for someone to save her vulnerable heart from splintering into a thousand pieces. Savannah wanted to blurt out the words that would soothe her soul, but they weren't hers to voice.

"Well, I guess it's time you learned the truth," Pablo said. "I have two truths to share, and then I have a question. Are you paying attention?"

Paying attention? Savannah wanted to throttle Pablo. Now was not the time for him to hide behind his discomfort by being glib. Savannah tossed a warning glance to Roberto, who cleared his throat. Pablo's gleeful expression evaporated.

"Carmita, the building is for my future. My wife. My family. It is my hope that the first person to step over the threshold of my new home is my wife. Will you let me carry you through that door? Will you?"

Pablo's two statements and his question hung in the silence like a heavy cloud. Seconds, uncounted but accumulating, ticked by without a word from Carmita. She sat, as if transfixed by Pablo's question. Her eyes darted from Savannah to Benita, to Roberto, and back to Pablo, where they regarded his passionate plea.

She blinked and asked, "You're building a house for you and me? For the family you want to have with me?"

Pablo, already kneeling in front of Carmita, grasped her

hands. "Please, will you be my wife?"

"You're doing this for me?" she asked again.

"It's always been for you. I thought you knew. Will you? Will you marry me and let me carry you into that home?" He gestured toward the courtyard and said, "That mess of lumber and cement will be our home."

Carmita didn't try to hide her tears. She opened her arms to Pablo and said, "Come here." With her arms wrapped around his neck she said, "Yes, I'll let you carry me over the threshold. Will you carry me there now? Please?"

Roberto's sigh was audible, as was Benita's gasp. Savannah closed her eyes and whispered a prayer of gratitude. Randall, who held Cedro's little hand in his, signed something to Cedro.

"Love?" Savannah asked. "You're telling Cedro that Carmita and Pablo are in love?"

Randall nodded. "I am. And I'm teaching him how to say, 'Pablo loves Carmita.' "

When Randall stood, Savannah joined him at the edge of the veranda. "Thank you. You don't know how much we appreciate your kindness."

"You're wrong about that, Savannah. I see the gratitude in your eyes. I'm happy to do something that brings joy to others. It's about time, don't you think?"

With a nod of his head and a sweet smile, Randall ambled away.

Chapter Thirty-Three

May 1945. Micah gathered his lesson plan and a stack of test papers that he needed to grade, and turned out the light in the classroom. The hallway was gloomy. Damp air harbored the scent of human sweat, a testament to the thermometer hitting the ninety-seven-degree mark today. Micah pulled a handkerchief out of his pocket and mopped accumulating moisture from his forehead. Regardless of gossip to the contrary, the likelihood of another summer in this place loomed. Micah lifted his gaze to the ceiling and winced. He was so sick of Crystal City, Texas.

A few high school students huddled in a circle in front of the building. Strident voices peppered the animated discussion. Micah coughed, announcing his presence and offering an unspoken suggestion that the group relax.

"Just ask him," one of the students said under his breath.

Micah kept walking.

"Why don't you ask him?" another asked.

Micah wanted to get out of his shirt and trousers, put on some shorts, and dive into the swimming pool. Too bad it wasn't open on school days. After he got over his initial qualms about re-entering the pool following his incident there more than a year ago, he cooled off at the pool at every opportunity. He enjoyed jawing with the students who gathered there, and the exercise made for a better sleep.

Today, his after-school contact with the students fell under the haze of a hot sun, where the humidity lay heavy enough to thwart any attempt the intermittent breeze made to ease the discomfort. He slowed his pace while someone gained enough nerve to be the spokesperson.

Brenda—whose crush on her teacher disappeared when Richard, the most popular member of the drum and bugle corps, showed an interest in her—called out to Micah. "Mr. Keller?"

"Hmm?" he answered as he retraced his steps.

"Is it true? You know, the stuff about them letting us out of here next month?"

Rumors and unfounded reports about freeing internees, en masse, passed in rapid succession from one end of the camp to the other. Although the news might turn out to be less than the perfect-world scenario that filled classrooms, offices, shops, and homes with conjecture, Micah, like most residents, held onto the hope that something good would happen soon.

In a long-awaited game of good versus evil, German forces fell in quick succession, much like a line of falling dominos. After American troops crossed the Rhine River in May, Soviet troops captured Berlin, and Marshal Tito unseated the fascist Ustaša regime in Croatia.

While Hitler's suicide took many by surprise, Micah considered the act in keeping with that of a cowardly leader who possessed a soul as heartless and cold as granite. What the man inflicted on others, he knew he couldn't bear. Before others managed to dehumanize him, an act Hitler systematically employed millions of times over—maybe more;

reports of atrocities and mass murders were ongoing—Hitler stole the world's ability to mete justice.

"I'm sure it's just a rumor," Micah said.

"Why? Why can't it be true?" Brenda asked.

"We're still at war with Japan, you know."

Brenda hung her head, "Yeah, we know. It's just, well, we want to believe the rumors."

"They're not realistic. When this war does end, you can be sure that President Truman won't rush to release people from the internment camps." He shrugged. "They may choose to keep—"

"I told you," one of the boys said. "Nothing will change when this stupid war ends. They still want to deport all of us." His voice, like Micah's worry, settled in the air like a sickly green sky that foreshadowed a tornado.

"Guys and gals," Micah said, "you won't gain a thing by holding onto gossip." He lifted a shoulder and said, "All of us want to pack our bags and get out of here, but listen to your comments. Some of you think you'll be back home in a month. Some think you'll end up in Germany or Japan. Keep your imaginations in check and your attention on your studies. That's your job right now."

"Spoken like a teacher," grumbled Richard.

"Spoken like a realist," Brenda said. "I know I won't have to stay here after I graduate, but until they let my dad go, I can't leave." She delivered a woeful glance to Richard. "I just can't."

Richard leaned over and took Brenda by the hand. "You have another choice," he said as he escorted her away from the others. Brenda's grimace didn't tender much credibility to Richard's comment.

"You think they're going to do it?" Amy asked nobody in

particular.

"Do what?" Micah asked.

"Nothing," one of the boys answered.

"He wants Brenda to marry him and go to California so he can enroll in college," Amy said.

"They're free to do that," Micah said. An unlikely couple, in his estimation. Richard's attention to Brenda didn't sit well with Micah. Although he couldn't name it, something in Richard's person disturbed Micah. The boy came to the Bible study from time to time, but hadn't committed his life to the Lord. It was as if something dark held Richard in its grasp, and instead of running away from it, he seemed eager to explore the compulsion.

"She doesn't want to leave her folks," Amy said. "I think he wants to get married so she'll get a job and take care of him while he goes to school."

Well, that comment gave something of a name to Micah's reservations about Richard. Amy wasn't pleased with her girlfriend's new beau either.

"Shut up," one of the boys said. "It's none of your business." He tilted his chin toward Micah. "Or his business either."

"Don't you all have homework? Something better to do than share rumors and spread gossip?" Micah arched his eyebrows, raised the hand holding math exams, and said, "I know I do."

As Micah walked away, the students murmured for a moment, and then dispersed.

"Mr. Keller?"

Micah turned around and waited for Amy to catch up to him.

"We have to do something. Talk to Brenda's folks, or

maybe tell the OIC that Richard is trying to take advantage of Brenda. Maybe they'll move him and his family to another camp."

"Richard hasn't done anything illegal. He and Brenda, when they're both eighteen, have a right to get married in the state of Texas. It's not our place to make decisions for them."

"But he's awful. He's worse than awful, and Brenda's such a pushover."

"Brenda didn't look as if she were ready to ride into the sunset with Richard. Neither of them is of age yet, so the best thing anyone can do for them is to pray."

"Pray that Richard goes away?" Amy asked.

"Why don't we both pray that Brenda sees Richard's true heart?"

"That'd be good. If she saw him for what he is, she'd run," Amy said.

"And . . . let's pray that Richard gives his heart to the Lord."

Amy huffed at that suggestion. "Is this where you tell me I need to pray for my enemies?" She underscored her protest when she shoved her hand against her hip and huffed again.

Micah grinned at his math student and disciple. "Yes, missy, that's exactly what I meant to say. See you tomorrow."

His grin evaporated while he made his way to his room. He contemplated the student's reminder that although the war might end soon, each detainee still held the distinction of being an enemy alien. The most accurate of the rumor mills at Crystal City said President Truman was of the opinion that the United States should deport all remaining detainees, from not just the U.S., but from all of the Western Hemisphere. After all this time, was that to be Micah's fate?

~

Carmita stood in the doorway of the veranda and crossed her arms over her chest.

"By the time Pablo finishes that little house, I'll be too old to have children. We'll all sit out here in our chairs and tell stories about what life was like . . . back in 1945."

Savannah wiped Paloma's sticky fingers before she handed the stained washcloth to Carmita, who dabbed blackberry juice from Alegría's chin.

"More?" Savannah signed to Cedro. She pointed to the last of the berries resting at the bottom of a bowl.

He shook his head, pointed to one of the dogs, and signed, "Water."

"The dog needs water?" Savannah signed.

Cedro pointed to an empty bowl. "Water," he signed.

"Get water," Savannah responded with her hand signals.

In the span of a year and a half, everyone in the household learned the basics outlined in the French sign language dictionary. More often than not, the participants adapted the gestures to one that fit their circumstances.

Cedro ran into the house. From her seat on the porch Savannah heard the five-year-old scoot a chair over the tiles, and a moment later the sound of water running from the faucet met her ears. By the time Cedro carried his water pitcher outside, it was half empty. Savannah didn't care. Not today. She'd mop the wet floor later.

This was one of those Costa Rican afternoons that healed every hurt, shoved away every worry, and buried every regret. Glorious was a fair description of this warm day, where the sun shone on the bounty of crops on the hillside, the breeze scented the air as it borrowed the fragrance of flowers, and a household full of children all determined to get along—all day long. A rare treat.

"I need to get started," Roberto said as he stood. He refilled coffee cups for Benita, Savannah and Carmita without asking if they wanted more, and topped each cup with a generous splash of warm milk.

"I'll wipe up the water," Savannah said as Roberto walked inside.

"I've got it. Just relax for a while."

The inseparable Rolf and Brigitte, not keen blackberry enthusiasts, giggled when Roberto started singing. The man volunteered to make empanadas, a Misión de Cacao favorite. Tonight the corn turnovers wouldn't hold just beans and cheese, but potatoes and chicken. When Roberto's deep bass voice sounded down the hallway, the siblings took that as an invitation to help him, and they scurried inside.

"How can I make Pablo hurry?" Carmita asked. She lowered herself to the seat Roberto vacated, leaned her elbows on her thighs, and with a wistful expression, stared at the paltry progress on what Pablo dubbed the "Hacienda de Vargas." The small structure was a far cry from an estate, but Pablo's excitement failed to diminish despite the frustrating shortage of materials and time.

Cedro raced around the side of the house and gestured frantically. "Truck. Randall. Come."

Savannah put her coffee cup down when she heard the sound of an engine approaching. Unlike other visitors, this driver didn't stop when he reached the rutted portion of the drive. Surprised to hear the daring—or foolish—driver continue toward the mission buildings, Savannah walked around the side of the building. She needed to warn them off.

Randall jumped out of the open bed of the type of utility truck used primarily for hauling crops. The doors on the truck cab bore faded letters that identified the vehicle as one of those owned by the fellow who took over Shuler's coffee plantation.

Cedro ran to his sign language tutor, signed a greeting, and raised his arms. As he always did, Randall hefted the boy into the air, twirled him long enough to make him dizzy, and gave him a hug before putting the woozy child back on his feet.

Randall called to the three men who waited in the back of the truck. "Over there," he said as he pointed to the area in front of Hacienda de Vargas.

Carmita grabbed Savannah's arm and whispered, "What are they doing? Where's Pablo?"

Roberto and the rest of the children joined Randall and the puzzled women at the center of the courtyard.

Savannah, as perplexed as Carmita, didn't want to interrupt the men as they unloaded stacks of lumber and sundry building materials from the truck. It looked like a miracle to Savannah. She could save her inquiry until the men finished.

"Hey," Pablo shouted as he crossed the courtyard. "What are you doing?" Angry eyes accented his flushed face. With his hands fisted and his jaw clenched, he set out to throttle his target.

Carmita raced toward Pablo and grabbed his arm. Savannah couldn't hear their exchange, but Pablo stopped long enough to give the scene a proper assessment, and released his balled-up hands.

Randall gestured to the others to join him as he walked over to Pablo and Carmita.

"What's this?" Pablo said. He'd buried his accusation, but his initial anger simmered.

"You ever hear of an Amish barn raising?"

"A what?" Pablo asked. Clearly, the young man wasn't in the mood for pleasant chatter.

Randall turned to Savannah. "Tell them who the Amish are, will you?"

"The Amish. Um, they are a religious sect—I suppose you would call them that—who live simple lives. They are Christians, to be sure, but they don't use modern conveniences like electricity or cars. They tend to keep to themselves. They're good people who look out for each other." Savannah slipped a sideways glance to Randall, hoping for some acknowledgment that she answered to his liking. She, too, wanted to know about this unexpected delivery.

"Right enough," Randall said. "Especially about the 'look out for each other' part. Since those folks don't use modern equipment, it's an ordeal for one person to put up a building. The Amish—at least the ones who lived near where I grew up in Pennsylvania—help each other by having a barn raising. They gather all the materials needed and then all the men come together and build a barn. Usually in one day."

Carmita's eyes widened. Emotion flicked over Pablo's face as understanding stole the anger, made way for a dose of embarrassment, and rested in gratitude.

"This stuff," Pablo asked as he gestured to the growing pile of building materials, "is for our house? But where did you get it? I cannot pay—"

"Don't you recognize this mess?" Randall asked Pablo.

"No. Why would I?"

"This is what's left of the outbuilding we tore down last

month. Instead of burning the rubble, like Ramirez wanted us to do, I asked if I could have the pile. When I told him why I wanted it, he offered me all of it."

"This is free?" Pablo said. "The boss let you have this free? For me?"

"Yep."

When Carmita turned her dumbfounded face toward Savannah, she said, "I don't believe this. I don't know what to say."

Randall's actions, once again, left Savannah speechless. Since he took Cedro under his wing, Randall had become something of a resident at the mission. Although he still lived in the workers' quarters at the plantation next door, he attended every Sabbath meeting and joined the mission residents afterwards for a meal. Often, generous gifts of food or supplies accompanied his visits. Now this?

"We'll be back first thing tomorrow for our house-raising," Randall said. "If you could have Roberto fill their bellies tomorrow with some of his famous sopa negra, we'd appreciate it."

"You and these men are willing to erect a house in one day in exchange for black bean soup?" Savannah asked.

"Yep. That's what neighbors do." Randall strode to the truck, where the men waited, and climbed aboard. He waved his hat at the stunned crowd still standing in the courtyard, and signed, "Goodbye my friends," as the driver pulled away.

Roberto wrapped his arm around Benita. "You know what this means?" he asked. Dimples heightened his delight when he said, "A wedding. Soon. Then grandchildren."

When his comment evoked bewilderment from Carmita, Roberto looked at Benita and asked, "What? What did I say?"

"First, the wedding, Roberto. We have plenty of children

to share here already. Be patient. Don't rush them."

"That's true." Roberto pointed from one child to the next and started counting, "One, two, three—"

The rumble of an engine interrupted the lighthearted celebration.

"Did they forget something?" Pablo asked.

Unlike the last visitor, the approaching driver stopped some distance away. Savannah heard a door slam. A solitary man, dressed in professional while shirt and dark trousers, approached the group.

"Which of you is Roberto Vargas?"

"I am."

The visitor extended an envelope to Roberto. "You are to appear in court on Monday."

"What?" Roberto asked.

The visitor ignored the question, marched to his car, and drove away.

"What is it?" Benita asked.

Savannah's heartbeat picked up its pace as she considered the possibilities. Did someone figure out that Paloma didn't belong to Benita and Roberto? How could that be? No one knew. Dr. Gutierrez wouldn't tell under threat of torture. But, could he or his wife have let it slip? No. It couldn't be about Paloma.

Just as daunting was the possibility that someone might have decided to challenge the transfer of the mission property from Savannah to Roberto. No. The transfer happened too long ago. Anyone who cared would have raised his objection before now.

After Roberto read the letter, he wiped his mouth and chin with the palm of his hand, as if contemplating how he might break the news.

"Simón, please take the little ones into the kitchen. Give them some juice. Read them a story."

At eleven, Simón was old enough to understand his father's grave tone, yet young enough to contest his exclusion from grown-up talk. Something in Roberto's solemn eyes induced Simón to obey without comment.

"What?" Benita asked. Her face had grown ashen.

"Let's go into the chapel and sit. Then we will pray," Roberto said.

They left the door to the courtyard open and took seats in the dimly lit sanctuary. A shiver ran over Savannah's arms, although the temperature wasn't the basis for her discomfort.

"The letter is addressed to me, as the courts have my name on record as the owner and administrator of Misión de Cacao. The authorities scheduled a hearing regarding custody—"

"No," Benita wailed. She doubled over in her seat and grabbed herself around her middle. "No. Not Paloma."

"No," Roberto said. "It is not about Paloma."

Benita gasped as another sob shook her shoulders. She swatted tears away from her face. "I don't understand," she cried.

Roberto turned his face to Savannah. "I'm sorry. The parents have returned. They want their son and daughter back."

Savannah stared at Roberto. If she could just hold back the tears welling in her eyes, she could make his statement go away. If she could just stop the shudder that promised to engulf her, she could pretend the letter didn't exist. If she could just hold her hands over her ears so that his words couldn't penetrate her understanding, she could start tomorrow just as she had today. If . . .

Chapter Thirty-Four

"Did you hear?" Amy asked as she sat down.

"Hear what?" asked Brenda.

"Look. He's coming. He can tell us himself."

Micah twisted his torso and craned his neck to follow the students' line of sight. Richard marched toward the group that had assembled for Bible study. In his hand he held a piece of paper, which he waved at his classmates. The teenager looked as if he wanted to jump up, click his heels together, and take a bow upon landing.

"Is it true?" Amy blurted her question before Richard took a seat on the dry patchy grass.

"Depends. What did you hear?" His upturned mouth widened, revealing unabashed pleasure.

"Did you enlist? Did you?"

"Maybe." Richard winked at Brenda when he answered. Brenda, wearing a pained expression, disengaged herself from Richard's ego when she dropped her gaze to her hands.

"Your dad's gonna kill you. You'll end up fighting your own family," one of the boys said.

"No, I won't. Germany surrendered. Besides, I'm an American citizen, like my mom, and my dad's the last of the Germans in his family. So we're not really 'German German,' if you know what I mean. Anyways, I don't have to ask him if I can enlist. Turned eighteen earlier this week. I don't need his permission for anything anymore."

"Why would you go and volunteer? Why now?" one of the girls asked.

Richard raised a shoulder and curled up one side of his mouth when he said, "Why not? By the time I finish my basic training, Japan's military will be history. My service will be no sweat. Two years from now, I'll have that GI Bill ticket to the university of my choosing. Seeing the world during my tour of duty sounds pretty copacetic to me."

"Copacetic? Cleaning up the mess overseas? You think that'll be exciting?"

"It won't be like that. Quit being a killjoy," Richard said. "The only catch is I gotta get 120 days of active duty before the war officially ends. I'm good as long as we don't sign a treaty with Japan too soon. Everything's jake. Swell."

Was Micah the only one present to realize Richard wanted to see a protracted conflict with Japan? Micah would not be the one to stir that pot. Instead, while students gabbed about Richard's plan, Micah mulled over its impact on today's Bible study session.

He had one participant, Brenda, who apparently made a difficult decision to refuse Richard's offer to marry and move to California. Or, perhaps Richard didn't want to wait until Brenda's eighteenth birthday. Maybe he rescinded the invitation. Richard, who talked as if he learned a decade's worth of slang during the short weekend he spent out of the camp, made a decision that removed him from the protection and security provided to him by his parents.

Brenda, though wounded, was a disciple of Christ. Richard didn't hold that distinction. His future, despite his

271

grandiose plans and his verbose claims to the contrary, was insecure.

Micah didn't relish the circumstances any of these teens faced. Those years between adolescence and adulthood were precarious and filled with a host of temptations. The relocation to Crystal City, the forced abandonment of friends and all things familiar, and the challenges each faced when they took their first steps into Federal High School had the capacity to obliterate their fragmented existence.

Micah ran his thumb over the well-worn lettering on his Bible's cover. Although more mature than his students, Micah conceded that he wrestled with the same unknowns as these teens did. If not for his faith, he may have ignored the urge to climb out of the swimming pool that night.

Given an opportunity, Micah shared his testimony with fellow internees. Each telling stirred memories of his own path to salvation, and reminded him that God's purposes prevail for those who know Him. Where might Micah be if he hadn't followed God's bidding? He shuddered at the possibilities. On some level, sharing his belief was selfish, as the act buoyed his faith and supplanted discouragement and fear. He never knew when he might need an extra portion of God-given fortitude.

Micah cleared his throat. "Let's get started, shall we?"

~

Pieter coughed, rearranged himself over his mattress until he found another comfortable position, and soon resumed snoring. Micah envied his roommates, one who slept as if dead, and the other who tossed and turned each time gusts of wind rattled against their window.

As he lay in bed, Micah rested his head against his entwined fingers and stared at shapeless dark shadows that loitered in the crowded quarters. The room, with its window tightly closed against the storm, was stifling hot. The sour odor of human sweat filled Micah's nostrils and worsened his sleepless state. Exhaustion gripped him, but his mind was as alert as the sentry who manned the front gate.

What, Lord? Micah tried to slow his breathing, but when the wind intensified the sound of rain pelting the window, it rendered his efforts futile. Micah raised himself to a sitting position, put his elbows on his knees, and rested his chin on his fists. *Show me.*

The vision of Savannah standing alone in the chapel at Misión de Cacao pressed the air out of Micah's chest. Whatever her circumstances, her face bore an anguish he never witnessed in the days they spent together. A tremor of terror played over Micah's shoulders and forced him to his knees—where he realized he belonged. *Lord, give her all she needs.*

~

It was with great reluctance that Savannah let Simón take Brigitte by the hand and lead her to school. How could she let the child out of her sight, much less send her to class as if everything were normal?

Brigitte's feet skipped and danced as the two children walked down the lumpy rutted driveway. Her flaxen locks shimmered in the early morning sunshine. Savannah's throat tightened as she regarded the girl's innocence. If she dared look at Rolf at this moment, the unfathomable trepidation that weighed down her spirit and etched fear across her face might terrify the boy.

Since the moment Roberto shared the contents of the official letter, the sound of a ticking clock accompanied Savannah's every move. Each miniscule advancement of the second hand, each meal shared as a family, each goodnight prayer and morning greeting, pilfered an equal amount of their futures.

No matter how sincere and often she prayed, Savannah failed to form a suitable argument that would induce the court to act in their favor. She had no doubt the children would thrive as long as they stayed at the mission. She had every reason to denounce the upheaval the children would suffer when the courts took them away.

"Are you sure you don't need help?" Savannah asked Carmita.

"You all need to go." Carmita turned to Alegría, Paloma, Rolf, and Cedro and signed as she said, "Who will help me clean the chairs?" She picked up a towel and demonstrated a wiping motion. "They'll help me dust the benches in the chapel. When they get bored with that, I'll have them help me hang laundry. They'll nap most of the time you're in San José. Don't worry about us."

Benita slid into the middle of the bench seat of the old truck and made room for Savannah to sit beside her. Roberto put the truck into gear and headed toward town.

"I'm nervous about this," Roberto said. "I'm not very good at collecting my thoughts and explaining myself."

"You need to let Savannah be the spokesperson," Benita said.

"How can I do that if they address their questions to me? Or to you? As far as the authorities know, we own the property."

"Just tell them that I take responsibility for the care of the children. Tell them I have a greater understanding of their needs, or something like that," Savannah said.

"I want what's best for Brigitte and Rolf. I can't imagine the courts would return them to their parents. After all the time that's passed, how could they?" Benita sounded as if she were rehearsing her argument.

Savannah didn't answer. In none of her prayer time did she sense that she would win over the parents. She was ill prepared, nonetheless, for what she deemed the likely outcome. Her heart refused to entertain the inconceivable.

Once Roberto parked and they entered the municipal building, an attendant directed them to some chairs in a hallway. In near proximity sat a man and woman, both fair and blue-eyed, and both wearing stricken expressions on their pale faces. Their physical features left no room for argument regarding the parentage of the two children who arrived at the mission three years earlier. Savannah squeezed her eyes shut and swallowed the lump that rose in her throat.

Under a clerk's direction, the parents and their representative followed Savannah, Roberto, and Benita into an office. It wasn't a courtroom, but a small area in which a variety of business and personal transactions were processed.

As the young man sitting at the desk looked up, a flicker of recognition flitted across his face. Savannah didn't need to look at the nameplate resting on the corner of the desk. In the two years since she transferred the property to Roberto, Jorge Diaz, son of the Municipal Executive, advanced from inexperienced court clerk to his current position as some sort of mediator.

The young man made introductions and stated the case rather simply. "This is a formal hearing in which the court gives notice to Roberto and Benita Vargas that Werner and Helene Berghoff have requested that their son and daughter be returned to them. We believe it is always in the best interest of a child to remain with his family, but because of the extenuating circumstances, this hearing is required. Señor Vargas, do you wish to make a statement?"

"I do, "Roberto replied, "but may I please designate Savannah Keller as our spokesperson? She is more educated than my wife and I, so more able to speak plainly. Also, she is the person who is most responsible for the children."

Jorge looked at the representative and asked, "Do you object?"

"Not at all."

"Señora Keller?"

"We found Brigitte and Rolf, alone and abandoned at the mission doorsteps almost three years ago. I don't know what caused their parents to leave them, but they left nothing behind. Brigitte knew enough to tell their names, and that she was three years old. We guessed Rolf was about one-and-a-half. We never knew their last name. I don't disagree that parents have rights, but I don't think the court should permit the children to return to parents who rejected them and didn't bother to fetch them for three years."

The representative leaned over to his clients and spoke quietly and at great length. When Savannah detected foreign words and accents, she gasped.

"You mean to say the parents speak only German?" Savannah blurted out of turn.

Jorge looked at the representative. "Is that correct?"

"Yes."

"How do they expect to communicate with the children? Brigitte and Rolf were toddlers when they arrived at the

276

mission. What little German vocabulary they possessed back then is gone. They speak English, a little Spanish, and they know Fr—." Savannah swallowed the words, *French sign language*. Her stomach churned at the thought of going through this same process with Cedro's natural parents. She gagged, coughed, and then cleared her throat.

"Never mind. My point is that the children don't speak German. How much trauma must these innocent children endure?" Savannah didn't mean to raise her voice, but Jorge had to see that the parents tendered their bold move to retrieve their children far too late.

The representative adjusted the collar on his shirt and looked at Jorge. "May I explain what happened?"

Jorge nodded.

The representative looked apologetic as he turned his attention to Savannah, Roberto, and Benita.

"Werner and Helene understand the severity of their request and the challenges it presents to the children. Nevertheless, they never intended to abandon Brigitte and Rolf. Werner and his brother, Gustave, owned a plantation together. Werner, as the elder brother, controlled the business. Gustave, who spoke Spanish, interacted with the local businesses and government authorities anytime they had the need.

"When Gustave learned about the Black List, he warned Werner and Helene that both of their names were on the list. He blamed Werner's inclusion as an enemy alien on some sort of association Werner had with a local social club.

"Fearing arrest, they made arrangements to relocate to Brazil, a country that refused to comply with the United States' directive to detain certain citizens. After the family boarded the cargo boat that would take them to Brazil, the captain left the dock. Not far off shore, a small fishing vessel pulled alongside. Several men boarded the cargo ship, seized the children, and took them back to shore."

"That's preposterous," Savannah said. "You expect us to believe a story like that?"

The representative raised his hand. "What were Werner and Helene to do? Swim several miles to shore? Once they arrived in Brazil, they believed they could not return to Costa Rica, for fear of deportation to Germany. Werner had enemies in Germany, but that's another story altogether.

"They corresponded with Gustave, who promised to find safe passage for the children, and who reported that he had hired a local woman to care for them in the interim. Gustave sent letters regularly, in which he fabricated stories about their progress and good health. He told Werner and Helene repeatedly that he couldn't find trustworthy people who would take the children to Brazil. It wasn't until Werner sent word of their plan to retrieve the children in person that Gustave admitted that they were not living with him."

"You expect us to believe they were victims in this?" Savannah asked. Indignation wrapped around her anger. How much did the Berghoffs pay this man to produce such a ridiculous defense?

"It is my opinion that they are victims. Gustave knew Werner wouldn't leave Costa Rica without the children; he knew the captain wouldn't take two young children all the way to Brazil. Gustave bribed the captain to take the family far enough away to prevent Werner and Helene from returning. He also conspired with the owner of the smaller boat to retrieve the children and return them to the dock. Once the children were back on shore, Gustave took them to your mission. He returned to the plantation and enjoyed full ownership."

"Can we back up a moment? What did you mean when you said, 'they *believed* they could not return to Costa Rica'?" Savannah asked.

A drawn-out sigh prefaced the representative's response. "The Berghoffs contacted me after Germany surrendered. They thought it was safe to begin the process to return to Costa Rica. It was then that I learned neither Werner nor Helene were ever on the Black List. They were never suspected of being enemy aliens."

Savannah pinched her brow together. "What do you mean?"

"Werner and Helene never saw the list. They trusted Gustave to tell them the truth. Instead, Werner's brother stole his property and sent his brother and sister-in-law away. His most grievous act, however, was separating Brigitte and Rolf from their parents."

Helene sniffled and wiped her eyes at the mention of the children by name. For her part, Savannah didn't think she'd ever cry again. The tale managed to render her being as cold and impermeable as steel. If she thought to break down the molecular structure, she'd fail to exist.

Chapter Thirty-Five

August 1945. "I still don't know why you talked Steinbrenner into giving you his mail route while school is out for summer. Couldn't you find anything to do with your free time? It must be 120 degrees out there today. It's probably worse than that in here. Where is the wind? I need a breeze."

Melinda—nee Young, now Melinda Carter—picked up a paper fan and waved it in front of her face. She glared at the hand-painted artwork before she folded the fan and huffed. "Nice gift from one of the Japanese internees, but what I need is a wall of electric fans set on high."

"Why don't you bring your swimsuit, jump into the pool instead of eating lunch, and then let your cold wet hair drip all over you while you work during the hot afternoon?" Micah waggled his eyebrows and added, "Hmm?" just to annoy her.

Melinda jumped when a door in the hallway slammed and footsteps pounded the floor. One of the guards ran into the office, skidded to a stop in front of her desk and gasped.

"Turn on the radio. Hurry."

"It's already on. What's up?" Melinda asked.

"Get the news sta—" When the announcer interrupted the broadcast, the guard said, "Never mind. Turn it up." He turned to Micah. "Get him out of here."

"No," Melinda said. "Not until I know why."

Too late for that. As soon as the voice introduced President Truman, Melinda and her co-worker forgot Micah existed.

Sixteen hours ago an American airplane dropped one bomb on Hiroshima and destroyed its usefulness to the enemy. That bomb had more power than 20,000 tons of TNT.

Hiroshima? Micah clutched his chest as his lungs collapsed. 'Destroyed its usefulness'? What did that mean? Was the whole city gone? What about Sam? Kai? Their son?

. . . The Japanese began the war from the air at Pearl Harbor. They have been repaid many fold. . . . It is an atomic bomb. It is a harnessing of the basic power of the universe. The force from which the sun draws its power has been loosed against those who brought war to the Far East.

Truman sounded almost giddy when he declared the success of the scientific advancement. Advancement? Micah choked as visions of death and massive destruction riddled his imagination. Yes, the Japanese were enemies, but what of the general population? The men and women who awoke to a normal day in Hiroshima were no different from the residents who lived in war-torn Warsaw, Berlin, Mannhcim, Paris, and the like.

What of the children among them? Innocents. Victims. Most were powerless people whose leaders enacted policies that led every citizen to a place that stole part of his humanity. How could anyone, any government or military leader, issue a death warrant to an entire city?

. . . With American and British scientists working together we entered the race of discovery against the Germans. . . . We have spent two billion dollars on the greatest scientific gamble in history—and won.

But the greatest marvel is not the size of the enterprise, its secrecy, nor its cost, but the achievement of scientific brains in putting together infinitely complex pieces of knowledge held by many men in different fields of science into a workable plan. . . . What has been done is the greatest achievement of organized science in history. It was done under pressure and without failure.

Why did the president direct his broadcast to science? Was it just a matter of convenience that the war offered an opportunity to test the new weapon? With untold thousands dead, did he expect the world to celebrate this feat? This event changed the face of the planet, the face of humanity. What about the people? The people!

Micah's gut roiled as the address continued. Visions of devastation, scenes that he knew were beyond his imagination, drew a mixture of bile and rage into his throat.

We are now prepared to obliterate more rapidly and completely every productive enterprise the Japanese have above ground in any city. We shall destroy their docks, their factories, and their communications. Let there be no mistake; we shall completely destroy Japan's power to make war.

More? The president intended to repeat this inhumane execution? Melinda's expression was one of horror. The guard fidgeted and said to no one in particular, "Wait until the Japs in camp hear about this. They'll start a riot."

Melinda's eyes widened when she looked at Micah. He nodded and mouthed, "I need to go."

As he slipped out of the door, Truman's voice carried through the hallway.

I shall give further consideration and make further recommendations to the Congress as to how atomic power can become a powerful and forceful influence towards the maintenance of world peace.

Micah gasped for air when he closed the door and stepped outside. Peace? A weapon so powerful it annihilates entire cities? He wanted peace as much as the next person did. As much as those people who lay dead in the streets of Hiroshima wanted peace. Peace? At what cost?

~

"It seems you have too much empty space," Carmita said as she looked at the bed she would no longer occupy. With the exception of what she intended to wear later today, her personal belongings sat in two small stacks on top of the dresser.

A stranger listening to Carmita's comment might question the young woman's use of the word empty. Three people still occupied the bedroom in the caretaker's quarters. Mattresses still nestled close to each other, creating something of a miniature maze in which one had to pass in order to retrieve nightshirts or daywear.

Savannah's smile was bittersweet. It's not as if Carmita was moving far away. Her new home stood a mere forty paces from Savannah's front door. It was the departure of another family member from Savannah's nest that clawed at her wounded spirit: first Rita, then Brigitte and Rolf, and now Carmita.

Before she entered the municipal building with Roberto and Benita, Savannah knew. It seemed as if God, with His merciful heart and perfect justice, guided her inside, sat beside her while she learned the truth about Brigitte and Rolf's abandonment, and held her hand while she witnessed the regret and subsequent joy wash over the faces of the children's flesh and blood. How could she argue with the outcome? It was the only proper conclusion.

Savannah didn't die when the parents arrived, nor did she faint away when Werner and Helene bundled the confused children into their car and drove away. Most surprising, though, was the steady, determined beat of Savannah's own heart. It didn't falter. Each gentle throb within her chest spoke of the blessing of unbridled love, something everyone at the mission showered over those two dear children— something that came back to each of them.

The greatest void was the one that accompanied Micah's arrest. Though the description seemed contradictory, his ever-present absence never abandoned her.

It seemed as if Carmita read Savannah's thoughts when she asked, "Will you be all right? You seem to have managed well since the children left. Have you? Really?"

"Do you know why I'm all right?"

When Carmita tipped her head, pressed her lips together,

and rested her solemn eyes on Savannah, the girl's beauty produced a lump in Savannah's throat. Her love for Carmita was as vast as the ocean was wide. Life at Misión de Cacao wasn't something Carmita planned either. Yet, Savannah fell in love with the girl the moment she arrived. Carmita, in turn, smothered everyone with her grace, her gentle spirit, and with tireless, hard-working hands.

"I asked myself a question. If I had known the outcome, would I have opened my home and my heart to Brigitte and Rolf? I wouldn't have traded a single second. Not one. I remember the day those blue-eyed beauties stared up at me. They were scared, but maybe a little brave because they held each other's hand. I remember Brigitte's relief when I asked her, 'Was ist dein Name?' Somehow, we knew we'd be all right at that moment, and we were."

Savannah studied Carmita's wrinkled brow and revised her last statement. "We are. Things will be difficult for them, but only for a while. I hope they remember us as they get older, that Werner and Helene will take out your beautiful drawing, point to each of us, one by one, and recall us by name. Most of all, I hope they remind the children how much we love them." Savannah reached around Carmita's shoulders and pulled her into a hug. "Thanks so much, you sweet girl."

Carmita sniffled and pulled away. "Don't make me cry. Not today. A bride should not have puffy eyes." She stepped back as she stretched her arm in front of her and pointed a finger at Savannah. "Stay here. I'll be right back."

When she peered into the doorway a moment later, she held a large package in her arms. "If it isn't a custom for the bride to give her parents a thank you gift on her wedding day, it should be. You have been so good to me. You've mothered me, encouraged me, and loved me as much as any parent ever could."

She inclined her head towards the courtyard and wore a radiant smile when she said, "Before I move far, far away, I want to give you a remembrance. Pablo made the frame for this, and we hope it prevents you from feeling this little home is too empty." She handed the parcel to Savannah. "Go ahead. Open it."

Savannah's finger's trembled as she studied the sketch of Brigitte and Rolf, holding hands and grinning at each other, as they often did.

"I'm speechless," Savannah whispered. Carmita incorporated her new collection of colored pencils in this treasure. Blue eyes and pink-tinged lips and cheeks warmed to the yellow-gold hair of the brother and sister. The likeness was uncanny, from the bow in Brigitte's hair to the pair's dusty bare feet. So real was the effect, Savannah could hear the echo of small feet dancing on the floors. She ran her hand across the fine finish of the wood frame, as striking and perfectly formed as the portrait it held.

She wiped a tear from under her eye, lifted both shoulders in a show of—what?—fake detachment? "I thank you now, from the bottom of my heart. I'll let the tears of joy run sometime after you say your vows."

Carmita flicked a damp spot off her cheek, nodded, and enveloped Savannah in a hug. "I love you, Mamá."

Chapter Thirty-Six

November 1945. "Gerald can't promise anything, you know." Melinda tucked a lock of hair behind her ear and glanced at Micah before she slipped a picture frame into the box sitting on top of her desk.

"Can I reimburse him for his postage costs with camp tokens?" Micah asked, only half-serious. It's not as if he had any genuine dough.

"Afraid not. His invoice will require an act, not financial recovery." Melinda straightened up and massaged her lower back. She put her nameplate into the top of the box and said, "I think that's the last of it."

Micah cleared his throat. "What act?"

"If—no when—you get out of here, you have to send us a letter, postmarked San José, Costa Rica. And you have to send us a family photograph. Make that a group photograph. I want to put faces to the names of everyone at Misión de Cacao."

"That's all?" Micah asked.

Melinda lowered her head and looked at Micah over the edge of her new eyeglasses. "That's all? Keller, those requisite pieces of correspondence will mark the end of an event that never should have happened." She lowered her voice and leaned forward when she said, "I shouldn't have said that out loud. If anyone heard me, it wouldn't be good for Daddy's career."

The Officer in Charge found himself in an uncomfortable situation once again. Melinda didn't have words to explain the impact that the atomic bombs dropped on Hiroshima, and then Nagasaki, had on her father. In the aftermath, he had to look the Japanese internees in the face as he carried out his duties at the camp. He had no choice but to support his country's wartime efforts, yet the unspeakable horror of those two events sobered the most stalwart military personnel.

"Does your father know Gerald is helping me?"

"He pretends not to," Melinda replied, "but it's not as if Gerald is doing anything that shouldn't have been done a long time ago. He just wants you to have your day in court. No one can argue that you all deserve that much."

A day in court? To answer charges of entering the U.S. illegally? Four years later, the notion resembled nothing more than a farce, but if it held the slightest chance it would lead him back to Costa Rica, Micah would enter the courtroom on his knees. But what were the chances of presenting his case? How were the odds any better than when they were at war? He, along with almost 3,400 other internees still living at Crystal City, wasn't holding his breath.

"Truman's latest proclamation didn't mention anything about justice and court hearings," Micah said. "He, and the rest of those people who met at that Problems of War and Peace conference don't just want us out of the U.S., they want us out of the Western Hemisphere. I wouldn't be surprised if Truman asked those brilliant atomic bomb scientists if they might invent a smaller version that could purge the contents of a few camps. They could celebrate another scientific advancement while they washed their hands of our inconvenient existence."

"Sarcasm is not one of your endearing traits, Keller."

"Sorry."

"Gerald heard that an ACLU attorney is representing some of the Japanese Americans interned in California. He's trying to see if the organization might consider representing the Latin Americans who ended up here. Who knows? Don't lose faith now."

"Easy for you to say, Miss Former-Mail-Censor. Will you miss this place?"

Melinda patted the small bulge hidden beneath her maternity dress. "I'll miss some of the people." When Micah waggled his eyebrows, she said, "A few people."

"I'll miss your leftover Thanksgiving turkey, you know."

"You'll miss me for my paltry once-a-year leftover delivery?"

"Naw. It's not about the turkey. You've been a good friend. I'll miss you," Micah said, his voice sobering and threatening to crack.

Melinda swiped at her eye. "No fair, Keller. I am not a crier, but this expectant mother doesn't have full control of her emotions. Don't get mushy on me. If you behave until you turn around and walk out of this office, I'll send you a Christmas card. I promise. And if you're still here in February, I'll send you a picture of the addition to the Carter household. But for now, just give me a hug and be on your way."

Micah zipped his jacket as he exited the administration building and headed toward his quarters. An occasional breeze nipped at his bare ears, a prelude to another winter in a place that—right this moment—held as much warmth and gaiety as a wasteland.

As he considered Melinda and Gerald's good fortune, the joy they shared in their expectation of a family, he fought those melancholy demons once again. It was the comment about the turkey that started it. Micah kept walking after he reached his residence. He shoved his hands into his pockets, pulled up his collar, and headed toward that unposted boundary between the German and Japanese homes.

The little neighborhood was spotless, every building well kept. Late blooming blossoms, a contrast to the brown landscape, bent their cheerful, vivid petals to the breeze. The varied home improvements could almost lead an unwary visitor into believing this was just another little city. A place where people worked, where children studied. A place that families called home.

Not in evidence were things that had gone missing. The pile of rocks that once hid an agitated rattlesnake was long gone, as were Sam and Kai. No one was outside his friends' former residence, but a light in the window announced the presence of the confined family who moved in to take their place.

Emptiness squeezed Micah's chest. How he missed the self-acclaimed Samurai warrior and his delicate, kind wife. He could only hope God had redirected their paths and prevented them from returning to Hiroshima. Would Micah ever learn their outcome?

He retraced some of his steps until he stood at the corner of the street on which Benjamin, Ella, and their daughters used to live. Micah walked down the dusty road and stopped in front of the little property. The front door, once assembled over a pair of sawhorses to hold the fixings for a Thanksgiving feast, stood at its rightful place at the entrance to the house.

Micah closed his eyes long enough to hear the girls' giddy laughter and to envision Sam's silly theatrics as he pretended to slice the meager serving of leftover turkey with a long Samurai sword. What an unlikely assembly they comprised that day: the Jews, the Gentile, and the Buddhist couple, gathered together to give thanks.

Micah turned away from the stranger's home and studied the copious little dwellings that dotted the vast flat land. Although thousands inside the structures went about their end-of-day routines, the specter of futility cast a shudder over Micah's shoulders.

Savannah shared in this emptiness, this loss. She invited children into her home and her heart, only to have them yanked away from her. He believed her letters, the ones that promised she would have done it again, even if she'd known the outcome. She spilled her broken heart into the letters probably unknowingly, but quite clearly—to the man who loved her most.

In retrospect, should he have brought her here? Should he have insisted Savannah and Alegría spend his internment with him? For some reason, Micah's second guessing always ended with the same answer: No. Something in his heart told him that the three of them faced great danger, had they all been in this camp. This separation, however, was insufferable. His absence during his mother's illness was unspeakable.

Micah knew to hold the things of the world loosely. But when war and government agendas ripped his family and his friendships out of his everyday existence, the theft left a hole so big and so deep that it threatened to steal his last breath.

~

In the weeks since Brigitte and Rolf left the mission, each of the remaining occupants suffered bouts of sorrow. It seemed no one required an explanation or demanded a happy pretense whenever anyone exhibited a downhearted manner. Preparations for Pablo and Carmita's wedding provided a welcome salve to the ache of separation, but the solitary resident who seemed incapable of coping was Cedro. Where Cedro slipped into a group activity for five children, he found himself an outsider when the count fell to three.

Alegría and Paloma, so close in age, drew to one another like magnets. Simón's schooling took him away from the mission on weekdays. When chores didn't demand his attention and energies, his friendships with a few boys in the area occupied much of his free time.

Randall's appearance for church and his short sign language sessions lifted Cedro's spirits, but the visits were too short in duration and frequency. Cedro wasn't screeching and in need of the Cedro March around the property; instead, the boy was visibly depressed and withdrawn.

On this pleasant November morning, Savannah arranged to take leave of the mission and set out with Cedro for an early picnic. Since he often fussed at breakfast, postponing his meal was of no consequence.

Cedro scampered alongside Savannah as they ascended the dark green blanket that covered the hillside's rich soil, and so far, he remembered to stay within her reach. If he focused his sights on some airborne creature that flew beyond his grasp, Savannah might have to run a long distance before she could get his attention again.

The two wandered to the highest point on the Misión de Cacao property, and traipsed through a broad field that belonged to the old Shuler plantation. On these few hectares grew clumps of bushes and wildflowers that attracted butterflies and hummingbirds. She'd found this spot during one of those days when her overwrought spirit screamed for solitude. Savannah could only hope the target of her picnic afforded Cedro the sense of peace and completeness that escaped him at home. God's presence smothered Savannah here. Might it do the same for her troubled boy?

"Are you hungry?" Savannah signed.

Cedro nodded, and when he sat abruptly on the blanket Savannah spread on the uneven ground, he lifted one side of his posterior and rubbed. "Ow," he signed.

"Sorry," Savannah signed back.

Cedro's brown eyes, dark as ebony, darted as he tried to track the paths of the busy insects that flittered over the landscape. He pointed his chubby finger at a butterfly and signed, "Orange."

"Monarch," Savannah signed. "You like?"

When a pair of larger butterflies with iridescent wings of neon-blue cavorted and danced around a nearby bush, Cedro signed, "Blue."

This one was more difficult to explain. The insect, one of the loveliest and most common of the Costa Rican beauties, required she spell the name. She signed, "blue m-o-r-p-h-o."

Cedro wrinkled his forehead and didn't bother to try to repeat the letters. Savannah's emotional wants aside, she needed Micah to return to the mission for a myriad of practical reasons. Cedro needed an education, and since the special school in San José could not accommodate him—not that it was a viable solution—the necessity rested on

Savannah's shoulders. How was she to spend time teaching when she already had too much to do?

Savannah didn't want to lose this little boy, this sturdy six-year-old who savored his inclusion in every event, no matter how routine or how small. Cedro, though deaf, was as much a social butterfly as the multitude of winged insects that held his attention this morning.

Several weeks after the meeting about Brigitte and Rolf, Savannah returned to the municipal building and requested a hearing with Jorge Diaz. Perhaps it was her decision to abide by the court's recommendation to return the children to their parents that won the young man's respect. Although he did not tender a decision to her new request, he pointed out those items Savannah needed to address before she submitted a formal petition. She memorized the scene:

"How did the boy come to be in the care of the mission?" Jorge asked.

"A man and a woman took him to Dr. Gutierrez for treatment."

"Who were they? What type of treatment?"

"They claimed to have found him wandering alone on the road, but the doctor said the boy resembled the couple. He believed they were his parents and that they had some reason to lie to him."

"Why would they need to lie?" Jorge asked.

"The boy had a broken arm. While the doctor treated the child, the couple ran off."

"They abandoned him?"

"Yes."

"So, in your mind, this is a case of abandonment, and you have someone who can corroborate your story."

"Correct," Savannah said. "It may also be a case of

neglect. The boy was not able to explain how he broke his arm."

"He was four at the time? Why couldn't he tell you?"

"The boy is deaf," Savannah said. During the long pause, Jorge dropped his gaze to the papers resting on top of his desk. He twirled his pen end-over-end.

"How do you manage with a child who cannot hear?"

"We've taught him how to use his hands. It's called sign language."

"I think I've heard of that." Jorge's pinched brow suggested that his having heard about sign language was more wishful than factual. "Let me ask about your personal circumstances."

Savannah nodded.

"You want to adopt a Costa Rican child, yet you are American. You have no husband."

"I do have a husband. He is an American, but also a Costa Rican. He was born here. His mother was Costa Rican."

"Señor Keller is not here. What might you do if he fails to return?" Jorge asked.

Savannah forced her shoulders to ignore her body's reflex to let them slump. After so much time had passed since Micah's arrest, it was a fair question. She failed to find a response.

"I fear it would be difficult for you to win permanent custody of the child while your husband is . . . absent."

"In your opinion, might *we* have a decent chance to adopt the boy?"

Jorge dropped his writing implement to the desk and leaned back in his chair when he said, "It is unfortunate the boy is deaf; however, his condition may render your request more acceptable, especially if you show the child is capable of communicating and that he has assimilated into a family situation."

"So, all things in their proper timing," Savannah said.

"I suggest you submit your request at a time when you are most likely to find favor."

Savannah closed her mind to the incident and returned to the present. She leaned back on the blanket and propped herself up with her elbows. The fresh scent of damp earth, and plant life cleansed by a recent rain, soothed her spirit. With the dreadful war behind them, all of God's sweet creation seemed to rejoice. Splendor surrounded the two adventurers.

Cedro wiped his chin, pointed to the tree line, and signed, "I go?"

"Where I can see you," Savannah signed.

He raced toward a thick throng of dark green bushes and lowered himself to the ground. From her perspective, she could see Cedro as he raised his face and watched the unpredictable spectacle performed by tiny green birds. The little avian wonders zipped over the top of the plants between brief moments in time when their little bodies froze, suspended long enough for them to pull sweet nectar from flower blossoms.

When Cedro ran back to Savannah, his cheeks were rosy and his eyes wide. He flapped his fingers up and down.

"Hummingbird," Savannah said as she signed the letters.

Confusion lined Cedro's brow again. Another long word. She motioned for Cedro to stand in front of her, and she placed the fingertips of both of his hands above her mouth. When she hummed, he flinched when he felt the vibration.

She signed the letters, "h-u-m," put his fingertips to her

mouth again, and hummed. Then she pointed to the birds, duplicated his up and down hand motions, and spelled, "h-u-m-b-i-r-d."

Although she heard nothing, the silent laughter that folded Cedro's face into a hundred tiny crinkles, wrapped around her heart as tightly as a fist. No, she didn't want to lose this boy.

Micah, we need you.

Chapter Thirty-Seven

December 1945. It seemed odd that Micah found himself standing in a queue at the visitation building. During his long stay at Crystal City, he'd not had occasion to entertain a visitor. Why now? Who in the world asked to see him? Melinda, maybe? It's not as if she could summon him to her old office, but with holidays approaching and motherhood not far behind, Melinda had to have better things to do than look up Micah for a chat.

As Micah reached the head of the line, he heard chairs scraping the floor in the adjoining room and the low murmur of voices engaged in not-so-private, but quiet, conversation. As he stood in the doorway, the guard pointed to a table near the corner of the room, where an unfamiliar man waited.

As Micah approached the table, the stranger rose and extended his hand. "Micah Keller?"

"Yes, sir," Micah replied. The man was in his mid- to late fifties, with streaks of gray running through his light brown hair. The pale gray eyes told Micah everything he needed to know.

Micah didn't release the man's hand, nor did he redirect his gaze. "Sherwood Hamilton. How did you find me here?"

The visitor drew his mouth into a wide grin. "The girl

didn't inherit her daddy's wanderlust, but she did get my pretty face, didn't she?" He pointed to the table. "Sit. Talk to me."

"I don't know what to say." Micah scratched the side of his face. He didn't. Who was this man who was his father-in-law, and why was he in Crystal City, Texas?

"Took you by surprise?" The man shrugged. "Before we get to business, tell me about Savannah. Stubborn girl wouldn't leave Costa Rica. Is she well?"

"Her letters are full of good reports. Did you know you have a granddaughter?"

"So they said," Sherwood replied. "Alegría. Joy. Pretty name. Is she a pretty child?"

Micah coughed at the question. "I haven't seen her since she was an infant. But she was perfect then, and one photograph and a drawing sent here prove she still is." He looked at Sherwood and locked onto his eyes. "I guess we've both missed a lot."

"Yes. About that. I don't know how much Savannah told you about me, but it's obvious I haven't been a very good father. I suppose I can excuse my abrupt departure from Costa Rica, as she was an adult when I left. I didn't leave things in good shape. I'm a bit embarrassed about that."

"I'm not one to judge," Micah said.

"I don't have a line of defense for my lack of correspondence either. I didn't know about you. My absence is inexcusable, so I'll start my apologies with you."

"Apology accepted," Micah said. "What brings you to my humble abode at the Crystal City Internment Camp?"

"Seems as if some attorney is looking for personal references. When I got a call asking for my opinion, I had to pretend we had a bad telephone connection so they didn't know how uninformed I was about my daughter's husband. I kept asking, 'You're calling about who? About what?' until I thought I understood enough to provide some sensible response. So I'm here so I can give them my honest opinion."

"Who's looking for references? I don't understand."

"Some attorney with the ACLU. Said something about internees like you having their day in court."

A flutter of possibilities lifted Micah's countenance. In his wedding day note to Micah, Gerald Carter penned, *I wish I could do more.* True to his word, Gerald forged ahead in his efforts to help Micah get out of this place. Could it happen? Really?

"I'm a pretty good talker, especially around the ladies. Know what I mean?" Sherwood asked as his thick eyebrows lifted toward his hairline.

In response, Micah raised his own. No, he didn't know.

"No, not like that," Sherwood said. "I'm just a good jaw-er. That's all. Anyway, I got to be good telephone buddies with the attorney's secretary, and she spilled everything. Said they already received fine letters of reference from the university where you worked. Back in Austin. Right?"

"He's contacting my former colleagues?" Micah asked.

"Guess so. I decided to hop on the bus in Bartlesville, Oklahoma and come down here to meet my son-in-law. So here I am."

"Thank you. I'm not familiar with Bartlesville. What took you there?"

"Oklahoma? Oil, my man. Oil. The odds aren't a sure thing—not like they were back in the day—but folks still enjoy a gusher every now and again. I've invested my share; now I'm waiting for the team to tease that crude to the surface."

Micah watched Sherwood rub his hands together. Was it the same gesture he used when he contemplated the "odds" of his failed coffee and cocoa venture in Muy Bella, Costa Rica?

"Enough of me. You know," Sherwood said, "the dossier the government has on you is more about your father than you. Filled with notes about his less-than-reputable patients and their assumed political influence on him. Looks as if your old man left you holding the bag. Ah ... the sins of the father."

"Innuendos to the contrary, my father was a conservative and religious man. Had anyone sought the truth, or bothered to analyze his activities, his position on important matters would have been obvious."

Unlike the Tico guards in San José who limited visits to mere minutes, or maybe because this was Micah's first visitor, the uniformed officers let the two talk for more than an hour. By the time Sherwood prepared to leave, Micah decided to hold the man responsible for some of Savannah's most challenging traits. He recognized, however, that her obstinate perseverance was probably what held the mission together, both before Micah arrived on the scene, and after his forced departure.

Sherwood made no promises to contact Savannah, to visit Micah again, or to plan a trip to Central America in his future. His one request?

"When you see her next, please tell Savannah I've always loved her. I haven't been the father she deserved, but in my own way, I love her fiercely. Although we've not met, the fact that you and my girl gave me a granddaughter, means Alegría's the apple of this granddaddy's eye. You tell 'em both that I love them, will you?"

"Why don't you tell them yourself? Whether you hit oil or not, go visit."

Sherwood's pleasant demeanor took a hit and ended up with a click of his tongue, the precursor to a pained expression. "You think Savannah wants to see her old man? After all he didn't do? I tried to make amends with her brother a couple of years ago. Turned into a disaster."

"I'm sorry to hear that."

"My former wife remarried. Did well for her and the boy. Got a nice house. Started a second family. But both were angry as hornets when I showed up. I don't think I can pay the price of my poor parenting another time. Better to leave things alone. You know?"

"No, I don't know. Savannah's got a heart that's ready to sweep up the least of us. Don't you think her grace extends to her own flesh and blood? She'd welcome you. We all would."

Sherwood's face morphed into something hopeful. The edges of his lips lifted when he said, "I don't know about that."

"I think you do. Let us know when you plan to come. We'll prepare the celebratory lamb, so to speak."

"Something to think about. Especially the granddaughter part. For now, I have to go. One of the local boys has been sitting in his jalopy all this time. He's probably ready to head back to town. Take care, Son."

Sherwood seemed to choke on his farewell, and when he extended his hand, Micah pulled him into a hug.

"Thank you for coming all this way. Your visit means the world to me. I know it will to Savannah and Alegría too."

"My Savannah chose well. I thank you, Micah Keller. Godspeed." He offered a parting smile, and headed out the front door.

Micah didn't know what to make of Sherwood Hamilton any more than he knew if his own future held much promise. Time—something Micah couldn't control—would tell. As he walked back to his quarters, he looked up. What he could do was pray.

Chapter Thirty-Eight

January 1946. Roberto stood at the front of the chapel and prayed over the congregation. Except for the moment when he lost his place and tripped over his words, he shared his sermon with candor, and with the passion of one who loves Christ, God's Word, and God's promises.

It took considerable effort this morning to focus on Roberto. Often it was the wriggly four-year-old Alegría who distracted Savannah. Today, it was the letter she opened the day before.

After all the grievous acts the U.S. and Costa Rican officials imposed on blacklisted families, their horrendous treatment of the victims continued to battle an unparalleled sense of injustice. The war ended in 1945, but as the calendar ushered in a new year, neither country planned to return the deportees to Costa Rica. Instead, they meant to send them back. In Micah's case, "back" was Germany.

A handful of detainees managed to hire legal representatives to help them earn the ear of the government. Micah was one of several hundred detainees who refused to leave the camp. He remained at Crystal City while attorneys and courts challenged each other. Micah wrote of the stalemate in his letter dated December first. Nothing else followed. No one in San José knew a thing.

Roberto's guitar interrupted Savannah's anxious thoughts, and when Benita's soft voice led the others in a song of praise, Savannah choked down her sorrow and squeezed Alegría's hand. The tears that washed her face spoke of gratitude in the midst of suffering. Their situation, though it wasn't over, could have been much worse.

The vegetable garden that Micah instigated produced a bounty season after season, and the fruit trees yielded generous crops. The young coffee and cocoa plants thrived and became more reliable sources of income, and although they risked being accused of conspiring with those on the Black List, people brought food and supplies in the dark of night and left it at the mission gate.

Savannah, standing with the congregation as they worshipped in song, stood taller at the remembrance. During all of Micah's absence, God blessed them with everything they needed. And more. He surrounded Savannah and Alegría with Roberto and his family, people who showered the two of them with love.

Savannah closed her eyes as Benita's praise lilted through the morning air. She heard the footsteps of several people as they walked toward the front of the sanctuary, a place where they sought Roberto's prayers. When someone jostled her, Savannah opened her eyes, but kept her gaze on the floor. Maybe she should go up for prayer, too. Before she could excuse herself and sidestep the person who stood beside her, an arm reached around her and pulled her into a hug.

She heard his voice before she saw his splendid face. "Savannah, love, I'm home."

~

Micah couldn't have heard Savannah's response even if she'd managed to pick up her gaping jaw and voice her astonishment. The crowd that surrounded this ransomed father and his family clapped, praised the Lord, and shouted "Hallelujah" as Micah lifted Savannah off her feet. He hugged her, kissed her, and wrapped his arms around her again.

The wide molten gray eyes of the girl who held fast to Savannah's hand, searched his face. Stunned at the sight of a face that resembled the reflection he saw in his mirror, Micah steadied Savannah and kneeled in front of his child.

"Alegría," he whispered. "Are you my Jojo?"

She tilted her head and parted her lips, but looked to her mamá before she spoke.

"You know who this is, don't you?" Savannah asked.

Alegría turned her inquisitive and serious eyes on Micah, released her mother's hand, and lifted both arms toward him. He thought his heart would burst from the flame that shot across his chest. So many emotions, he couldn't gather and name them all. When delicate hands wrapped around his neck, and a small kiss brushed his cheek, Micah gave in to his overwrought state and sobbed.

His beautiful daughter didn't recoil. Instead, she said, "Don't cry, Papá. I knew you'd come."

"How—" Micah's voice cracked. "How did you know?"

"Because you love me. You had to come."

She knew he'd come. This child, cheated from the security and presence of her earthly father. She knew he loved her. She knew he'd come. If he hadn't already been on his knees, the evidence of God's love for this child—his child—

would have rendered him face down.

Micah looked up and regarded the strangers who gaped at him. A solemn-eyed boy, about six years old, peeked around Simón, an adolescent Micah might not have recognized had he not conveyed the youthful image of his father. The younger child looked confused; he grasped the hand of a comely young woman who stood next to Pablo. She had to be Carmita, Pablo's new wife, the artist.

A lump rose in Micah's throat. How much he'd missed. How might they redeem the time? God willing, they'd manage.

Micah, still kneeling, locked his gaze on the young boy, and gestured the sign for hello. He lifted his hand, positioned his thumb on the edge of his mouth, and tapped his index finger to his thumb two times.

Cedro's eyes widened. He pointed to Micah and repeated the thumb-tapping gesture. *Père*, French for *papa*. When Micah nodded and held out his arms, a wide grin replaced Cedro's tense features. He raced into Micah's embrace.

Micah swallowed his sob, but couldn't dam the flood of tears. Finally surrounded by his flesh and blood, an adopted clan, and his friends, relief and joy wrapped around him with the same sure force and promise as God's grace gripped him and his family.

The celebration that followed the church service, which Roberto ended with a mighty shout of thanksgiving to the Lord God, surpassed every scene of reconciliation that Micah imagined in the months and years since the unfounded fears of a few powerful men separated him from his loved ones.

As the afternoon melted into evening, and the moon began its ascent into the skies above Misión de Cacao, Micah picked up his sleeping daughter and turned toward the hallway leading from the kitchen to the bedroom.

"I'll just put her to bed. I'll be right back."

"But that's not—"

Benita interrupted Simón. "Not for you to say. Come, let's check to see that the chickens have enough feed."

"But—" Simón replied.

"Come." Benita offered an apologetic smile to Savannah as she picked up Paloma and left the room. Roberto, Pablo, and Carmita followed after them.

"What?" Micah asked.

"We live in the caretaker quarters now," Savannah said.

She had more to say, he could tell. If all of the others left them to themselves, they knew Savannah and he needed a private conversation.

"Let's go then," Micah said as he redirected his exit.

He followed Savannah into the small bedroom and lowered Alegría to the bed. She didn't stir when her mother removed the child's dress.

"She can sleep in her petticoat. It's warm tonight," Savannah said. She turned toward Micah, reached for his hand, and said, "Come."

She led him to the main room, which also served as a second bedroom. Micah looked around the space. It was tidy, uncluttered, and small. He'd never had occasion to be inside this building before. It seemed more like a cottage than a house. The double bed looked as it if was used for storage. A pile of folded clothes and a stack of books rested on top of the quilt.

"We don't own the mission any longer. I transferred the property to Roberto."

"You what?" He must have misunderstood. That didn't make sense.

"I had to. Whenever they arrested the Germans, someone—whether it was the police or government officials, I don't know—took everything."

"They took everything? What do you mean?"

"They emptied their houses. They expropriated German properties and businesses. If the authorities didn't ransack the properties, sometimes the towns people rioted and emptied the confiscated shops. I couldn't let them take the mission. I gave it to Roberto instead."

"They let you give it to Roberto?" Micah asked.

"I told them I owed him wages, that I wasn't able to pay, and that Roberto agreed to forgive my debt if I signed the mission over to him."

"But they never earned much of a wage. We bartered the residence, food—"

"The government didn't know that." Savannah rubbed her thumb over his hand. How he'd missed her touch, her lovely face, her sweet smile. "Roberto said he intends to return the property to you, but that doesn't seem right to me. Should he make the offer again, perhaps we could consider owning equal shares with him. Honestly, it's not something that's cost me sleep."

Micah ran his hand through his hair and contemplated Savannah's assertion.

"After all that has transpired, the title to a piece of land doesn't seem as important as it might have a few years earlier," Micah said.

"After Roberto took ownership, things changed," Savannah replied. "Things were better for all of us. People no longer turned away when they saw me on the street. They started coming to church—you saw how many came this morning. As long as I owned the mission property, people were afraid to associate with us."

"It's not the property that beckoned me home." Micah raised his hand to Savannah's face and stroked her cheek. Her kiss was sweet, wanting. He leaned away when a rush of awkwardness seized him. "I need to tell Roberto that he delivered a very fine sermon."

"You heard the sermon?"

"I walked into the church at the same time he lost his place in his notes. When I signaled to him to be quiet about my entrance, he managed to pick up where he left off."

That comment earned a warm smile. "Did you like his discourse?" Savannah asked.

"Yes. A very strong message. Powerful."

"Thank you," Savannah said.

"Why should I thank you?"

"Because," Savannah answered, "I am the sermon writer. Roberto is the sermon deliverer." She finished her proclamation with a satisfied smirk. When she stood up, she reached her hand toward him.

"Come sit with me on the veranda."

When they stepped outside and Savannah closed the door, the moon, partially hidden by palm trees, cast dark shadows over the porch. Micah heard her breathe in the cool night air as she took her seat.

"Do you remember how I described this place when you first arrived?" she asked.

Micah lowered himself to a second chair, which sat on the other side of an upturned barrel. "I remember a setting quite like this, only on another porch." He pointed in the direction of the main house. "That way."

"But do you remember my word for Costa Rica? For the mission?"

"Magnificent."

"Yes," Savannah whispered. "Magnificent. This place is magnificent. A gift."

"Do you remember our first meeting?" Micah asked.

"You mean the one where I tumbled down the hill and landed in a heap at your feet?"

"Yes. A memorable introduction. You told me not to touch you, and then you said you saw stars."

Savannah got up from her chair and nestled into Micah's lap. She kissed his neck and his throat, and lingered when her lips met his. When she leaned back, with her head resting on his shoulder, she pointed.

"Look at the sky. It, too, is magnificent. Glorious. Look at the firmament, Micah. This is how I held onto hope while you were gone. The God of the Universe, who set those splendid lights in the sky, held us in His holy hands. Whenever my faith wavered, or despair claimed hold of me, I'd come outside and search the heavens. When I saw God's stars, I saw you. Welcome home, Micah Keller."

Author's Note

While I Count the Stars began as a lighthearted short story for inclusion in an anthology compiled by my writers' group. When early research into visa and immigration laws uncovered the actions of the U.S. and Latin American countries during World War II, it sent my tale on an unexpected and sobering detour. It also prompted me to expand the original short story into a novel, as Micah and Savannah's circumstances occupied my attention and stoked my imagination.

Historians have written little about the events surrounding the internment and deportation of thousands of Latin Americans who found themselves on the Black List at the onset of World War II.

While the Costa Rican city, mission setting, and characters in this story are fictitious, their predicaments are those that targeted individuals may have faced as governments enacted their war policies.

Numerous stories, newspaper articles, government reports, and information gleaned from various websites framed my depiction of day-to-day life in Crystal City Internment Camp, but Micah's journey, and many of the details of his situation and conditions in the camp are fictional.

The internment camp held 3,374 individuals at the time the war ended. Those individuals whose countries denied their re-entry, suffered deportation to Japan, Italy, or Germany. At the close of the war, a contingent of Peruvians protested their expulsion and remained at the camp for almost two and a half more years.

With help of ACLU attorneys, 364 Japanese Peruvians gained parole status, which permitted them to work as undocumented immigrants at a food processing plant in New Jersey. It wasn't until immigration laws changed in 1952 that those former internees had an opportunity to secure U.S. citizenship.

My research did not suggest a timeline someone in Micah Keller's circumstances may have endured in an attempt to return to Costa Rica at the end of the war. In my fictional world, I preferred to pen a shorter separation. Four years seemed far too long already.

ACKNOWLEDGMENTS

Many people blessed me on my writing journey, as my characters' hearts found a means to prevail over the distance between Muy Bella, Costa Rica and Crystal City, Texas. Although I've not stepped foot in Crystal City, I had the honor of visiting the beautiful country of Costa Rica during two short-term mission trips.

I relished the beauty of the landscape: the grandeur of the emerald green crater at Poas volcano; the wonder of innumerable varieties of flowers, butterflies, and hummingbirds. I enjoyed the soothing aroma of local coffee mixed with steamed milk, an abundant selection of luscious fresh fruits, and my fair share of rice and beans. The precious relationships formed with the people, however, I savored even more. Penning this tale kindled sweet memories.

I wish to thank my mother, upon whom I levied my first draft, chapter by chapter, until I concluded my yarn. Her encouragement, feedback, editing expertise, and her uncanny ability to pick up every misused word are priceless, and help me look smarter than I sometimes think I am. As my stories unfold, I often answer her, "How in the world do you plan to untangle this predicament?" with, "Uh, I dunno. I'll send you a new chapter tomorrow." And so, we've turned my haphazard methods into a fabulous team effort that brings me great joy.

Thank you, Fran Naumann, Brian Krause, Sue Copeland, and Trudy Garland, my faithful reviewers, for your time, your opinions, and your friendships. You shore me up when I need encouragement and remind me to endeavor to produce a work that is worthy of those who read the first page and continue to the story's conclusion.

I am grateful, too, for the tenacious women who welcomed this Florida newcomer into their writers' group. The name of their just-published anthology, *Birds of a Feather Two*, epitomizes the kinship that exists among these lovely ladies. I am humbled to have a place in their proverbial nest.

In all things, I give thanks to my Creator, to Yeshua, Jesus, whose love is pure and whose timing is perfect. Always.

～

A note to my readers. Thank you for stepping back in time with me. If you enjoyed this story, please consider writing a book review. Every author appreciates, and needs, those priceless gold stars and reader comments. I look forward to sharing another adventure with you soon.

ABOUT THE AUTHOR

VALERIE BANFIELD, a long-time resident of Central Ohio, headed south and planted her toes into the sandy soil near Florida's Gulf Coast. She is a basket weaver and instructor, an avid reader, and a passionate supporter of microfinance. She counts her participation in international short-term missionary campaigns among her life's most blessed and humbling journeys, and firmly believes that when we give God control, He rocks our world.

Valerie shares some of her lighthearted insights—those things learned from the human end of the leash—within the *Walking the Dog Blog* tab on her website. Visit her online at www.valeriebanfield.com.

Don't miss these riveting tales by Valerie Banfield:

Deluge: When Yesterdays Collide

Checkered: A Story of Triumph and Redemption

Deceived: A Case of Mistaken Identity

Gifted: A Basket Weaver's Tale

Anchored: A Lamp in the Storm

Sidetracked: If Yesterday Steals Tomorrow

~

While I Count the Stars, the short story,
is available in print form in:

Birds of a Feather Two: A Pasco Writers Anthology

Keep reading for a gripping preview of

Anchored

A Lamp in the Storm

When the tempest roars, where lies the safest course?

Chapter One
Safeguarded

DECEMBER, 1895. Thomas Burton squinted, as if a heightened degree of focus could push back the haze hovering over the surface of the choppy expanse. He dared not blink for fear of losing sight of the ship altogether. When a hot white plume and a spray of red and orange specks burst through the low-lying cover and spewed into the clouds, he drew back, sputtering. The sound of the explosion reached his hearing moments later, drawing a lump to his throat and forcing him to gasp for air.

With his eyeglass fastened on the horizon, and the view eerily distorted by the mist, he watched the glow of flames as it licked the fabric of the three sails that led the schooner to its treacherous end. As the fog bell sounded again, Thomas said a silent prayer for those in the distance who would no longer hear its mournful toll.

Mate Alfred Reynolds joined Thomas on deck as a second round of small explosions vaulted into the atmosphere. He tugged the glass from Thomas' hand, and hefted it to his right eye.

"At least it weren't a passenger liner," Reynolds said.

"S'pose they were transporting gunpowder along with their other goods."

"Looks like a shipment of whale oil. The ring of flames around the vessel is moving outward." Thomas turned his head toward the mate. "Any sign of survivors?"

Reynolds shifted the glass across the horizon, left to right, up and down. "Don't see anything except fire."

Reynolds handed the glass back to Thomas. "If you ask me, we've no reason to stay on deck."

"I'll keep watch a while longer, sir."

"Too cold for survivors, and you know it. Folks so dimwitted to venture out this time of year, almost serves 'em right."

Thomas turned just long enough to send a disapproving glance to the captain's second-in-command. "I'll stay, sir."

"Suit yourself. You want to keep Bannister company whilst he rings the fog bell, s'up to you." Reynolds leveled his well-worn scowl on Thomas, his loose jowls jostling with his downturned lips. When a wave tossed against the side of the lightship, he shook the spray from his face and headed to the officers' quarters.

The frigid air amplified the fog bell's clanging each time the clapper smacked against its iron shell. The familiar sound, delivered relentlessly in two-minute increments, assaulted Thomas' eardrum with each peal. His body, like those of his mates, was so accustomed to the seafarer's warning that he could anticipate each resounding gong at precisely the moment it rang into winter's unforgiving air. At this moment, each time the bell tolled, the hope for survivors diminished.

Captain Roy Garvin bunched the fabric circling his thick neck with one hand and blew his warm breath into his other hand. "Anything out there, Burton?"

"Not that I can see yet, Captain."

"Yet? Unless someone was already in the water when the first explosion hit, you won't find anyone."

Thomas allowed a brief recess from scanning the area between ships. He studied the solemn countenance of the seasoned sailor—the man relegated to the dreaded lightship for the duration of his maritime service. Thomas found fatigue, sorrow, and defeat in every deep line in the old salt's face.

"I know that, sir."

He lifted the eyeglass again, leaned forward, and blinked several times. "Captain?"

When Thomas heard the Captain turn, his footsteps heavy on the deck boards as he returned to the port side, he offered the glass to him.

"Something out there, 'bout halfway between the wreckage and the *Nautican*, sir."

"Probably barrels of oil." Captain Garvin turned, as if to go.

"Beg to disagree, sir. Looks more like a raft, or maybe a small lifeboat. Request permission to lower the lifeboat, sir."

Thomas heard Garvin snort back the first response that rested on his lips. "Haven't you been on ship long enough to lose your optimism? We have better things to do than look at empty waters and worthless debris."

"But, what if . . . sir?" Thomas respected his captain. He did. But the man would rather pretend no one survived the sunken schooner than to conduct a search that might put his crew in harm's way. Captain had every right to protect his crew.

"Storm's heading this way. I can feel it."

"Then let me head out now. I feel an urgent need to

VALERIE BANFIELD

reach the boat, or raft, or whatever it is." Thomas paused before he added, "Sir."

Thomas stared hard into the captain's eyes, even as the mariner drew them into thin slits. "Is this one of your prophecy sightings, Burton?"

Thomas knew Captain didn't mean to taunt; the man chose his words carefully and deliberately. How was Thomas to explain himself when he didn't know why God sometimes nudged him to do something, or say something that originated outside of his own mind? All Thomas knew, God spoke to his heart. Others knew it too. Captain, included.

"If God spared someone's life, and the waves are tossing him about while he holds onto that chunk of wood floating out there, we best retrieve him. God Almighty may have saved someone for a special deed and purpose. I aim to do my part."

Captain released his hold on his coat, rubbed the back of his neck, and said, "I won't send other men out with you. You may go if you have two volunteers." This time, Captain strode to his quarters without leaving room for Thomas to comment.

Thomas ran the eyeglass lens over the dark waters. Where did it go? He closed his eyes, blinked them tightly once, and scoured the horizon again. Nothing. This time, when he closed his eyes, he said, "God? If you have a reason for me to lower the boat and turn those oars, You have to show me where You want me to go."

When he looked again, the drifting mass was in plain view, moving closer to the ship.

Thomas scrambled to the galley and shouted, "Need two volunteers. Might have survivors. Anyone?"

His request earned silence and disinterested faces.

4

"Men, this is why we're here. To save people from drowning. I need two volunteers."

Thomas caught Andrew Miller's eyes and fastened on them tighter than the chain holding the lightship's anchor. Andrew peered over his playing cards and lowered his hand just far enough for Thomas to see him chewing his lower lip. Andrew emitted an annoyed, "pfft," and dropped his cards to the table. He slapped Henry Simpson on the shoulder.

"Let's go."

Thomas clapped Andrew on the back as they waited for the crew to lower the lifeboat into the icy waters.

"Thanks, Andrew. You too, Henry."

Thomas and Henry strained at the oars while Andrew searched for the floating mass.

"You're crazier than I am, Burton," Andrew hollered.

"Then why'd you volunteer?" Thomas yelled.

"I figure I can either die from boredom, or die in the Atlantic. Ain't got much to lose, either way."

"That's not true," Thomas answered. "We talked about it before."

"Yep, and just like before, I ain't listening to you."

"Just row, Burton," Henry said.

"I see it. Small lifeboat," Andrew yelled. When a spray of water caught him full in the face, he hunched down. "Couple more swells, and we're on it."

"Come alongside," Andrew said. He grabbed the side of the small lifeboat and whistled. "Burton, how'd you know 'bout them?"

Thomas ignored the man—his most authentic friend among the crew—and scrambled to the other boat. Water in the bottom of the tiny craft swamped Thomas' legs, almost to his knees.

A dark-haired man, sprawled facedown on the bench, didn't move when Thomas pulled at his arm. When he flipped him over, the gash across the man's chest confirmed Thomas' expectation that they were too late to help him.

"Hurry, Burton," Henry said. "That boat's taking on water faster than any of us can bail."

Just as ominous as the rising water were the frigid waves and blasts of cold air. They had little time in which to act.

Thomas picked up the smaller form. Just a lad. Couldn't be more than eight. His lips were blue, but he had a heartbeat. Thomas hefted the small load to Andrew, who straddled the joined vessels and placed the boy in the center of their lifeboat.

A tarp covered the last figure, and when Thomas pulled back the protective layer, his feet all but fell from under him. A woman? Out here? That wasn't a passenger ship. Why would a woman travel on a cargo ship in the middle of winter? Why risk it? The lad? He wasn't a stowaway or a street urchin trying to make his way to America. He had to be this woman's son. The man likely was her husband.

He leaned over the man's body, pulled open his coat, and reached into his pocket. A watch. Surely, a means of identification. The woman would have to have it. Otherwise, she might not believe what happened to the man—the man whose body they had to leave in the sinking boat—whose grave was the mighty Atlantic.

When he tried to wrestle the woman's body upwards, he found she clasped a bundle under her coat. With no time to worry about the belongings she held in her grasp, he picked her up and delivered her to Andrew's open arms. Andrew's eyes caught Thomas' gaze and widened as he studied the limp frame resting in his care.

"Let's go, men," Thomas said.

"I'll row. You minister to them," Andrew said. "It's fitting. Go on."

It's fitting? Why? Because sometimes God's voice tugged at Thomas' soul? Most of the crew mocked him, dubbed him the Sea Preacher. Or, was it fitting because he was the only crew member among the three who had a wife and a family? Thomas felt a pang in his chest, sharper than the wet water clinging to his legs and feet, and deadlier than the waves threatening to take their lifeboat to the ocean floor. He did have a family. Once.

~

Captain Garvin carried the lad to the officers' quarters and lowered him to Mate Reynolds' berth. The captain tipped his chin in the direction of his own bed and said, "Put her over there. I'll tend to the boy."

Just as Thomas lowered the sodden woman to the mattress, Reynolds burst into the room. In his hands he clutched a pile of linens, blankets, and clothes. He stared, open-mouthed, from one man to the other.

"Th-th-th-that's my bed," he said.

"That it is, Mate," the captain answered. "And, the woman is in my bed. Would you rather have me put them in general quarters?"

"But, sir, the men will be in an uproar if we bunk with them."

"Why? Because their captain will see all of their shenanigans? Do you honestly think I don't know every one of them already? Every bad habit, foul mouth, and deep, dark secret? How much do you think any of us can hide while we rot away on this thing called a lightship?"

Thomas unlaced the woman's narrow shoelaces, but waited for Reynolds to excuse himself before taking the coverings off her feet.

As he spun around and left the officers' quarters, Reynolds raised his shoulders, set his jaw, and answered with a piqued, "Very well, sir."

"Thank you, sir," Thomas said.

"Why are you thanking me? What else can I do?" the captain asked.

"You didn't want me to go out. I know that. I take responsibility for putting everyone in an inconvenient position."

The long drawn-out exhale delivered by the captain caught Thomas by surprise.

"I may act like a cranky old salt, Burton, but I treasure life as much as you do. If I'd been certain we had survivors, I would have sent the whole crew to retrieve them. I admit I'm taken aback by your returning with a young lad and his mother, but you don't need to apologize to anyone."

Thomas pulled the shoes and stockings off the unconscious form. The woman was ghostly pale, but her lips were gaining some color. Her fingers, which he rubbed all the way back to the lightship, were frightfully cold, but frostbite hadn't gained hold on her, or the boy either.

The boy emitted a weak moan and whispered, "Mummy," but eased back into sleep.

When Thomas unbuttoned the woman's heavy woolen coat, his lungs contracted. He covered his mouth and leaned forward, all the while trying not to retch. He'd broken the most sacred of unwritten nautical statutes when he, unwittingly, brought the woman's cargo aboard.

"Burton, what is it?" The captain looked up briefly while he massaged the boy's feet.

"Baby. It's a baby," Thomas whispered.

Captain Garvin rushed to his feet and walked to the other bed. He clutched his chest and said, "A corpse—on board ship? You know what this means. We're doomed. Doomed."

"Captain, surely you don't believe in superstition."

The captain ignored him. "I know I'm hardly a perfect man. I've sinned, I've been selfish, and I've not always been honest, but whatever did I do to deserve this? We're doomed. This entire crew. This ship."

Captain Garvin's eyes darted from one side of the room to the other. He put his finger to his lips. "We cannot say a word. Not to anyone. Nothing. Do you understand?"

Thomas nodded. He touched the plump cheek of the baby. A girl. A small pink bow graced her pale gold hair, which was just long enough to start to curl on the ends. He closed the blue eyes and touched the perfect cherub mouth with his fingertip. Such grief this mother did not yet know.

"What will we do with her?" Captain Garvin paced across the short length of the room.

"Please, sir, we can't just toss her overboard."

"We have to. Superstition aside, we can't keep her on board."

"May I make a suggestion, sir?"

"By all means," Captain answered quickly.

"I have a basket in my quarters, one large enough for the baby. Let me put her in it, and once the sun sets, I can lower her off the side. No one need see me. I'll take care that the waves carry the child away from the ship."

Captain stopped walking, swallowed hard, and said, "Go get the basket. Be quick. And, make certain a wave takes that body out to sea. Should it find a place under this ship, no amount of your praying will save us from the luck that will haunt this vessel."

After he removed the mother's sodden garments—with as much discretion and respect as he could offer under these conditions—and wrapped her in warm, dry blankets, Thomas lined his basket with a linen towel. Before he lowered his charge into her final earthly home, he clipped the lock of her hair held by the pink bow, unfastened the tiny bracelet gracing her wrist, and folded the remembrances into a piece of paper. As he folded the linen over the tiny form, he whispered, "I'm sorry, little one. May the angels watch over you until He comes to take you home."

Made in the USA
Columbia, SC
14 April 2017